THE JULIA NYE MYSTERY SERIES

Book One
The Good Old Summertime

Book Two
St. Louie Slow Drag

Book Three
Heaven Will Protect the Working Girl
A Novel of Suspense

Book Four
Bread and Roses

In-Between Murders: Stories that LINK and
ILLUMINATE the Julia Nye Mystery Series

Book Five
Train Song
A Novel of Suspense
Expected Summer 2017

The Good Old Summertime

Betty Jo —
Enjoy the 1910s
and best wishes
for the 2010s —
Jo

JO ALLISON

OLD
UNDERWOOD
PUBLISHING

Copyright © **2016 by Jo Allison**
Copyright Second Edition, 2017, registration pending

ISBN-10: 0-9973145-0-8
ISBN-13: 978-0-9973145-0-2

115 Timberbrook Drive
Bristol, VA 24201
oldunderwoodpublish.com

Printed in the United States of America

Design by Rebecca Sharkey, rebeccasharkey.weebly.com
Editing by MS Editing, mandyschoenedits.com

Please visit:
joallisonauthor.com
1910-stlouis-by-jallison.com

To the memory of my father, a lawman in a wet county

1

*From the **St. Louis Globe-Democrat**, Tuesday, June 4, 1910*

> *Opponents of prohibition are charging that some Anti-Saloon League members actually hope the amendment prohibiting liquor statewide will fail in the November vote.*
>
> *The charge says that members of the League benefit from getting paid in the campaigns to convert counties to no-license jurisdictions one by one. More than half the state's counties and towns currently prohibit the sale and use of alcohol.*

Sheriff Claude Picard lit himself a cigar, got comfortable on the fresh grass of early summer, and studied the creek that used to be the Mississippi River.

The shallow water still marked the boundary between Missouri and Illinois. But these days it wandered through the rocks of the wide, steep-sided bed that had been forsaken by the big river. The Mississippi flowed several miles to the east.

Every time he came here, Claude thought about the flood of '81, most of thirty years ago now, when the Mississippi River covered the town of Kaskaskia, Illinois. He knew an old-timer who claimed he'd gone out in a rowboat and could see the chimneys of the town below. Everyone had waited for the river to return to the state line, but it had receded to its new path and was still there, where it might swirl over the old settlement forever. The narrow bridge in front of him, spanning high over the creek, was the only way off what was now an Illinois island with a handful of residents. Tragedy at the time, but it suited his present needs right well.

Claude contrived to arrive ahead of Ettie on the nights they met, watching for her wagon's cautious approach over the bridge onto the island. Two-foot-wide board tracks lay over the crosspieces, and Ettie always hit them straight on. This evening, he had watched her leave the same careful way, watched her turn precisely onto St. Mary's Road, watched the wagon and its cargo disappear. As usual, he was biding a while after she left. Didn't want to offend the sensibilities of any stray traveler going her way into Perry County, no more than two miles down the road.

It had been an easy meeting tonight, but the sensibilities between him and his two old police buddies were another matter. John in particular. Claude had made it clear to John Nye that he wasn't about to quit the trade, and if John and Micah saw fit to be offended, so be it.

Nonetheless, the memory of John's reproach during his visit at the jail last week, complete with the hasty retreat of Claude's two young deputies who had sauntered in at the worst moment, made this evening less pleasant. Claude realized he'd bit down on the cigar sufficient to taste tobacco. Fine. He was ready to get home, and Ettie should be far enough down the road. He squashed the lit end of the disfigured cigar on the ground and strode back to the wagon.

"None of their business, anyway," he said out loud.

Neddie, the Belgian on the right, shook his head and whinnied—in agreement, Claude fancied.

"You're right, old boy. Let's get on home." Claude tucked the money belt under his right thigh and snapped the reins. The horses moved out smartly, and he knew the empty wagon was no more than a featherweight to the big draft animals. By the time the team approached the bridge, he had them trotting like buggy horses.

They took the leading edge of the tracks with ease, and Claude braced himself for the bump when the wagon's wheels hit.

There was a bump, O.K., and a loud crack. The left front of the wagon seemed to sag; the metal rim abandoned the front wheel to travel off on its own.

The spokes cracked in turn, sounding for all the world like a Gatling gun was mounted under the wagon. The horses bolted, and the combination of the lost wheel and even more speed made the wagon skid to the right. Toward the edge of the board tracks.

Through the almighty noise, Claude heard a thud, the money belt hitting the floorboard. Cursing, he lunged to his right for the damn thing. He got hold of the buckle just as the strangest vision took his attention, Marjorie screaming, "Let it go!"

His wife's image was still before him when the wagon slammed into the low railing.

Claude grabbed for the top rail, but his momentum ripped it from his grasp. All he had in hand was the money belt as he went headlong over the edge. One moment he was thinking that, all in all, it would have been a might softer landing to fall into the Mississippi. The next, he was hearing his last curse turn into a scream.

2

A t first glance, I figured the book wedged between the cushion and arm of the chair must belong to Amelia Ingle. It was under the jacket Amelia had abandoned, along with the dusting, for me to deal with. If Dad weren't arriving any minute, I'd have left the mess so she could do her agreed-upon chore. But truth to tell, Amelia could ignore dust for a considerable spell, and I couldn't put up with it much longer.

The folks on the front porch had urged me to join in our favorite pastime, denouncing the sins of the last century and plotting the shining new order of the Twentieth.

Carl Schroeder called to me through the open window. "You'll want to hear this, Julia." I glanced out to see him toss his derby on the small table, smooth his thick red hair, and balance on the railing. One of the small corps of young men who shared our passion for debating over progressive notions, Carl was a reporter for the *Westliche Post*, the big German paper in the city. But this evening, he carried a copy of the *Times*, the *Post's* English-language sister.

I knew he had news to share about prospects for the suffrage vote coming up in Washington State. I'd listen through the open window while I dusted and considered my father's imminent visit. I had no idea why Dad saw fit to come all the way into St. Louis to see me this evening. If he wanted to make a surprise inspection of my city living arrangements, he wouldn't have telegraphed.

The book could lie on the table that stood under the open window, once I dusted the surface. I could hear the discussion as I worked. We had high hopes for Washington in the upcoming election. The news article wasn't about optimism, of course. It was about the cost of having police at elections if women actually made it to the polls.

"As if the police would be any help at the polls." Without looking I could imagine Amelia's spiky blond locks flaring around her head as she spoke, punctuating her disdain for the police in Seattle. Amelia was one of the few women in our circle to go all the way for a modern hairstyle. I wore my curly chestnut hair in a braid and that defied convention. But Amelia had cut hers too short for either a braid or the conventional up-do.

Carl was saying something along the lines of who would help if the police didn't, and then I heard the quieter voice of Amelia's brother. Henry Ingle had stopped by on his way home. I missed what Henry said, though, because the book claimed my curiosity. The dust cover declared it a volume of American poetry—but the dust cover extended beyond the edges of the book itself.

Ah. *The Girl of the Golden West.* Disgusting romance unworthy of the new women in suffragist household. For a moment, I feared it might be the copy I'd smuggled into my room last month, but I'd returned it to the library on time. Surely it wasn't Amelia's. I had never known her to read romance. Or engage in any light reading, for that matter. One of the women must have hidden the book when Amelia appeared—and then watched in frustration as Amelia tossed her jacket over it. I tucked the book back into the cushion and returned the jacket to cover it. "Your secret is safe with me," I whispered to the imaginary line-up of faces among my other five housemates.

On the porch, Henry was responding to something Amelia had said. Henry was as soft-spoken as his sister was brash, and the warning in his voice surprised me. I wasn't sure what I'd missed, but another glance out the window told me Carl was surprised as well. He leaned more sharply toward the Ingles, head tilted toward Henry, mouth opened, ready to speak. For his part, Henry was turned to stare directly at Amelia beside him on the porch swing.

"The police don't enforce laws they don't like." Amelia sounded as if she were repeating herself. "Sometimes they break laws they don't like."

"Don't let's get into that." Henry must have been repeating himself as well.

Our group of friends agreed on the issues most days. We all supported suffrage, of course, along with city beautification and good government and public parks. But there was the one sticking question: prohibition. Amelia was even stronger on the virtues of temperance—enforced temperance, that was—than she was on getting the vote. When I listened to her argue, I could hear her sympathy for families destroyed by drinking fathers, men driven to violence they wouldn't stand still for otherwise. Amelia and Henry belonged to the Anti-Saloon League. She was an officer in the Women's Christian Temperance Union.

And then Carl would retort that visiting beer gardens was what all his neighbors did, and there had never been cause to associate a family beer garden with violence.

I usually came down on the anti-prohibition side, but I admired the Ingles' passion for a cause, so I didn't press it with Amelia or Henry.

Carl pressed it. "I'm curious what you're suggesting, Amelia. Are you talking about bribes? Is that what you're getting at?"

Our housemate Fran had joined the group so Amelia wouldn't appear to passersby to be alone on the porch with two men. I heard her groan at the prospect of another prohibition debate.

Henry saved her, jumping in before Amelia could answer. "Do you think police would interfere with women voting—if suffrage passes?"

I moved the curtain to see Amelia turn to Henry and smile. It was the smile that made men look past the hair and the sometimes-excessive passion for her causes. This smile lingered longer than most. Maybe it was something she reserved for her younger brother, offering dimples and perfect teeth in acknowledgment of returning to the original topic.

"That's a possibility. Cops probably aren't among the men who'd vote for us."

Carl snorted and turned to get more comfortable on the rail. But he'd no more than settled when he jumped to his feet. "Sir? Can we help you?"

A voice outside my view said, "Interesting topic: cops who oppose suffrage. I can scarcely countenance it."

At the sound of my father's voice, I let go any pique at his visit. Maybe I'd missed him more than I'd realized.

"Dad!" I opened the screen door and was surprised to get a weak version of what everyone called our ear-to-ear grins.

Dad pulled himself up the steps. We hugged, and I heard noises behind me. My friends rose to greet Sheriff John Nye.

I did the introductions, and we all stood about making small talk. Finally, Fran and Amelia moved inside, Henry headed home, and Carl started back to work but announced he would phone me later, which was odd. Dad and I took over the porch swing.

"So, why have you come to the city, Dad? And are you going to tell me what's bothering you?"

He considered me a moment. "No. Not what's bothering me, Julie. But, I'd like you to go somewhere with me tomorrow."

"Take off work? To go where? I can't even ask Chief Wright. He's out of town."

"I know. I telegraphed Micah in Chicago. He can't get back for the funeral himself, but he said I could take you away from the office. Claude Picard is dead, Julie. I want you to go to Ste. Genevieve with me."

I heard a gasp from the window. Dad and I leaned forward to peer through the muslin. Amelia had the dusting cloth in one hand, her jacket over an arm, and the deceptive poetry book in the other hand. Not that she needed to dust, but she was using my technique: wipe the table, listen through the curtain. She waved the cloth weakly and swallowed twice before she managed to say, "Oh, Julia, I'm so sorry it's bad news."

3

From the **St. Louis Globe-Democrat**, *Friday, June 7, 1910*

> *Special Dispatch from Ste. Genevieve, Mo. – Funeral services are to be held here today for Sheriff Claude Picard, 57, who died in a wagon accident earlier this week.*
>
> *The Sheriff's wagon was found with a damaged wheel and horses still in their traces on the bridge that leads into Illinois. The Sheriff's body was located below the bridge in the shallow creek that separates Illinois and Missouri at that point.*

D ad didn't take his eyes off Claude Picard's casket once during the long, unfamiliar service in the big Roman Catholic church.

They'd been friends years ago, cops in St. Louis, and that explained a certain amount of grief. But I'd read more than sorrow in Dad's demeanor. When I'd raised an eyebrow at his mutterings on the train ride, he'd made one phrase intelligible: "Damn, useless, shame. Should've stopped him." And then, he'd refused details. Shielding his daughter from a reality he found too grim for more words. As if I'd stand for that.

We'd gotten a ride to what they called the new cemetery, a mile or so from the church, in one of the flotilla of wagons and buggies the townspeople provided.

New cemetery. Indeed, new times.

A Model-T sputtered and barked its way through the crowd, spooking the Belgians pulling the hearse along with the other horses standing about in their traces. Someone in the family must've thought it would be a credit to Sheriff Picard's memory to have his widow and the two teener sons arrive in an automobile. The Model-T stopped on the other side of the grave and issued one last boom from deep in its innards.

Beside me, Dad let out a rough sigh, as if his distress with the whole affair were reduced to annoyance with the machine.

I patted his arm to distract him from the Model-T, and he squeezed my hand that rested near the crook. But then he stood there at attention, not even bowing his head during the prayers.

When the graveside service ended, the auto cranked to life and edged away. Dad and I shuffled with the rest toward the horse-drawn vehicles.

A tall red-haired man moved against the crowd and, when I realized who it was, I knew he was headed for Dad and me.

"Julia. Sheriff Nye." Carl touched the brim of his derby in greeting. "We've got some space over here. Would you care to join us?"

We nodded and followed him. Once Carl's back was turned, Dad raised his eyebrows at me. I didn't want to explain that I'd told Carl about the funeral last night when he'd telephoned, as promised, to ask why my dad was in town. I shrugged.

But, Carl's presence surprised me, as well. Surely he could have reported the fact of the Sheriff's death without coming to Ste. Genevieve.

We got close to the long wagonette, and now I wondered why Henry Ingle was here. He sat at the rear of one of the benches that ran the length of the vehicle, talking to a youngish man who leaned on the big back wheel of the rig. The man didn't look to be boarding.

Carl did introductions, and the man turned out to be Amelia and

Henry's cousin, James Ingle.

"James is one of your fellow lawmen," Carl said to Dad, "chief deputy of the county here."

James was slender like Henry, but taller, his hair a darker blonde—but likewise parted to a nicety—his eyes more green than blue. Not much about him looked like Amelia. He shook hands with Dad, smiling and nodding. Dad nodded as well. Both faces registered recognition: they'd met before.

Dad said, "I'd like to talk to you a space, son, after we pay our respects."

James Ingle's smile faded. Maybe I misread the man I'd just met, but I imagined he wasn't looking forward to that conversation.

Dad nodded again to Ingle, helped me onto the single step at the back of the wagonette, and took a seat on the bench with Henry and me.

Carl stepped in behind us and indicated the man sitting behind the driver. "William McConnell, my friend and fellow reporter, writes police news for the *Globe-Democrat*."

Dad exhaled. McConnell had no doubt written the story Dad had groaned over this morning, on the train from St. Louis.

William McConnell held out a hand to my father across the tight space. He said the usual things to Dad and then added, "I haven't been formally introduced to Miss Nye."

True. I knew him from a distance, one more face in the daily stream of newspapermen reading my typed reports in the downtown Police Headquarters. Most of the men muttered about a woman in the police station—can't talk free, you know. The tall man with the dark blonde hair had nodded and smiled at me once, but I suspected he shared the common opinion.

Carl did that introduction as well, ending with, "Careful, Will, there's only a few appropriate things to say to women like Julia."

The men chuckled to the extent allowed by the occasion. William McConnell didn't register concern, but then he didn't have much to say to me, either. He did have something to ask my father.

"I gather you knew Claude Picard well, Sheriff Nye."

Dad stared at McConnell, who assumed a pleasant face and waited. Dad made up his mind.

"Well, Claude Picard and Micah Wright and I were cops together, and good friends, in the City. Twenty years ago."

"Aha" flashed in Carl's red-haired complexion as he pieced it together. John Nye had returned to Callaway County and Claude Picard to Ste. Genevieve County, to be elected sheriffs. The one cop who'd stayed in St. Louis had made it to the top. And twenty-some years after they'd parted, St. Louis City Police Chief Micah Wright had offered his old friend's daughter an unconventional position.

McConnell nodded and seemed ready to ask something else, but Dad hastened to add, "It's a two-hour train ride from St. Louis out here. Any particular reason you and your friend find Claude Picard's death so newsworthy, Mr. McConnell?"

"Yes, sir." If McConnell was surprised to be on the business end of a question, he didn't show it. "By the nature of his job, Sheriff Picard is a public figure. And one whose wagon wrecked, for no reason we've been told, crossing from Illinois to Missouri. Or vice versa."

Carl jiggled his foot, which was what he did when he was waiting to jump into a debate. But he pressed his mouth shut, for a change. Henry didn't take his eyes off Dad.

Dad said what he always said to me when he didn't want to argue any longer: "I expect so."

Henry's sigh was loud enough for me to hear, but, before I could

14

wonder at it, a mechanical commotion distracted me.

The Model-T pulled up beside us, the driver trying to keep it from sputtering out at the low speed, our driver trying to control his horses, which stomped and tried to shift away.

Marjorie Picard turned in the passenger seat, pale and composed, and said, "John, will you stop at the house before you leave?"

◆ ◆ ◆

I didn't remember Marjorie Picard, although she'd likely been at my mother's funeral, seven years ago. It didn't matter. I would offer condolences as an old family friend and gather what answers I could to explain Dad's reaction.

In the house, we made our way past knots of people eating and shaking their heads over events. I stopped to pick up a tiny sandwich. Mrs. Picard stepped out of a room off the kitchen and gestured an invitation to Dad and her sons to join her.

I flushed. Not that I thought it showed on my skin. It was the old anger I'd learned to control when necessary, set off when someone didn't give me the respect any man would have gotten. When someone treated me like a girl. I'd somehow trained Dad and my precious older brother not to dismiss me like that. Dad nodded at Marjorie Picard and held out a hand to escort me into the room.

The door led to a screened lean-to that served as the back entrance. People were milling on the deep porch that wrapped around most of three sides of the house. Another crowd stood about in the back yard amidst the lilac remains and the recently trimmed forsythia. Roses and other flowers bordered the lean-to, and we probably couldn't be overheard across the fragrant moat if we kept our voices down.

Mrs. Picard blinked at my presence and then smiled as she searched for any resemblance to my mother, no doubt. Instead, she could only have seen a tall, thin young woman with a longish face, lacking in the style, grace, and handsomeness she surely remembered in Anna Nye. Like others before her, she said, "Oh, my dear, you look so much like your father—prettier of course." I smothered my pique and smiled back at her. Dad gave me a sideways hug. I had indeed grown into what my mother feared: my father's likeness.

Her sons, David and Samuel, asked about my working for the police in St. Louis. I suspected their curiosity about the city meant she wouldn't have them with her much longer.

Marjorie Picard looked down and started biting her lower lip. The pleasantries ended.

"John." She dropped her voice to a whisper. "I don't think it was an accident, as they are saying." In contrast to her public calm of a quarter hour ago, she trembled.

Dad took Mrs. Picard's hands. "What's the coroner saying?"

Nothing came out of her mouth, although it was moving. David, the older son, put an arm around her and faced Dad. "He says the wagon skidded on that bridge. The tracks and railing held the wagon, but Papa went over." He drew a breath and continued. "Papa was supposed to have hit his head on a rock when he fell, and then he drowned."

Tears ran down Mrs. Picard's face. Dad tightened his lips a moment before he said, "And why do you not think it an accident, Marjorie?"

Her whisper was even softer. "There wasn't any money."

4

Carl Schroeder took off his derby and smoothed his thick red waves. He glanced at William, hoping his friend approved of his easy kindness. Carl had just told Henry Ingle to go ahead and run his errand, and he and Will would be happy to save a seat for him on the crowded train back to St. Louis. William tilted his head in acknowledgement, also wondering, Carl assumed, about the package Henry was shepherding to the City. It was another intriguing angle on an odd story.

Carl and William made their way among the black-clad visitors headed toward the Mississippi River and the train depot. As they got a bit of space around them, Carl thought it safe to say, "Ste. Genevieve is a wet county. If James Ingle shares Henry's prohibition stand, why would Claude Picard ever have hired him?"

William smiled and shook his head. "Not everyone worries the prohibition question all the time, Schroeder."

Carl wanted to argue, but a family moved close. Besides, Will might have a point. William McConnell was one of the most respected reporters to cover police news in the City, even though he hadn't turned thirty yet. And one reason was that he always searched for all sides of a story. Carl loved to work a story with William and learn from him. And since the German and American papers weren't strictly in competition, he could seize the opportunity now and then.

"What kind of package do you suppose Henry Ingle is taking

17

home to St. Louis from a funeral in Ste. Genevieve?" William asked.

Good question. Carl didn't have any idea, and he didn't have to admit it because he heard his name being called.

Carl used his six-foot-three-inches to look back over the crowd and see Julia Nye moving in their direction. He waved his hat and settled it back on his head.

Julia came striding toward him in her tailored black skirt and jacket, her thick braid no doubt swinging across her back, her slender waist free of conventional corseting. Carl found himself wondering, maybe for the hundredth time, what the more stylistically eccentric suffragists like Julia wore under their shirtwaists if they didn't wear corsets.

And then he noted she was walking from the direction of the Picard house. Julia might have answers, as well.

The trick would be to make sure he eased into the conversation, didn't just demand information. Julia could go mulish if she imagined some fleeting insult to her independence.

Carl broke into a smile picturing her reaction to that line of thinking.

But Julia seemed to see the smile as a greeting, and the frown between her eyes eased.

"Carl, may I ride with you back to the City? Dad's staying here overnight to help Mrs. Picard."

"Well, you'll need a man to see to your safety, I'm sure."

"Fine, Carl, I'll go sit with a stranger."

He chuckled. "Will your father be here a while?"

"Don't know, for sure. He'll want to get home as soon as possible. He always thinks the hooligans come out of the woodwork in Callaway County if he's not there."

Carl heard William moving up behind him. "He must be close to the Picard family."

Julia peered around Carl and regarded William as if she weren't sure she had to respond to that. The frown reappeared between her eyes, and she said, "I expect so."

William had heard that before. Judging from his friend's sigh, he appreciated the non-answer less from Julia than from her father. Carl decided to wait until he could get Julia alone to ask about Picard.

The three headed for the platform, and William managed small talk. "So, Miss Nye, did you enjoy the old buildings and such?"

Ste. Genevieve was the oldest settlement in Missouri, and William had led Carl on an enthusiastic tourist-walk while they'd waited for the train.

Julia glanced back at the town, where the huge church towered over old houses and stores that had been there at least a century.

"No," she said. "They're . . . old."

Carl burst out laughing and then felt bad when he realized he'd startled the somber folks around him. He tried to regain his own solemnity by reminding himself that there was something odd about this accident. If it did, despite William's jibe, involve prohibition and politics, Carl was determined to sort it out.

5

O n a crowded car, I sat next to Carl and across from McConnell and crossed my legs at the knee. I'd learned the gesture to judge men's reactions to unconventionality, but it had become natural, and I didn't think much about it. Marjorie Picard occupied my thoughts. William McConnell stared at the ankle that appeared, though, and I wasn't about to retract it. Henry Ingle slipped into the seat beside McConnell and must have noticed the ankle as well. He gave me the half-amused, half-embarrassed smile he directed at Amelia when she was forward for the cause.

McConnell raised his eyes to my face, and I had a pleasant smile ready for him. His eyebrows, precise and expressive, angled nearer the bridge of his nose as he looked at me. He had high cheekbones and vertical dimples that materialized and deepened when he grinned—as I remembered. He wasn't grinning now.

Instead he turned deliberately toward Carl, who jerked into speech.

"So, Ingle," Carl said, "is your cousin as actively prohibitionist as you and your sister?"

Henry was still smiling over my crossed-legs political display, but he lost the grin and said, "Yes indeed, Schroeder. James shares our concern about the evils of alcohol and the urgency of prohibiting it, preferably in the November election."

Carl snorted, and the debate was on. I let the clacking of the train wheels cover the arguments I'd heard so often.

Marjorie Picard had said James Ingle was investigating her husband's death. James Ingle favored prohibition. Sheriff Claude Picard had almost certainly disliked prohibition. Beer was available at the wake at the Picard house, easy enough because Ste. Genevieve County was wet. Even Perryville, the county seat of adjoining Perry County, was wet while the rest of the county was dry.

I knew that because I'd heard Carl discuss such things for hours on end. For my part, I'd never cared to drink beer or liquor, so opposing prohibition was an intellectual position my part, not an emotional one. Differing positions on liquor should be a silly reason for two men not to work together, but many people didn't see it that way.

For Carl and Henry, it might have been a problem. They were off to the races with the question, leaning toward each other, Carl gesturing widely, Henry's blue eyes bright. Economic ramifications were the current topic. Their energy pulled me back to listening.

Henry, who worked for a bank, said, "I fully realize St. Louis depends heavily on its brewers, but the city will just have to deal with the fact it profits from poison."

"That's ridiculous," Carl said and flung an arm in my direction.

I tried to hide my smile, as I moved out of the way.

Carl was good-looking as long as he was doing something. If he was sitting still, you might notice his hawkish nose, his large mouth, his crooked teeth. But when he was moving, talking—and certainly when he was debating prohibition—he glowed.

I glanced at McConnell, who watched his chum with a smile. He caught my glance and nodded. I wondered if, like me, he was waiting to find an opening into the conversation.

"Henry," I jumped in, as he drew a breath. "I'm confused about something."

He and Carl swiveled to look at me.

"Why would Sheriff Picard have hired James as his Chief Deputy? I'm sure your cousin is quite competent, but the politics of alcohol might rule out hiring anyone who was the least outspoken on the matter."

Carl shifted his stare to McConnell—who offered a wider grin. Maybe McConnell and I had the same question.

"Well." Henry smiled at me. "I believe James is indeed quite competent. His wife's family has lived in Ste. Genevieve for years, and I think Sheriff Picard was delighted to have someone of James's caliber when he took up police work several years ago. And I don't know that they ever debated the matter of prohibition on the street."

Maybe Carl couldn't imagine not debating the issue. The joy of the argument caught him up again, and he and Henry took off.

I shook my head and smiled at McConnell. He nodded again and turned to study the fading landscape. I glanced out but had no interest in the scrubby trees and gray outcroppings.

A wet county. A sheriff with a politically unlikely chief deputy who might well succeed him. And no money. No money to show for . . . what?

When Dad got back to St. Louis, I intended to make him talk to me about Claude Picard, old buddy or not, fellow sheriff or not. Dad had nurtured the detective in me, and, if he thought it was something he could turn off with a simple dismissal, he could think again.

6

From the **St. Louis Globe-Democrat**, *Saturday, June 8, 1910*

> *Special Dispatch from Ste. Genevieve, Mo.—Ste. Genevieve County Chief Deputy James Ingle will be taking over the duties of the late Sheriff Claude Picard, according to County Judge Arnold Crichton.*
>
> *Sheriff Picard, 57, died Tuesday in a wagon accident. Funeral services were held here yesterday.*
>
> *A former St. Louis City policeman, Picard is survived by his wife, three daughters, two sons, and a grandchild.*
>
> *Judge Crichton said a new sheriff will be elected in November to fill the remaining two years of Picard's current term.*

I waited in the dining room of the Wohler-Grand Saturday evening, past ready to hear what Dad had learned down south.

Chief Wright and I had been putting in an honest Saturday's work at Headquarters when Dad telephoned to say he'd meet us for dinner. The Chief reserved a back room. We'd been waiting on benches outside the elegant restaurant on North Sixth a quarter of an hour when Dad arrived.

Now though, the Chief kept wandering from the path our waiter had planned, darting over to shake hands four and five tables away. Dad and I waited and smiled at people we didn't know. I tried to figure out where the wavering shadows came from and looked up to see that the ceiling fans were at the ends of long iron poles, like upside-down daisies, circling below the white mushrooms of the lamps. I admired the effect for a few moments and snapped out of my country-girl gawking when the Chief joined us, his abundant, graying hair bouncing with his steps. The waiter sighed, and we were underway again.

For three thin people, we put away a fair amount of food. The Chief suggested we wait dessert until we discussed "matters," which was fine with me because I had plenty of questions stored up.

Dad pushed his chair back from the table, folded his hands over his waistcoat, and frowned.

"Well. Tuesday evening, it was. Getting late. Marjorie expected Claude home earlier and figured the news was bad when the deputy, Ingle, arrived at the door. Said he'd gotten word that Claude's body and the wrecked wagon had been found."

"Where exactly was it?" The Chief was frowning.

"Close to the village of St. Mary, where a bridge goes over into that piece of Illinois that got cut off by the flood years ago. St. Mary is in Ste. Gen County, but just a mile or so from the Perry County line."

The Chief wrote in his memo book. It must be to hide his grief about his old friend. He would surely remember everything Dad said.

"Ingle told me Marjorie said she thought Claude might have been going to Perryville on business—and that he, Ingle, saw fit to believe her."

Dad and the Chief nodded at each other as if they read something significant into James Ingle's statement.

"You met this Ingle when you were down there a fortnight ago?" the Chief asked. Dad noticed my head jerk at the realization he'd visited Ste. Genevieve, going through St. Louis and not stopping to see me. He sighed, nodded, and continued.

He'd asked Ingle about the wagon and been told it was a standard vehicle for transporting substantial goods, drawn by a pair of sturdy Belgian draft horses. "Ingle said the wagon and horses belonged to Claude, not to the Department. When they found it, a front wheel was broken. No one's sure why. Horses were in harness, and the wagon itself had crashed into the railing, but stayed on the bridge. Claude must've been pitched off the seat into the creek. Which is mostly rocks at that point, Ingle said."

The Chief considered that and shook his head. He put down his pen, leaned back, and did that weird thing so many men with mustaches do. He began combing it with his lower teeth. I usually tried not to look.

It was my turn. "Which way was the wagon headed? Onto the island, or off?"

After staring for a couple of seconds, Dad smiled. "That's a good question, honey. Ingle didn't say, and I didn't think to ask."

Chief Wright agreed. "It'd be nice to know which way the wagon was headed, and why the wheel broke." He began doodling in the memo book. "Who found the body, again?"

Maybe he was picturing his friend. I stepped into what I imagined to be his fancy. A young John Nye, taller in his helmet, characteristically leaning a bit back of vertical, walked a Victorian version of Market Street. Micah Wright, shorter than his buddies, was out in front and challenging them to move faster. Claude Picard, stouter, blond, with a firm set to his jaw if the picture in the *Globe* this morning was any indication, wore his double-breasted uniform with pride.

Dad shifted in his seat, getting my attention and the Chief's. "Paul Carrey, the sheriff in Perry County found him. I went to

Perryville this morning. Seems Carrey got a telephone message from someone in St. Louis."

The Chief blinked.

Dad nodded. "This is why an accident doesn't seem so likely. Someone told Carrey there'd be . . . spilled cargo . . . along the St. Mary's road. He didn't find anything in his county, but he was curious, so he decided to ride a ways into Ste. Gen. He was surprised—and of course, dismayed—to find the wagon and then the body."

Feeling good about my first question, I tried again. "Why would anyone here know about spilled cargo in Perry County? Or Ste. Genevieve County, for that matter?" I thought a second, and added, "Had Sheriff Picard been to Perry County?"

Dad frowned at me, and I couldn't figure why. Those were obvious holes in someone's story.

I looked to the Chief to see if he had answers. His frown said he wished I hadn't asked.

He turned to Dad. "So, what's next, John?"

"We need to decide that, Micah. There are questions, I'll grant you, but asking them won't bring Claude back. Or get Marjorie's money back."

Chief Wright shook his head and leaned onto the table. "John, you mean to tell me you're willing to let it go? Claude didn't fall off that damn bridge by accident. Because of a shattered wheel? On a wagon Claude Picard maintained? That's ridiculous on the face of it. And someone knew there'd be a breakdown?" The Chief snorted.

Dad nodded. "Yes, but here's the bigger question. If we try to find out if it was . . . more than an accident, we open the whole issue of what he was doing."

The Chief's sigh ballooned over us. "I've been thinking about that,

John. And I think Marjorie's answered it for us. She's got to know what will happen if we investigate. She and Claude were convinced he was doing the right thing. I figure everyone in her world knew about it and was fine with it. And if she was willing to suggest to you it wasn't an accident, then her priority is to find out what happened."

What in the world was Picard up to? "What are you talking about?" I asked Dad.

He frowned at me and turned to Chief Wright without answering me. Again.

"O.K. then. We do it. We need a whole new tack, though. I may have asked all the questions I can. I was extended a courtesy, as Claude's friend, but I can't keep at it, not enough to do any good."

He twisted in his chair and leaned closer to Chief Wright. "Maybe you can find out a bit more, if you go down to extend your sympathies, but Ingle says he investigating, and we'll look like we doubt his ability. Or his integrity. And there's no guarantee the prosecutors would use it if we found anything."

"I agree." Chief Wright was chewing his moustache between words. "But if you and I can't ask, who can?"

"What do you think of going outside police channels?"

I forgot my pique at Dad's behavior when he turned away from the Chief's raised eyebrows and said to me, "Are you willing to help, honey?"

My first thought was how much time I'd wasted planning to override his objections. Chief Wright leaned forward, looking from Dad to me, with another frown. "What do you want her to do?"

"I want her to recruit a couple of investigators."

"Recruit!" I jumped in my seat, and it was a good thing we were in a private room. "I want to investigate. I don't want to recruit someone else."

"Now, honey, you can't go asking questions down river. They won't talk to you."

"How do you know that? If someone is hiding something, who are they going to talk to? At least let me try!"

I could tell he was close to saying, "Forget it."

Chief Wright jumped in. "Who did you have in mind, John?"

"Julia's reporter friends. They can investigate it as a story, and, if they raise enough stink in the papers, the district attorney will more likely pay attention."

The Chief hmmed as if he was going to have to think about that one.

I thought about it. Quickly. "Who are you talking about? Carl? You think Carl Schroeder can handle this and I can't?"

Dad gathered patience. "I believe Schroeder can certainly pitch in. He's a reporter, isn't he? The police reporter for the *Westliche Post*? And I thought you could also ask the *Globe-Democrat* reporter, McConnell."

The Chief nodded. "McConnell's good, and Schroeder might be helpful. He has a reputation as a screaming anti-prohibition militant. I don't know how that will go over with the drys down there, but maybe he could work the wet angle."

Prohibition again? Well, it didn't matter. If they thought I was going to ask Carl, let alone William McConnell, to investigate, and then just sit back and watch . . . in my first chance to detect in the city. Not hardly.

I opened my mouth to argue, but Dad said, "Maybe it's not a good idea. I'm not so sure I want you involved at all, honey. I just didn't want Ingle to know I'd asked them myself—but it's not likely he'd find out."

It occurred to me, in one of those moments of devious clarity, that I could say one thing to Dad and something else to Carl. The problem would be the Chief. What would happen if I got involved asking questions, missed a train, and was late to work one day? Well, I'd have to take the chance and be careful.

So, I agreed to talk to Carl—and McConnell, for Pete's sake. "What do I tell them about this matter of cargo?"

Dad abruptly decided he didn't want dessert, and the Chief hurried off to pay. I was rising as well, irritated but determined, when Dad turned in his chair and caught my hand. I sat back down.

"Julie, I want you to understand that this is not the kind of investigation you've done with me back home. I don't know what happened to Claude, but it well could be that someone intended his death. That means the investigators themselves could be in danger."

"So, you want me to ask Carl to put himself in danger while I sit home and worry about him?"

"The men are in less danger than you'd be, honey."

He read my reaction. I couldn't have kept my face neutral if I'd wanted to.

"I mean it, Julie. Someone might try to stop you where they'd hesitate to confront the men. You just tell the men you've heard there are doubts about the death, and let it go at that."

I was trembling. This was the man who had taught me to shoot, taught me to detect, taught me that I was as worthy of his respect as my brother. Taught me all that despite my mother's objection and rejection. The idea that Carl Schroeder and William McConnell could do something I couldn't do was not acceptable.

By the time we parted at the boardinghouse, not having said much to each other on the way there, Dad felt it necessary to repeat himself. "Let the reporters work on it, Julie. Stay out of it yourself."

I tried my best to nod as if I agreed. His sigh said he wished he'd never said anything to me—or in front of me. *Too late, Dad.* I vowed silently that I'd find out every last thing he wasn't telling me as I trailed—or led—Carl and William McConnell to one heck of a story.

7

From the **St. Louis Globe-Democrat**, *Sunday, June 9, 1910*

Special Dispatch from Ste. Genevieve, Mo. – Coroner Daniel Stanger has ruled that the death last Tuesday evening of Sheriff Claude Picard was accidental. The Coroner said that Sheriff Picard hit his head when the wagon he was driving wrecked on a narrow bridge.

Coroner Stanger said the Sheriff seemed to have fallen into the shallow stream and drowned before regaining consciousness.

No one answered the telephone at Carl's house. It was a beautiful, June Sunday so Carl was probably out defeating prohibition in person at a beer garden. I had no choice but to go to the Soulard neighborhood.

I looped my rich-reddish-brown braid at my neck and tucked the long wings behind my ears. I considered makeup. A lot of bachelor girls were starting to use it, but it just didn't do much for me. My hazel eyes were sufficiently outlined by dark lashes, and I already had a good blush over clear, olive skin. Makeup wasn't going to change my high forehead or shrink my large mouth or create a dainty, upturned nose.

And really, Carl was likely to help me regardless of how I looked today, so I took the straw from the hat tree and was on my way.

I'd been to a beer garden with Carl once, and I tried that one—

among the plentitude of beer gardens in Soulard. Sure enough, I found his widowed mother and younger sister there.

His mother tilted her head at me as if she sniffed romance. "You look for Carl?" she asked, in her heavy accent, as I approached.

"Yes, ma'am, I need to talk to him about a story."

His sister smiled. "He's meeting a friend at Weider's Garden." I was grateful she was the one to offer directions. I might not have understood their mother.

Along the way, I admired the neighborhood. Neat houses crowded the sidewalks. But there was an openness it took me a minute to identify. It was the sky.

Downtown St. Louis streets were filled with wires. Electricity wires ran alongside the streets, telephone wires from two different companies crisscrossed above the streets, and the ever-present trolley lines trailed down the middle of the streets. When I first arrived in January, I'd stood staring up at a downtown intersection, watching smoke from coal fires swirl in the sky and imagining that an angry child had made vivid pencil marks on dirty paper. Summer had improved the view in that we'd lost a fraction of the coal smoke.

Not only were there fewer lines out here, away from downtown, but ivy had covered a back fence at Weider's and was making its soft way up one of the electric pole guy wires.

Music came from inside the establishment: a piano, a mandolin, and men singing. As I listened, they finished rhapsodizing about the banks of the Wabash and moved across country to the sidewalks of New York. I hadn't associated beer gardens with popular ballads, but I approved.

On the porch of Weider's, folks sat at round slabs of polished wood balanced on squatty barrels. The smell of beer was much stronger at this garden, and it stopped me at the sidewalk. I didn't mind people drinking. I just hated the smell of beer.

The majority of the faces staring at me were male, ranging from a five-year-old-maybe with a bow at his neck to the elderly regulars. Only a few women were outside, and that counted a heavy-set serving-woman with her sleeves rolled up over muscled forearms. She hefted a tray with eight or nine glasses of dark brew and smiled at me. Good enough. A fluffy black dog came over to me, and I petted it and waited for the woman to serve two tables. I ignored the men whose glances were more than casual.

When she approached, I asked the serving-woman if Carl Schroeder was there. She chuckled.

"Oh, *ja*, he is here." She gestured inside with her head.

I was surprised past speech by the scene I walked in on. Thank goodness, the musicians didn't have a direct view of the doorway.

Carl balanced on the edge of a straight-back chair, mandolin at the ready. William McConnell perched on the stool of the old upright.

A hesitant young female voice suggested, *"In the Good Old Summer Time?"*

"One of my favorites," Carl said.

They were good together. Carl had sung and played at the boarding house before, on wintry Sunday afternoons. But it was the last thing I expected from William McConnell. He returned to his distinctive grin between numbers, and I suspected he was enjoying himself—and was slightly embarrassed at the same time. I imagined he didn't do this often, and Carl had jollied him into it.

I was torn between wanting to put them to work on my investigation and listening for a while. Listening won. I did go back out to the beer counter to order an iced tea. Most establishments in St. Louis served iced tea in the summer as a matter of civic pride because it had been popular at the Fair in 1904.

"Tea, miss? You want tea?"

"Yes indeed."

The man behind the counter muttered, "Waste of good ice," but he served up a nicely sweetened drink in a beer stein.

I sipped at it for a quarter hour or so, at a table near the door. They were working through the popular repertoire of the last decade and having a great time. I wondered if I'd make their day better or worse.

But, time was wasting. I carried my sweating beer stein closer to the upright. McConnell saw me, and his fingers faltered. I smiled and tried to gesture that he should continue, but he brought the song to an abrupt end. Carl looked at him, saw the direction of his gaze, and swiveled around.

I raised my stein to him, and his grin widened. He clapped McConnell on the shoulder, said something in German to the room at large, and walked over to me.

"Julia! What in the world are you doing here?"

"Looking for you. Can you break off the concert to talk for a while?"

"Of course. Did you like it? We're pretty good, huh?"

I raised my stein to William McConnell as well.

McConnell wasn't one for blushing, I thought, but he came close. "If you'll pardon me, I'll get something wet myself." He tried to slip off, and Carl looked content to let him go.

"Actually," I reached out with the stein, "I need to talk to the both of you." That stopped him. But, we had an audience left over from the music, which wouldn't work for what I had to say.

"Do you suppose we could go for a walk?"

McConnell's eyebrows went up, and even Carl hesitated a moment before he said, "Uh, sure, why not?" And turned to bundle up his mandolin.

McConnell seemed pretty sure why not. But he gave me half a smile, a hint of the dimples. It served, I supposed, to point out the obvious, that a lady walking with two gentlemen instead of one would be inappropriate. Victorian rules.

Past the staring crowd, Carl moved out to the street side of the walkway. He was going to brush the lower branches of the trees that grew in the narrow grassy strip between street and sidewalk. If I'd had on a long, full skirt I'd have brushed the steps that led up into small yards. McConnell fell in behind us.

"Is there a problem, Julia?" Carl said.

"Sort of." I'd put thought into how to broach this, and I directed my opening over my shoulder toward McConnell. "I read in the *Globe* this morning that the coroner in Ste. Genevieve ruled Sheriff Picard's death accidental."

"That's what the man told me." McConnell's tone was curt.

"I know. But Mrs. Picard doesn't think so."

They both stopped walking, and I turned as McConnell put his hands on his hips. "How do you know that?"

"She told my father."

"And what is your father doing about it?"

"Asking us to investigate."

"Us?" Carl twitched his shoulders.

I nodded, and McConnell said, "Your father is a sheriff. Investigation is his department."

"Well, he's not a sheriff in Ste. Genevieve or Perry County. They won't appreciate him asking any more questions."

"And you think they'll appreciate us asking questions?" McConnell shook his head. "I can't believe he'd ask you to get involved."

"Well, believe it. And if you're too shy to ask questions, I can find someone who does want the story."

For some obscure male reason, that made McConnell and Carl stare at each other instead of at me. I folded my arms and waited for them to sort it out.

"You know, I hadn't planned on finding you here together. We could go down there this afternoon."

"Hold on, wait just a minute, Julia," Carl said. He pulled my left arm loose, tucked it in his, and began to stride down the sidewalk, his mandolin bouncing on his back.

McConnell caught up and managed to fit on my other side. "I, for one, have serious doubts about what we can accomplish—and who exactly is going to talk to us—on a Sunday afternoon. Tomorrow we can talk to Ingle." He looked around me at Carl. "We can be down there first thing in the morning."

I pulled away from Carl. "Think right now, Mr. McConnell. A sheriff elected by the people of Ste. Genevieve County is dead under strange circumstances. No one in law enforcement can investigate except James Ingle, and he might choose not to do it. Aside from the fact it sounds like a heck of a story to me, don't you think you have a civic duty to look around, at least consider Mrs. Picard's concern? What if it was murder, Mr. McConnell?"

He stood staring at me as if I were the problem, not mayhem in Ste. Genevieve.

Carl asked McConnell—not me—"Do you think James Ingle is involved? Could it be a temperance matter?"

Honestly. Everything was a temperance matter with Carl.

I repeated myself. "I think we should go this afternoon. Not," I glared at William McConnell before he could interrupt, "to ask questions, though."

"Then what would we do there, Julia?" Carl sounded more than a whit patronizing.

"Well, I want to see this stream where Sheriff Picard died. I want to see the bridge before they repair it."

"And how would we get there?" McConnell didn't even bother to hide the patronizing tone.

"We could visit Mrs. Picard and borrow a buggy. Take the train to Ste. Gen, go to her house as if I were making a sympathy call, and borrow a buggy. We'd have to wangle all sorts of excuses during the workweek, but today is perfect." I directed my words to McConnell. "But then, I'm not the investigating reporter. Do you have a better idea?"

Carl made a choking sound. McConnell frowned, and I watched the muscles clench along his strong jaw line. Then he started walking on down the sidewalk. Carl moved closer to me, but I kept my eyes on William McConnell. If he said no, I didn't know who else to approach. The police reporter from the *Post-Dispatch* found my presence at Headquarters . . . "embarrassing" was the word, I believe.

I could see as McConnell turned that he was looking at his pocket watch. "We'll need to hurry," he said.

Carl sighed and looked down at me. "Are you dressed for this or did you want to find some men's trousers to wear?"

◆　◆　◆

Carl and McConnell had lots of questions on the two-hour train ride, and I didn't have enough answers. Finally, McConnell asked if I knew what Sheriff Picard hauled in the wagon. I was irritated all over again to have to say, "No." But Carl looked at McConnell and nodded, as if the question were an answer in and of itself.

Marjorie Picard was surprised when we showed up on her porch. But I suggested to her that Dad was still concerned about details of the Sheriff's death and that two of my reporter friends wanted to look around. She seemed fine with that, happy, as a matter of fact.

An evening breeze worked through the trees in her spacious yard, and I tried to impress on her our need to hurry. I figured the bridge was at least seven or eight miles south from Ste. Genevieve.

"I'm sorry to just ask to borrow the buggy and then head out, Mrs. Picard. But we need to return on the late train."

"Of course, dear. The gentlemen can take the buggy. We keep it over at a neighbor's stable now. But David can show them where it is."

From the corner of my eye, I saw that Carl was trying not to smile, presumably at Mrs. Picard's assumption that I'd stay with her.

I thought fast, and said, "The thing is, Mrs. Picard, I'd like to ride along so I can tell Dad what I see."

She was digesting that when David spoke up. "Really, Mother, there's no need for the buggy. Four of us can ride in the auto." He gave her a quick hug and headed for the door, grabbing a golf cap on the way out.

I reached for Mrs. Picard's hand, squeezed it, and hurried after the men. I hadn't realized the Model-T was theirs. To tell the truth, I didn't ride in automobiles all that often, and I welcomed the adventure.

David led the way to the barn where the auto had apparently replaced the buggy. I didn't see anything horse-drawn, and the smells of oil and gasoline were making inroads on the leather and other organic smells of your typical horse-shed.

"Have you gotten the wagon back yet?" I asked David.

"No," he replied, as he slipped the gear into neutral, made sure the brake was set, and fished under the seat for the crank handle. "Deputy Ingle said they had to ship the bad wheel into St. Louis to get it fixed."

Carl jerked his head to stare at the lad, and I wondered what Carl knew about the wheel.

I prompted David for the story regarding the wagon while he knelt and inserted the handle under what I had heard called a radiator.

"They had to put a new wheel on so they could pull the wagon back to town." He stopped talking while he cranked. On about the eighth or ninth crank, the engine coughed and caught. He smiled at me and started around to help me into the seat. I jumped into the front on my own. David blinked, took his seat beside me, and eased the car out of the barn, pausing for Carl and McConnell to cram into the back seat.

"Ingle went ahead and sent the broken wheel to someone in the city. Until that wheel's back on the wagon, it stays in the county barn." He was speaking louder now, to be heard over the engine.

McConnell's voice drifted up from the back seat. "So no one here could fix the wheel? Do you know where he sent it in St. Louis?" He sounded casual again, but as I glanced back, I saw an intensity in the quirk of his eyebrows.

David said, "No sir," and McConnell settled back with a slight frown. David pulled onto St. Mary's Road, according to a sign, and turned south. He developed a slight smile as he shifted to what I thought was called a higher gear. The auto produced even more noise, and we were all quiet. I was used to the creak of buggies. The Model-T rattled, all of its metal parts protesting their proximity to each other.

So, Claude Picard owned an automobile. Why would you use a

wagon if you owned an auto? And the answer, I realized, was cargo space.

Less than half an hour later, David parked the Model-T at the edge of the water. Carl and McConnell tumbled out of the back seat and made their way onto the narrow bridge, but David just sat there, staring out over the wide, rocky bed with a stream I could barely see. Maybe he wanted to be alone, but he looked so forlorn that I couldn't make myself leave the car. Instead, I considered him. He seemed to mature every time I looked carefully. His blond hair was his father's, along with the brown eyes that were narrowed as he looked at the stream.

"Has it changed much, do you think?" I asked.

"No. I came out Wednesday . . . after they'd found Dad. It looked like it does right now."

He got out of the car, and I hopped down before he could come around. He didn't seem to notice, just walked aways past the auto.

I gave him a minute, and then followed him close enough to ask, "Which way was the wagon headed when you saw it, David?"

"This way. He'd already done his business on the island." He pointed across the bridge. I saw some scrubby trees and flat land stretching behind them. We'd turned away from the Mississippi several miles back, and it was nowhere in sight.

Carl and McConnell were on the bridge, watching us.

They took a last look at the broken railing and joined us on land.

"So." I eased into the subject. "Was the wagon full or empty?"

David looked at me strangely, and said, "Empty, ma'am."

Carl snorted softly.

McConnell said, "Your father was thrown out of the wagon when it canted onto the railing, hit his head, and drowned—"

"That assumes his fatal injury came when he fell out of the

wagon," Carl interrupted. That was the most negative thing I'd heard—from the least likely quarter.

McConnell didn't react at all, and David didn't react much. One hand clinched into a fist. McConnell continued to consider the young man. "Do you have any reason to doubt the coroner's statement?"

"You could see a big gash on his head." David walked a few steps away and kicked at a clump of weeds.

I turned to Carl and McConnell. "So the Sheriff was on his way home."

McConnell nodded.

"Meaning that he had delivered this mysterious cargo to someone, here, and was returning with an empty wagon. Right?"

Carl nodded this time, as if to encourage a slow student.

I glanced at David, who'd turned to listen. I decided to ask the cargo question anyway.

"Delivered what? What does a sheriff deliver? To the middle of nowhere?"

McConnell sighed. Carl rolled his eyes as he said, "Booze, of course, Julia. Bootleg booze."

"What?"

"Either beer or something harder. I wouldn't know which."

"Beer," David said.

"Julia." Carl put an arm on my back and walked me away before David could say more. "Ste. Genevieve County is wet and Perry County, outside Perryville, is dry. I remember when the vote was held in the county. It was a small group of prohibitionists who managed to get the county to go. There are still people in the county who don't want to travel into Perryville to get a drink. Therefore, there's a profit in selling beer to someone who distributes it around the county."

Carl was warming to his subject. "These stupid prohibition laws will never work. If people want beer, someone will provide it."

I stepped away from him but dropped my voice to a whisper so David wouldn't overhear. "I understand that. What I don't understand is why a sheriff would be running beer. He was a good man, Carl."

"Of course he was a good man. He opposed these stupid laws. Lots of good men do."

"So what, Carl? You oppose these laws, but you don't break them."

"No. I'd be arrested if I broke the law."

I shook my head to settle this new notion and turned to walk back in the other direction.

Behind me, Carl said, "Who better to break the law, Julia? Who better to break a bad law?"

8

We boarded the late train to St. Louis. William McConnell doled out some extra cash to the conductor, and we moved into a closed compartment. There weren't enough people in the car for me to be embarrassed. This time I plopped into the middle of a seat, forcing McConnell and Carl to share the bench across from me.

"So, Sheriff Picard was murdered," Carl said.

I jerked my head up to look at him. I shouldn't have been surprised. My father didn't think Picard's death an accident. Neither did I. But murder was a strong, bleak word.

McConnell seemed to read my mind. "You didn't think it truly would be murder, did you?"

"No, I didn't—don't, for that matter. Although I don't think it was an accident, either."

"If not murder and not an accident, what then?" Carl asked.

"A robbery gone wrong, maybe." I looked at McConnell. "How did you know about the beer?"

His dimples deepened. "I overheard someone say that Claude had just moved a load out. Took me a while to put it together."

Oh.

"Which bothers you more, Julia?" Carl asked. "That he might have been murdered or that he was involved in moving booze?"

"Well, I'm shocked a law officer would do . . . that. I'm surprised there's enough money in running beer into Perry County for someone

45

to get killed over."

Carl leaned forward, earnestness making his blue eyes brighter than I'd ever seen them.

"Julia, some of the Anti-Saloon League people are fanatics. It's not the money. It's the booze itself that offends them."

McConnell smiled at his friend. "You know, Schroeder, I'm not a professional investigator, but I should think it's a mistake to assume you know who the perpetrator is—or his political affiliation—or even if there is a perpetrator—at the outset. I think we should just follow the evidence and see where it leads."

They stared at each other a moment, McConnell half-smiling and pleasant, Carl shaking his head.

"Fine, Will. We can go through the paces your way. But alcohol is involved, and Ingle is prohibition. Don't you think it would be a good idea to know why he had Henry come down and take that wheel to St. Louis? Why bother? Take up a collection and replace the damn thing." Carl jerked on the seat. "And don't you think it'll be a coincidence if a pleasant, credible, young prohibitionist takes over as sheriff, does a good job, influences a few votes, just before the election?"

"Ingle is obvious, Carl. I'll be down here as soon as I can, asking the best questions I can come up with. I'll surely ask why he sent the wheel to St. Louis. We'll keep an open mind, though, right? So we don't overlook the other possibilities."

"To be sure." Carl leaned back with a thud. "By the way, what are the other possibilities?"

McConnell and I looked at each other. "You first, Miss Nye."

I closed my eyes and tried to concentrate. "O.K. Maybe it truly was an accident. Maybe he had an apoplexy. Maybe it was a robbery that had nothing to do with prohibition politics. Maybe someone knew he'd have a lot of cash."

"Yes? Do we know if there was any cash found on the body?" Carl said.

His tone made me cross. "Several dollars. Not the kind of money Marjorie Picard expected."

"And you know this how?" McConnell said.

"My father asked."

"So he still had money. Maybe robbery is not so likely." The smirk on Carl's face was unbecoming.

Before I could say something equally unbecoming, McConnell said, "It could be robbery . . . by a smart robber who just took the larger amount." He shrugged. "You were doing a good job with your list. What else?"

Was he feeling sorry for me? *Stick to Picard*, I told myself.

"Maybe it is Ingle, but it has nothing to do with the booze," I said. "Maybe Ingle wants an extra couple of years in office. Maybe . . ." Now here was a scary one "Is there competition among beer-runners?"

Carl snorted. "The conflict, Julia, is between wets and drys."

McConnell was now frowning at Carl. "Follow the facts, Schroeder, not the politics. It should be easy enough to ask around about who's running beer. Although—a sheriff would be pretty stiff competition."

He stopped to look at me, and I said, "You're right."

Carl sighed and turned to stare out the window. McConnell pulled out a memo book and started to write. My thoughts turned to my father. If it had been my brother he needed help from, he'd have told him Claude Picard was a bootlegger. But of course, he would protect his daughter from such sordid affairs. I nursed my irritation to a healthy anger over the last half-hour of the ride.

◆ ◆ ◆

By the time I stalked into Union Station, I was in no mood to hear Carl and McConnell discussing which one should see me home. Truth was, though, it was dark. The streetcar was on its shorter nighttime route. I could certainly defend myself with my revolver, but shooting someone who happened to get close seemed overmuch, even in my present state. A man by my side would make the walk on Vandeventer at this hour safer—for me and maybe others.

It turned out McConnell lived closer.

We rode as close as we could get and then walked past businesses rising into the night. I let my anger lapse, pleased to enjoy the glimmer of the big five-globe lamps on the electric lines strung overhead. I glanced at McConnell, to see if my silence was a social blunder, and could tell he'd followed my gaze. He nodded.

At West Pine, he picked up the conversation. "Miss Nye, I must say that I'm worried about your involvement."

I was ready to be angry again, but I'd spent most of my energy in imaginary rants with Dad. I'd act as if I took him seriously. "Do you think I might be in danger by investigating?"

"You might."

"Wouldn't all three of us be in danger?"

"Yes, I suppose so."

"Then I should be concerned about you and Carl as well?"

He stopped by one of the smaller lampposts near the boarding house. "Are you worried about us, Miss Nye?"

"I hadn't thought to be, until now."

"That's a biased position—in reverse—isn't it?"

"You're right, Mr. McConnell. Perhaps I should have walked you to your lodging."

"Are you armed?"

"I am, as a matter of fact."

"Really? Would you walk me home if I asked?"

"No."

"Why not?"

"Because I have to be at work at six o'clock in the morning, and you'll wander into Police Headquarters in the middle of the afternoon."

McConnell laughed. "Actually, it might be later. I'll hope to make it in before you leave."

9

*From the **St. Louis Globe-Democrat**, Monday, June 10, 1910*

> *Special Dispatch from Ste. Genevieve, Mo. – The Globe-Democrat's sources have confirmed that Ste. Genevieve County Sheriff Claude Picard was engaged in transporting beer when he died in a wagon accident last week.*
>
> *The accident occurred near the boundary of Perry and Ste. Genevieve Counties. Perry County, outside the county seat of Perryville, is dry, while Ste. Genevieve is a wet county.*

I dreamed Sunday night that I was typing police reports in my tidy space between Chief Wright's office and the file room. The odd thing was that all the reports were about Claude Picard. I'd get one done, and then someone, Carl, William McConnell, several St. Louis detectives, Dad at one point, would come by and give me a new version of events. I was tired by the time I got to work Monday morning.

I'd worked an hour when Chief Wright arrived, came straight to my desk, and handed me a *Globe-Democrat*. I skimmed McConnell's story and looked at the Chief. He had to know that it was a very big stone to toss in the pond of public opinion. The ripples would last until the November elections for sure. But all he said was, "I guess you contacted your reporter friends."

Mid-afternoon, Carl came by. He stood still long enough to say hello and then bounded off to read the typed reports in the file room.

A few minutes later, I heard him talking—fast—in the nearby squad room. Off-duty patrolmen from the Central District and the detectives gathered there to drink coffee and chat. I could picture the cops rolling their eyes as he left.

It was after four when William McConnell pushed through the double doors at the head of the stair and made straight for my desk.

"Mr. McConnell. You were right. It's getting late. Have you rested well?"

McConnell sat in the chair in front of my desk. "Hello, Miss Nye. Long day?"

I softened. "I've been thinking and typing like mad. The good news is I've caught up on my work. The bad news is I'm exhausted, and even Carl running in and out is an annoyance."

"He never does anything by halves. And, I'm afraid I have more for you to think about."

"What have you been up to?"

"I've been back to Ste. Gen. The train ride is getting monotonous."

"You're not serious. Ste. Genevieve?" I stared at him. "Whom did you talk to?"

"Ingle. I'd planned on more, but it took a while. We sparred for forty-five minutes about the damn wheel." His eyebrows flicked. "Sorry."

"It's O.K., Mr. McConnell. The wheel belongs in the 'damn' category by now."

The apology changed to a grin. "Does the word not offend you because of your politics?"

I shrugged. "I don't think politics has anything to do with it. In fact, a lot of the women in the movement are . . . straitlaced. It's a good image because of the bad publicity we get anyway."

"Do you mean that strategy whereby your opponents refer to you as women of loose character because you use the streets for demonstrations and soap-boxing?"

I stared at him a moment. He looked back at me, a patient smile playing in the dimples, and I gave in.

"Yes. That's one strategy." I returned to the question. "What did you find out about the wheel?"

"Well, Ingle insisted he wanted the job done quickly, for Mrs. Picard, and the only one who would work on it in Ste. Gen County is some old guy who will take weeks. I couldn't shake him. He says he sent it to St. Louis in the keeping of his cousin Henry, who saw the package off the train Friday night, to be delivered on Saturday to Armbruster's Wheels, down on Third Street. And he'll have it back in a week." He paused. "Maybe it's that simple."

"I'm surprised the wheel can be fixed, judging from the impact to the railing."

"I agree. Ingle wouldn't answer any questions about how badly damaged the wheel was. Or much else. Seems Deputy Ingle is unhappy about my story this morning."

McConnell turned his hat in his hands and scooted to the edge of the chair. "I really have to get to work, explain where I've been. I'll ask this Armbruster about the wheel first thing in the morning. Can we meet for dinner tonight? I'll try to rein Carl in and get him to join us, and we'll go over Ingle's story."

A meal out with two men. Apparently he wasn't worried about the stroll in Soulard any more. Not to mention, he was including me in the detection. I wasn't sure Carl would have thought to suggest it.

I suppressed my smile and asked, "What time do you stop for dinner?"

"If nothing's happening, I usually go out about seven."

"So . . . do you want to call me at seven or what?"

"Why don't you come to the office?"

That's what a man would do, I realized.

"If I have a story working, you could maybe wait a few minutes? Then we'll meet Carl, who'll be late regardless of when we say we'll meet."

He did know Carl.

I smiled. "See you then."

He donned his straw, touched the snap-brim in a quasi-salute, and left.

A City Directory sat on the table behind me, and I fetched the big volume over to the light on my desk. I made note of the address of Armbruster's Wheels on Third Street, well into the industrial district.

I must have registered footsteps as I searched for the address, but they didn't cause me to look up until the sound ceased. In front of my desk.

Two of the detectives who'd been in my dream last night stood before me. Detective George St. Martin smiled. Detective Terence Kelley didn't.

Kelley looked down at the open City Directory and said, "Doing a little personal work on city time, are we?"

It was close to the truth, of course, but the last person I'd share that with was Terence Kelley.

Dad always said I made judgments on too little data. And that might have been the case with Detective Kelley. I didn't know anything about him, really. Maybe some tragedy in his past overshadowed his efforts at being civil. No one shared gossip about Terence Kelley.

He not only disapproved of my typing police reports; he never let me type his. When the Chief insisted everything be typed, Kelley started doing his own, on a machine that never delivered good quality. He'd drop the reports—or throw them—on my desk for me to file. Although . . . he excelled in the nasty business today.

"How do you know I'm not verifying an address on a report?" I wasn't terribly polite in asking, and I heard George sigh.

"Well, let's see," Kelley said. He turned the book with one hand and snatched the report I'd been typing with the other.

He couldn't have read all the addresses on the pages before him, but he pursed his lips, maybe in reaction to something he saw. He slammed the City Directory shut, tossed the officer's report in my direction, and turned to George. "Women working here," was all he said. The disgust in his tone finished the sentiment.

Kelley turned toward the doors as if he expected George to follow. The report slid off the side of the desk and fluttered to the floor. I followed its path and looked up to see a pained expression on George's face.

I knew of no other way to explain it than to admit that George St. Martin was interested in me. Exactly why he was interested wasn't clear. He didn't approve of my dress, my hair, my attitude, or my politics. It wasn't clear what was left. But he delighted in visiting me, sometimes daily, checking to make sure I hadn't converted to a more conventional mode. He hadn't asked to visit at Miller's boardinghouse—thank goodness. He simply let it be known that when I came to my senses, he intended to court me.

It wasn't that George was hard to look at. He had greenish-gray eyes ringed with dark lashes and dark hair that was never quite where it was supposed to be. He had small features. He was about my height, and when I stood next to him, I felt like an exaggerated version of him.

Just now, he leaned close on the desk and said, "You know, Julia, you really take this work too much to heart. You look fatigued." Then he fetched the paper and handed it to me, as if he were proud of himself.

"Bye," I said, and he wiggled his fingers as he followed his friend out the door.

I thumped the report back beside the typewriter, grabbed the Directory, and returned it to its spot.

One thing I could say for George: he befriended Terence Kelley, and that's more than I'd have done.

I got back to work. I had a stop to make on Third Street before seven.

◆ ◆ ◆

Armbruster's Wheels extended back a long, narrow way and opened onto the kind of alley that was more of a courtyard, convenient to working with wagons. I'd seen several parked there as I rounded the corner. In addition to servicing horse-drawn vehicles, Armbruster sold wheels and rubber tires for autos. He'd put together a shiny pile of hardware in a display window. Moving into the new century. I approved.

I tried the name, and the balding, diminutive man before me was indeed Mr. Armbruster.

"Yes, sir," I said. "I'm here to check on a damaged wheel that was sent to you from Ste. Genevieve County."

Mr. Armbruster narrowed his eyes.

"I'm asking for Mrs. Picard, you see, as to when the wheel might be done and," I hesitated to underscore my timidity, "exactly what the damage was."

Invoking her name seemed to help. Mr. Armbruster cocked his

head and regarded me. "And what did you say your name is, again, missy?"

I was going to have to swallow my usual reactions to familiarities like "missy" if I intended to do this job.

"My name is Julia Nye. My father, John Nye, is Sheriff of Callaway County. He and Sheriff Picard were old friends."

"Ah, the Kingdom of Callaway." He looked me over one more time. I tried for a smile that was all innocence and curiosity.

"And the widow sent you."

I hated to outright lie. "She does want to know what happened."

"I see. Of course. This way."

We went through an open door to the work area, lit by a bulb overhead. I unpinned my hat, so I wouldn't have to deal with the brim's shadow, and laid the straw on a worktable. I noted storage boxes and wheels of wood and metal propped about, and two large cans of Mobil oil. The area smelled of varnish. I was impressed that it was so neat and clean. Mr. Armbruster smiled at my expression and said the Picard wheel itself was in the dirt-floored area in back.

"You understand that all I got were pieces." He looked at me over his eyeglasses. "There is no fixing that wheel, of course."

I thought just fast enough to sound surprised. "Oh my. Then why did Deputy Ingle send it to you?"

He looked me over one more time, and when he answered, he was so intent that his words thickened with his German accent.

"The deputy wanted me to read what I could in the pieces. And I did do that, my dear. I read that someone had sawed the rim of that wheel partway through."

I drew a quick breath. Mr. Armbruster nodded, in approval of my realization, apparently.

"I do not know if the wheel finally failed because of a heavy load or a bad road. But I have the rim that separated and pieces of spokes. The weight of the axle would have made them go pop."

I stopped short of saying, "Damn." McConnell would've been proud. Apparently the look on my face was sufficient, because Mr. Armbruster nodded.

He said, "I will tell Deputy Ingle, of course, but maybe you could tell the Sheriff's widow."

Of course. Such a womanly thing to do.

"Here, let me show you, so you will understand." He headed toward the back.

I didn't like men opening doors for me, but I was trying to bend to convention for the sake of the investigation. Besides, Mr. Armbruster had told me more than I had any right to expect. I would embarrass him if I insisted he go first. So, I smiled and moved to the side as he twisted the knob.

I stepped through the doorway ahead of him and, for a second, I must have blocked his view of the amazing sight. Flames rolled from the large, open, back doors toward us. In the heart of the flames were two lanterns. They must have been lit and thrown not long before we opened the door. Flames sought out the sawdust on the workroom floor, and tiny explosions followed in the path of the broken lantern frames. And those little explosions ignited pieces of wood, packaging, and wheels.

The lanterns seemed to be headed toward us as if we were the tenpins and two bowlers had rolled their fiery balls simultaneously. Armbruster peered around my shoulder and screamed in my ear. Oddly, I flinched from the scream, not the flames. The flames fascinated me.

Just as Mr. Armbruster pulled on my arm, something hit the overhead light. I heard glass break, and the lighting changed from the electric glow to the dance of the flames. Almost immediately, I felt something explode in my hair, in the wing that hung in front of my left ear.

I grabbed at the lock and half expected to see a fistful of flame when I held my hand out in front of me. Instead, I saw a fistful of blood. I stared at it as Armbruster jerked me back and slammed the door shut. He pushed me toward the front office.

As we went by, he grabbed my hat. The motion took no time at all but it panicked me as thoroughly as if he'd stopped to locate something. We had no time for that. Someone had fired the back entrance. Lanterns might await us in front.

We staggered through the next door and then the front one. The street was empty. Mr. Armbruster leaned me up against a building next door and dropped the hat. The neighbors operated a tool shop that was sure to house lots of flammables. Armbruster flung their door open and screamed a warning. Then he ran back to me, grabbed my bag, and pressed it to my head. But, of course, my bag was not soft. The revolver in it clanked against my skull, and I winced.

"I must pull the alarm." His voice was distant, as if he were talking to me from halfway down the block already.

I did try to use the purse to stem the bleeding. It was as awkward as I'd expect. I decided to use my jacket for that purpose after I looked down and saw blood soaking the lapel. But to get the jacket off, I needed to slip the purse straps from my wrist. I stared at my bloody bag and couldn't figure out how to manage.

Armbruster was back in front of me. "Here, here, get away from the building." People from the tool shop were talking to me as well, but only Mr. Armbruster registered.

"Did you sound the alarm?" He seemed surprised I'd asked with some composure.

"No, no. The police officer called. He saw the flames flare as he walked the side street." He glanced at his shop and swallowed hard. "The back door may hold."

I nodded too hard and blood dripped on my arm. We made our way across the street where I leaned back against something solid and considered the wheel shop. I expected to see a tower of flame, but there was only shifting light through the front door.

Fire vehicles began arriving, the first ones taking the side street and pulling into the alley. I stared at the fire horses coming down Third Street. The one nearest me on the three-horse team snorted at the smell of smoke and rolled his eyes. But something in his horse language said he'd enjoyed the race through the streets, scattering buggies pulled by less important, probably inferior, animals. He and his fellows pounded the granite pavers and skidded to a stop almost in front of me.

I stopped considering the psychology of horses and listened to the men work. Excited voices were discussing how the fire had started. I let it wash over me.

A pat on the arm made me open my eyes. Mr. Armbruster was sweating but trying to smile. He turned to a familiar voice, one of the last I wanted to hear.

I looked away from the little wheelwright to see a tall, frowning shape. Terence Kelley's dark eyebrows lowered over glittering blue eyes and his solid, once-abused nose. He took my upper arm and turned me so he could look at my head.

"How did you get hurt?" I thought a greeting would be appropriate.

Mr. Armbruster answered. "She was hurt when something exploded."

Kelley finished his examination and let go of my arm. "It's not bad," he concluded. "Tell me, Miss Nye, why are you here?" Mr. Armbruster was making concerned noises, but Kelley ignored him as well as the blood that still dripped down my face and onto my clothes.

"I was asking after the wheel." I had some faint notion the strict truth wasn't necessary, but I couldn't think of anything else.

"What wheel is that? Do you examine wheels for a hobby, Miss Nye? Is that a new suffragist pursuit?"

I opened my mouth and nothing happened. Dear Mr. Armbruster came to my rescue. "She was asking about a wheel sent to me for repair. She helps out a family friend. This is poor payment, Detective, for her concern."

"Oh, Miss Nye is always helpful." He moved closer to me. "And what did you find out about your wheel, Miss Nye?"

Armbruster all but stepped between us. "We never got to it, Detective. When we opened the door, we ran into the flames. Will you investigate who started this?"

Kelley ignored him again and got closer to my face. "All this and you never saw the wheel you came to see?"

Mr. Armbruster said, "The wheel was in a shipment that had only come in today. We were ready to open the package."

I stared at the back of his head. That just wasn't what had happened. Mr. Armbruster looked around, willing me not to say anything, I thought. He turned back to Kelley and said, "She must see a doctor. Dr. Patterson will be in his office, a block over. Will you take her or do I?"

Kelley snorted. But he turned and called for a patrolman by the name of Jamison. The young officer took my arm and guided me out of the crowd that had gathered.

"Be careful, Miss Nye," Mr. Armbruster called.

I waved back in his direction and held onto Jamison. "Don't

worry, Miss Nye," he said. "We'll get you to Dr. Patterson, and he'll stitch this up."

That should have bothered me. But I was more concerned about why a senior detective was walking a beat in this particular part of town. Detectives didn't walk beats. Kelley would only be here if he were investigating something, or someone, in the area.

And why had Armbruster denied knowing the condition of the wheel to Terence Kelley—when he had told me everything I needed to know?

10

Carl had worried the question all day: how to connect the Ingles men to Picard's death, how to establish the prohibition link. Problem was, he had his real work to do.

The German Ambassador was freshly arrived from Washington D.C. Carl had started his day at a brunch, part of the first of two days' worth of activities.

It was the kind of event that made Carl realize how much he enjoyed rubbing elbows with dignitaries and serving their words back to the German community. It wasn't so much that he relished the power, although the German community was large and influential enough that there was some clout attached to the job. It was more a sense of being on the inside, knowing what was happening in the meeting rooms and chambers of the nation's fourth-largest city.

And then there was the freedom his job offered, freedom he was putting to good use today.

Having whipped out the Ambassador's story, he'd visited Julia, to see if anything was happening on the police front. Or, maybe, he admitted to himself, just to see Julia. Julia was energetic like him, but she could channel it into organizing her world—and Police Headquarters—and into her apparent passion for her work. Carl liked to sneak into the station and watch her.

On the way to Headquarters, Carl had toyed with the idea of finding out where Henry Ingle was on the day Sheriff Picard died. Or whether Ingle was a frequent visitor to his cousin James, perhaps to the end of working out a conspiracy to get rid of the Sheriff. He'd had trouble sleeping last night just imagining the prohibition-inspired implications of the sheriff's death.

Something about seeing Julia had made him think of the train trips they'd shared, and the thought of trains made him bounce back out of Headquarters. He intended to find the whereabouts of the wheel Henry had been dealing with Friday night.

Carl had headed to Union Station, searched out the porter who worked the cargo area, and struck up a conversation. It took five minutes to get around to talking about the awkward package the man had helped load onto a wagon headed for Armbruster's Wheels, over on Third. Apparently there was no easy way to bundle up a wagon wheel that felt as if it were in several pieces.

Armbruster's on Third Street. Carl thought he might make time to visit on his dinner break.

He'd have to make it quick, though. When he got back to the office, there was a message from William suggesting the three of them meet for supper at the delicatessen on Pine between the *Post* building and the *Globe* office.

Carl tried to stifle his impatience and write up some background on the Ambassador as a head start for tomorrow's full day. He was finishing up when his contact in the Fire Department called. Germans in the Department were few and far between, but the friend of a brother of a friend usually managed to alert him to any serious action. This action was serious, as far as Carl was concerned: a fire on Third Street.

11

Dr. Patterson was a nice man. His wife and assistant was a nice woman. That was saying a lot given that one wanted to put stitches in my head and the other wanted to cut one, just one, wing of hair. They finally convinced me to cooperate, not because of their kindness, but because she offered me a mirror.

It wasn't much more than a quarter of an hour before I had a half dozen black thread tracks in my forehead, covered by a tiny cloth bandage and held in place by ugly yellow tape. The bloody hair was gone, leaving a few ragged strands. I'd also washed my face and neck. I'd dabbed at my waist and jacket to no avail. The jacket was a summery green, and I looked like a Christmas display.

Not only had I lost two valuable pieces of wardrobe, but now I'd have to change clothes and I'd be late to the *Globe* to meet McConnell.

I paid the doctor and promised to come back next Monday to get the stitches out. I turned to leave, wobbling only a little, and thought I must have conjured William McConnell. He stood framed in the doorway.

He looked . . . worried, for lack of a better word. In my muzzy state, I considered why I thought that. His eyebrows were closer together than usual, I decided. I wasn't sure I could make mine do that. I tried and the stitches pulled at my forehead. I came back to the moment when he put his hands on his hips and said, "Damn. Is 'damn' an appropriate word now, Miss Nye?"

I smiled. "No, Mr. McConnell. Not that I'm offended, but damn is too strong a word. It's only a cut."

Dr. Patterson jumped in to say, "That's right. It's only a cut. But you're dizzy because of the blood loss. That's why you need to go home and take it easy." He interrupted himself. "Do you work?"

"Yes. Don't tell me I can't go to work."

"Well, you shouldn't. Stay home and rest for a few days. Let your blood build back up."

"I work sitting down. I'll manage."

McConnell didn't seem surprised at my attitude. He held the door for me, and I didn't have the energy to protest. I took a deep breath and stepped onto the sidewalk.

Smoke drifted about, but I saw no sign of flames. Noises from Third Street were louder than I'd expect for a workday, but this street was quiet. Everyone was no doubt taking in the excitement a couple of blocks over.

McConnell took my elbow without asking.

"I don't need your help." I tried to compose myself, which wasn't easy given the state of my clothes and hair. I couldn't remember where my hat had ended up. Soaked, or worse, I supposed. One more loss.

McConnell didn't let go of my arm.

"You need someone's help. It won't do either of us any good if you end up staggering down the street." He paused a moment and added, "You could take my arm if you want to."

I had a stock of sarcastic comments about women who couldn't walk around the block without holding onto a man. None of the remarks seemed appropriate just now. I tucked my hand in the crook of his elbow, for all the world like any conventional couple out for a bloodied stroll.

Once I steadied enough to walk without swaying, he asked what had happened. I took my first opportunity to picture it, to think it through, starting with opening the door to Armbruster's back room. I explained what I'd seen.

"Someone threw the lanterns, just as you stepped into that room?" McConnell's eyebrows were angled sharply toward his nose. If I'd thought that look meant he was angry with me, I'd have staggered off on my own.

"No, before we entered. I don't remember hearing them hit." As I explained it to him, I began to worry about more than my appearance. I tightened my grip on his arm.

"The lanterns were still rolling, though, so it must have been just before Mr. Armbruster opened the door. The light fixture broke as I was staring at the lanterns. That's what I remember hearing."

"And that's what cut you? Do you know what broke it?"

I thought another moment and shook my head. Which was a mistake. When I stopped swaying, McConnell resumed walking at a slower pace.

After a couple of seconds, he said, "Would you recognize a gunshot?"

I stopped walking. I wanted to say that of course Sheriff Nye's daughter would recognize a gunshot. But, as a matter of fact, it only now occurred to me that it might have been that. I thought back and just couldn't be sure.

McConnell had turned to me, still supporting my arm, as I pictured it. "It might have been."

I looked up to eyes that were registering concern along with anger. "Fire and a possible gunshot," he said. "Why? What were you about to do?"

"Mr. Armbruster was going to show me the remains of the wheel." I paused, trying to think. "The fire may have destroyed that."

McConnell was still looking at me, but he likely was trying to picture the scene, probably unaware that he had shifted to holding my hand now. "How far from the light fixture were you?"

It was a good thing he was patient. As I thought about it, he tucked my hand back on his arm and started us walking again.

"I'd say almost twelve feet. It was over a table, I think, and the ceiling was high."

"The shot wasn't aimed at you, then."

"No, if it was a shot, as opposed to . . . something exploding from the flames . . . it was meant to take out the light."

"Maybe so Armbruster couldn't see to grab up the wheel parts."

"Or," I was slowing almost to a stop on this one, "so we couldn't see the man who threw the lanterns."

"Was he inside?"

I turned to McConnell. "There was an opening in back, big doors, like you'd need for wagons."

We were, for reasons I didn't stop to consider, holding each other's hands again as he said, "So the man probably strolled on down the alley."

I was looking at McConnell as he checked behind us. He reacted to something, and I turned to see Carl, no more than half a block away. Then he was calling to us: "Julia! William!"

I let go of McConnell's hand to turn, and I wobbled. He grabbed my elbow again, but a second later, Carl pulled both my arms toward him, handing McConnell my hat in the same move.

"Julia, for God's sake, you look as if you've been in a butcher shop. Are you cut? Are you O.K.?" He was all but shaking me, and I was worried he was going to hug me right there on the street.

"I'm O.K., Carl."

"Why in the world did you do that?" He shook my arms again, and McConnell stepped in.

"Don't shake her, Carl. We don't need her collapsing on the street. And do stop yelling." He stood there holding my hat and looking peeved at his friend. "We need to get Julia to her house, or someplace we can talk. Let's decide while we head for the streetcar."

"She could've been badly hurt. Look at this!" Carl yelled anyway.

McConnell pulled me away from the redheaded fury and offered the hat, "Do you want to put this on? Someone must have rescued it before it got too wet." I nodded, carefully because I could feel each stitch holding its piece of my forehead together. The hat would cover the bandage and the lopsided hairdo.

I pinned it on, also carefully, and McConnell said, "Come on, Carl. Let's get going."

Carl made little huffing sounds, but he took my arm, pulling me away from McConnell. "Kelley said you were there looking at wheels."

He didn't wait for my reply. He looked at McConnell over my head. "Did you send her in there?"

"Of course not," was all McConnell said, although his tone might have told Carl not to be silly.

"Carl, I know you're concerned. But I decided to see if Mr. Armbruster had figured out anything before I met you two for dinner. Aside from what I learned, we know now that someone didn't want us to see the wheel. It's been a productive day. So, calm down. I only need to get someplace and sit for a while, O.K.?"

"It's your last productive day. I can't believe you've gotten hurt doing this. You know your father will be furious with us for letting this happen." In his anger, Carl was pulling me along faster than I wanted to walk. In my anger, I came to a complete halt, and we had a small tug of war.

"You didn't *let* anything happen, Carl. It happened because that's the way it is. If you think I'm stopping now, you're dead wrong. And my father doesn't need to know anything about it."

"Oh, you think he's not going to notice a scar on your face? You think he's not going to blame us?"

"I can't believe you're saying this, Carl." I stopped short of saying I'd expect this argument from William McConnell. "You will not tell me what to do."

Carl crossed his arms and rooted himself in place.

McConnell said, "I don't want to tell either of you what to do, but standing in the middle of the street yelling at each other is not accomplishing anything. Julia does need to sit down. Come on, Carl, let's get to the street-car."

McConnell was smart enough not to take my arm, and Carl wasn't touching me either. So I was free to turn and walk with as much dignity as possible toward the streetcar line on Broadway. The two of them followed me closely, not saying anything. Out loud, that is.

12

I wanted to tell them what I'd heard and get home. It looked like both men were going to escort me there, and I'd have time for the story because the car would make every possible stop at this time of day. I surely didn't want to tell the story in front of my housemates, particularly Amelia. The trick was to figure out how to be inconspicuous on a streetcar. With great luck, I found a seat at the end of the bench, and they stood in front of me, Carl still glaring. I decided to be as casual as possible and hope fellow-riders picked up on my tone, not the content.

McConnell's opening fit my plan perfectly. He was calm as could be, just chatting with friends. "Carl, you said Kelley told you . . . something. What Kelley?"

Carl stared at him a moment. "Terence Kelley."

"He called in the alarm," I added, matching McConnell's casual style.

Carl jerked, and it wasn't because the car stopped. He wasn't as good at this as McConnell.

"Did he say why he was there?" McConnell asked me.

"No. He just . . . appeared."

Carl and McConnell raised eyebrows at each other, and Carl muttered something about Kelley. The woman beside me stared at him and seemed happy to get off at the end of the block. Carl immediately took the seat.

I looked up at McConnell. "You know, the strangest thing happened. When Detective Kelley asked me why I was there, Mr. Armbruster insisted on answering him." I hoped I implied to anyone listening that men were just so complicated. McConnell stretched his dimples and nodded.

"In fact," I continued, "Mr. Armbruster told him we hadn't even seen the silly wheel, hadn't gotten around to opening anything in the shipment."

Carl said, "So . . . I guess we won't know how it was damaged."

"Oh, no, Carl. Mr. Armbruster really had opened it, you see, and he'd told me all about it."

I hoped that sounded . . . cute . . . or coy . . . to the folks around us. Instead of indicating the seriousness of the crime I was about to reveal. I also hoped William McConnell didn't think I sounded like this all the time, although I didn't know why I should care.

But, he probably didn't think that. Because I thought he was acting as well when he smiled and said, "So, you do know something, Julia. Are you going to tell us?"

I fluttered my lashes as if I had gossip to offer. Both men leaned in to hear.

"Well, I'll bet you didn't know the wheel was damaged before the accident."

Carl froze for a second and then leaned closer still. "Now, Julia. How could Armbruster know that?" He smiled, too. Lordy, I hoped no one I knew saw this flirting routine.

I had to get this out before I lost my wits entirely. "Armbruster said the rim had been sawn part way through, to break down on a bad road or under a heavy load."

The car stopped as we stared from one to the other. New riders settled in and stared at the three of us.

We rode in silence for part of the block, until Carl picked up the conversation, speaking in casual character to McConnell. "What would have made this wheel go? There was no cargo."

"Maybe just the bridge. If he hit the edge of those tracks . . ." McConnell could have been talking to himself.

"I wonder," I said, "if someone could have emptied the wagon . . . afterwards."

"And Ingle could cover up the timing." I could feel Carl all but bounce on the seat beside me. McConnell shot him a look.

We stayed quiet after that, until the car stopped two blocks from the boarding house. I was dizzy when I stood and had trouble making it off the platform before the car started moving again. Both men hovered close enough to grab an elbow if I tottered. I took up a gentle pace and resumed the conversation.

"Somehow I don't think James Ingle is behind this."

Carl had trouble moving at my pace, getting ahead of us, stopping, starting again. "Of course he is. He's Anti-Saloon League, his whole family is, and now he's in line to be sheriff. That's two motives. Why don't you think he'd be involved?"

"It's a hunch, I guess. He doesn't look the type to damage a wheel knowing it could harm the man who'd hired him. Or anyone else."

"Look the type?" Carl hooted in the freedom of the sidewalk. "Wait, tell me, Julia, what does a murderer look like? Dark hair, dark eyes, don't you think, Will? A drooping mustache. Hell, a drooping eye."

I rolled my eyes and that hurt. I was back to not having much patience with Carl.

McConnell, on the other hand, smiled. "I don't know about the drooping eye, Carl. After all, maybe whoever did it just wanted to stop the shipment. That's second degree felony murder at the most."

O.K. I was out of patience with both of them.

"Although," McConnell said, "I agree."

"Agree with what?" I asked.

"You. My instinct is to believe Ingle, too."

◆　◆　◆

We were almost to the porch when Carl did take my arm.

"Here's what you do, Julia: gather a few of the women outside. Fran will join me, won't she? And somehow you suggest that Amelia Ingle join us, too. See?"

"No, I don't see, Carl." I pulled my arm loose. "Why do you have to talk to Amelia tonight?"

"I want her to say something incriminating about her brother or her cousin. They're the obvious suspects, I tell you."

I sighed, and McConnell tried his hand. "Why don't we wait an evening, Carl?"

"Maybe Amelia doesn't know about the wheel—or the fire. We need to talk to her before she has a chance to talk to Henry." Carl was knocking, not even waiting for me to open my own door.

And wouldn't you know, Amelia Ingle came bustling up. I knew the business-like opening of the door: nothing casual, nothing days-end weary, just another task to do to keep the lambs in line.

She burst out of the door, her hair bristling. "Julia! Look at you. Come in here right now. What have you done to yourself? That jacket! Your beautiful sewing, dear, I'm so sorry. Whatever happened?"

Amelia didn't wait for an answer. She'd dragged me halfway across the parlor when she looked back and saw Carl and McConnell just inside her door. She smiled and said, "Thank you, Carl. I'll take care of her now." But she was looking at William McConnell.

Amelia's blue eyes sparkled when she was either pleased or irritated or intense, which, between the three, was almost all the time. She had a wonderful smile and a somewhat sharp little nose. Just now, her smile had an edge, and she looked like a pretty fox.

Carl didn't leave, of course. "Now, Amelia, Julia's fine, and we thought we might sit a bit before we head back to work. Is Fran here? I wanted to chat with her. Let Julia get cleaned up and then join us. Oh, do you know Mr. McConnell? One of my fellow reporters."

Fran did come in during the introductions, and so did Claire. Mary appeared from the kitchen, towel in hand.

Fran had heard Carl invite himself to a spell on the porch, and she was more than happy to oblige. Fran fancied Carl. And now her big brown eyes were smiling along with her petite mouth. Fran's features were individually pretty. They didn't seem to belong on the same face. Claire was much more conventionally pretty. Her nose tipped up, and her blonde hair went willingly into a Gibson girl every morning. All she lacked was Amelia's sparkle, something I couldn't define. Men seemed to understand Amelia's allure effortlessly.

I thought McConnell was looking back and forth between Claire and Amelia, but I could have been confused because of the dizziness. When everyone was done looking each other over, McConnell, Carl, Claire, and Fran moved to the front porch. Mary called after them that she'd bring some iced tea out after she got me fed.

"Julia, look at your bag," Amelia said, and I turned back to her. "It's all bloody." She lifted the bag from my wrist. "It's also heavy. What do you carry in here?"

I hesitated, but only for a moment. It didn't much matter that she knew.

"A revolver. Listen, Amelia, I'd really like to go change."

The fox was more evident. "Why do you carry a gun?"

I gently pulled the bag from her grasp. Not that the gun needed special care. It was a Hopkins & Allen .32 police positive, and one of the reasons I carried it was because it wouldn't fire if it were bumped or dropped.

"For protection, of course."

"Protection against whom?" Her frown made me more determined not to play into her concerns.

"No one in particular," I said lightly and changed the subject. "Are you doing some laundry tonight?"

"Oh, yes, I could do a bit of mine and a bit of yours. Do you want me to help you upstairs?"

"No, thanks, I'm going to get a cup of coffee and take it up while I change."

She moved between the kitchen and me. "Are you going to tell me what happened?"

Put that way, no. I liked Amelia, admired her, but sometimes she pushed and I dug in.

"It was nothing. I have a little cut and it bled a lot. Let me wash my face, and I'll be back down in a minute."

I gave up on the coffee and started for the stairs. Amelia took a sharp breath and was blowing it out noisily as she swooped up a *Post-Dispatch* and headed for the front door. The way she walked and the reception Carl had planned almost made me want to hurry.

I was halfway up the first flight when I heard Amelia say, "So, Mr. Schroeder, Mr. McConnell, do you gentlemen know any more about this story?"

The afternoon *Post-Dispatch* likely had picked up on McConnell's morning story about Claude Picard. Amelia was playing right into Carl's plan.

In my room, I peeled off the jacket and waist, now cooled and sticky with my blood, and tried to avoid smearing it on my skin. I dug out an old blouse that gathered and extended over my skirt by several inches. I glanced in the mirror and then grabbed scissors to even up my hairline before I could think about it. No choice, really. I headed down the stairs.

The scene on the porch spoke volumes. Amelia was pacing. Neither Carl nor McConnell was standing for her. Amelia must have started off in a chair but jumped to her feet to make a point.

Carl was leaning forward, elbows on his knees. His mouth was working as if he were readying himself for an opening in Amelia's diatribe.

Fran was deciding, I could tell, whether to side with Carl or with Amelia, looking back and forth between them. One response might smooth the path to romance but it would make life miserable at home. Claire fidgeted. Amelia's passion was making her nervous, as usual.

McConnell sat very still, eyes following Amelia as she moved around the swing to the steps and back, continuing a monologue I'd heard before. Amelia must have spent her school days making and wearing—and nagging other people to wear—the blue ribbons of abstention. She knew all the phrases.

"The beer that man carried greased the path to an inebriate's grave." Her voice rose, and she came to a stop in front of Carl, a finger jabbing the air in front of his face.

"That is beyond reason, Amelia," Carl said. "There're probably one or two people, at most three or four, in both Perry and Ste. Genevieve counties who drinks too much. Telling everyone they can't drink is a violation of personal freedom. It's un-American."

"Indeed, Mr. Schroeder? And you're an expert on what's

American? I believe my family knows a bit about that. Drinking is a plague on the land, it's ..."

"Just a minute, Miss Ingle," Carl interrupted. "Are you implying that I don't know the American justice system as well as someone named Ingle? Is that what you just said?"

Amelia had an answer for that, I was sure, but McConnell spoke up. "Miss Ingle, did you know that Sheriff Picard was transporting beer—before the stories ran?"

Carl thumped back in his chair, glaring at her. Amelia froze for a moment. Then smiled. Like a fox. "Why, Mr. McConnell, it's common knowledge in Ste. Genevieve County. My cousin is Chief Deputy there, and he's spoken of it, of course."

That was the opening Carl had wanted, I thought. Instead, he said, "Oh, really, Amelia? And if your cousin shares the family awareness of what's right for Americans, how come he'd work for a man who ... who helped redress that stupid law?"

Honestly, Carl. The question should have been phrased in a way that would get an answer, not an explosion. McConnell sighed and closed his eyes for a second. When he opened them, he glanced at me. I shook my head.

"Stupid law?" Amelia hissed. "Someday the whole country will wake up and know the temperance truth, and we won't have this nonsense about wet counties and dry counties."

Carl shouted, "And I suppose the government will tell people who they can marry and how many children to have, as well!"

That shocked everyone into silence. Even Amelia didn't have a comeback for the intimate question about families. So, I decided to air my own concerns.

"Both of you are missing the point here. Aside from prohibition, it seems that a law officer was helping someone else break the law.

That's a moral question I'd like to talk about." If I had more energy. "It's just as important as the law itself, no?"

Fran and Claire nodded vigorously, trying to change the subject. Fran started to say something but was drowned out by Carl and Amelia shouting, in unison, "No!"

McConnell chuckled, and they both turned to him and started in again. He just sat there, the creases beside his mouth suggesting amusement, and looked from one to the other. After several minutes, he looked over at me. I shrugged and slumped.

McConnell stood and widened his grin, just for me, and said, "You should get some rest, Miss Nye. You lost a lot of blood for a little cut. I'll see you at Headquarters tomorrow, I trust."

I managed to stand. "Thanks for your help." McConnell touched the brim of his straw, said, "Ladies," and headed down the steps. Carl made leaving noises and followed, sans smile for me or anyone else. Fran sighed.

When I turned around, Amelia was glaring at his back. And then she turned the glare on me. I headed for the door before she could continue her tirade.

I hoped the day's events had given McConnell something to go on. I feared Carl had only picked up more to be angry about. Once I got just a bit of rest, I needed to think through who could have gotten to a sheriff's wagon to do the kind of damage Armbruster had described. And who would want to. And what Terence Kelley was about.

13

Lord, these women were too much. Amelia Ingle was worse than her brother, if that were possible. The sight of the little shrew put Carl in a foul mood. Or at least it would after tonight. Looks only went so far. And Julia going on about the morality of running beer. Good Lord.

Carl stomped down the street and then realized William was almost a building-length behind him. He turned and caught William's tight-lipped grin.

"Go on if you want to, Carl. You could make it to the *Post* in a couple of minutes. Maybe I should telephone from somewhere"—he gestured at a corner store—"and warn the city room."

"Funny, Will. I'm telling you the Ingle family has stooped to murder, and you think it's funny."

"Murder isn't funny, Carl. Your letting Amelia Ingle provoke you is funny."

Carl stopped in the street, ignoring the approaching car. "I did no such thing. Provoke me to what?"

"Provoke you into losing the opportunity to ask a few good questions."

William swung onto the platform of the slowing streetcar. Carl might have liked the walk, but now he had to answer this charge, so he swung up beside his friend. Trouble was, William wasn't often wrong about such things.

He said, "Oh, for heaven's sake, Will," while he thought about a real answer.

William went on, though, staring back in the direction of the boarding house. "We need to talk to Kelley," he said and added, with more enthusiasm, "Maybe Julia can find the opportunity to talk to Amelia Ingle some more, ask her about her cousin, under the guise of concern about the beer-running. What do you think? Can Miss Nye be subtle, play it out?"

William glanced back at Carl, who faked a huge sigh and leaned into his friend.

"Look, Will, we can't get Julia any more involved in this. She's gone and gotten hurt. You know damn good and well her father didn't ask her to investigate. He asked her to ask us. It may be a good thing she's hurt, come to think of it. Maybe she'll stay home and out of our way."

Carl thought Will was trying to be serious but the grin edged back across his face. "You know her better than I do, but I have the feeling she's not likely to stay out of our way." The grin widened until the deep vertical creases formed into rough dimples. "In fact, her father might've asked her to work with us. He knows her better than either of us do—and she's a pistol."

Carl didn't argue because it was true. Not that her father would ask her to get involved, but that Julia was headstrong and smart and would keep investigating if she wanted to. Carl couldn't imagine she wouldn't want to. What bothered Carl more at the moment was William staring back down Market with that grin still on his face. So, in addition to worrying about prohibition-crazed conspirators and German dignitaries, Carl was going to have to decide about Julia. Was it time to stop imagining some future romance and ask for a date—before William McConnell beat him to it?

14

From the St. Louis Globe-Democrat, Tuesday, June 11, 1910

> *St. Louis city fire officials are investigating the cause of a fire that destroyed the rear of Armbruster's Wheels, on Third Street. A witness on the scene suggested that the fire may have been arson. A police investigation is being launched, as well.*
>
> *Fire crews managed to save two-thirds of the interior because of a timely alarm and quick response, according to Fire Chief Herbert Daniels.*

I got to Headquarters a little after six the next morning and tried to work on the night shift reports. My head hurt, but I didn't think that was the problem. I just had to concentrate on not moving fast, or I got dizzy. Maybe I could convince the Chief I was O.K. if he only saw me behind my desk.

I acted as the Chief's unofficial secretary, although typing reports was my only job most of the time. There was a real Department Secretary, a man, of course, who did official Department and Police Commission work. He kept busy in his own office and didn't have much to do with me. There was a clerk, also male, who worked for him, another clerk downstairs to help the desk sergeant, and several clerks who worked for the police department but had desks in Four Courts, over on Clark. All men. The Chief sometimes had me take messages when he was out—or had me run interference. I was good at that. It meant I had a telephone on a table just behind my desk. It didn't ring too often, but I was always thrilled when it did.

Just after eight it trilled, and I yelped. Very few people were around to hear me. Two heads popped out of the squad room, and I waved at them. I swallowed hard, stood after only two tries, and picked up on the third ring.

I'd have been surprised whoever it was, but a call from David Picard was welcome.

"Miss Nye, is that you?"

It took me a moment, but I assured him he'd made the right connection.

"Miss Nye, I can't seem to find out more about that wheel. Deputy Ingle is saying he won't know anything until the wheelwright in St. Louis gets it back to him."

Bless his heart. I couldn't decide whether or not to tell him what I knew. A voice in my head said that if Mr. Armbruster wanted to be careful, I should be too.

"Well, David—"

"Besides, there's more happening here."

I hadn't even had to respond about the wheel. "What's that?"

"I went in early this morning to ask Deputy Ingle about the wheel, and he was heading out to look for a man who lives here. He thinks the man might have been the one who tried to set a fire during the night over in Perry County."

"A fire? Where—and was anyone hurt?"

"A family named Kline. They were . . . associates of Papa's. They're saying no was hurt, but Mama is upset."

"When was it and have they told you who they think did it?"

"No, ma'am. He didn't say who. And I think it started toward dawn."

David was speaking quickly, sounding eager to get off the telephone. Long-distance connections were expensive.

"Thank you for calling, David. We'll be in touch."

I was eager to get off the line—and sit—as well. I turned to find Chief Wright in front of my desk. He had his hands on his hips and was staring at me.

I depressed the hook with one hand and waved the earpiece at the Chief. "David Picard."

That made his eyebrows pop up. "Join me in my office, Miss Nye."

I followed him, not as fast as I would normally move. He was behind his desk and watching me, lamps already lit, when I got into the room. "Do you need to sit down?"

I'd liked to have said, "Of course not," but the sad thing was that I did need to sit.

"What have you done to yourself?"

There wasn't much point in anything but the truth. The morning paper had said a young woman customer was slightly injured. And presumably Terence Kelley would type up his own report, some day. I tried to make it seem that I was asking after the wheel for Marjorie Picard out of courtesy.

"It's only a small cut. It just bled a lot, and that's why I'm tired. But I'm fine."

Before he could disagree with me, I added, "That's not the big news."

"Well, young lady, before you give me any more news, let me tell you that you're through here for the next couple of days. I suspect this Dr. Patterson told you to stay home and you didn't have the sense to telephone in and tell me. Correct?"

I realized I shouldn't have bothered to come to work—although I tried never to miss, on principle. This was my chance to head south to do some real investigating. Talk to Marjorie Picard some more, figure out what was going on with the barn fire. There were two problems with that. The Chief might look after me, and I wasn't sure I could even make my way to Union Station.

"You know your father and I never intended for you to get involved in this matter. Couldn't McConnell or Schroeder have asked after the wheels?"

"I thought it was a simple matter, sir." That was honest. Maybe I'd expected getting the information to be more difficult. I'd certainly thought it would all be simple compared to what had happened.

"Well, from here on, you take it easy, and let them contact people. The fire at the wheel shop was no accident, you know."

How dotty did he think I was? "I know, sir. I'll be careful. I've just been the one to talk with Mrs. Picard, that's all."

"Very well. What's your big news?"

"Someone tried to burn a barn in Perry County last night."

"A barn."

"David Picard says the barn was owned by a family named Kline. He thinks it had something to do with the cargo."

The Chief sat down at last. "I don't know the name Kline, of course. Paul Carrey is sheriff down there, and he does a good job of enforcing the law—all the law." The Chief rubbed his forehead and sighed.

I wasn't too sure what he meant, and he read it. "I mean he has to deal with Perryville being wet and the rest of the county dry. He enforces the law carefully, which isn't easy. This prohibition thing is more trouble than it's worth." He looked at me with a frown. "Not that you should repeat that to anyone."

I tried to shake my head and stopped because it made me dizzy. I pushed up on the chair arms and stood. "What about the reports? I'll get behind."

He waved away my protest. "My dear, we got by with hand-written reports for a good number of years. I know you take this seriously, but we can file hand-written reports for a few days. If you can make it in by the end of the week, we'll pick up there." He got up and rounded the end of his desk.

"Julia, you know how precious you are to your father. Don't get hurt. Go home and rest. Someone is pushing this. We can investigate the fire here, and Carrey can do it down there." He put his hands on my shoulders and looked me in the eye. He was about my height. "You understand me, right?"

"I understand you, Chief Wright. Thank you for your concern. I'll be back as soon as I feel like it, I promise."

He shook his head and escorted me out. I even let him get the door.

◆ ◆ ◆

As I left, the thought nagged at me. Maybe we should all three take the Chief's advice. Someone was willing to set fires if not do something more aggressive. Would Carl or McConnell pursue this because they thought I was set on doing it? They might suggest I quit, but they wouldn't want to seem to back down themselves. I did, despite my politics, understand men somewhat. So, the question was whether I should continue, risking all three of us. It wasn't a problem I'd envisioned in my detecting fantasies.

I wanted to talk to William McConnell. I didn't trust Carl's insistence on suspecting the Ingles because of their prohibition stand.

So, I returned home. We had a telephone in the parlor, with a neatly lettered sign that read, "No out-of-the-city conversations, please, ladies."

McConnell had given me his exchange—just in case. I was dialing it when Amelia came bouncing in. She has to be at work at nine o'clock, I think. I'm never there when she leaves.

"Oh, Julia, you're home. Are you not feeling well? I didn't think you should go to work." She paused. "Who are you calling, dear?"

Just then, McConnell picked up. I tried waving Amelia away but she stood fast.

"Hello," I responded when McConnell answered. At least I thought fast enough not to use his name—and to greet him like a woman friend. "It's Julia."

"Are you O.K.?" he said, and I could imagine the frown that went with that tone.

"I'm O.K., but the Chief insisted I come home." I didn't know what else to say in front of Amelia.

"Well, that's a good idea, Julia. Although I'm surprised you agreed to it." There was a pause on his part along with my own hesitation as I registered his use of my given name.

"Pardon me a moment, please." I lowered the mouthpiece. "I'm fine, really, Amelia. Don't be late to work."

I heard McConnell chuckle on the other end. Amelia put her hands on her hips, which said she wasn't going to move. "Who are you talking to?" she whispered.

McConnell all but whispered. "Amelia Ingle, right? O.K. Do we need to meet? Why don't you go lie down and let her leave for work? Then meet me, if you feel like it, at the *Globe*. I can be at the front door in an hour. Will that work?"

"You're right. Resting is a good idea. I'll take your advice and talk to you later."

McConnell chuckled again and said, "I'll see you soon. Be careful."

I slouched in the chair, suggesting I was going to nap right there. "Just a friend. I promised I'd let her know how I was, and if I'd be home." I closed my eyes and waved her away. "Really, Amelia, don't be late to work."

I opened my eyes maybe a minute later. She was moving toward the door but looked back at me. "You stay here today."

It sounded like a warning.

15

I fished out a combination purse and travel satchel and put the extra ammunition and a few toiletries in it. I grabbed clean linen along with a white waist, a gown, and a shawl. If I had to spend the night in Ste. Genevieve, the waist would go with the old skirt. And the baggage fit with the note I attached to my bedroom door, saying I was off to see my father in Callaway County for a couple of days.

I took the gun out of my skirt pocket and put it in an inside pocket near the opening of the bag. Even with petticoats underneath, the revolver banged against my leg and annoyed me when I hurried, which I had to do if I was going to meet McConnell on time.

I was panting by the time I got to the *Globe* building. Maybe blood loss did take something out of you. McConnell waited, chatting with a man who stared at me and then entered the building. I looked up at the big bays jutting out toward the intersection of Sixth and Pine. And got dizzy again.

When I managed to look at him, McConnell was staring at the satchel. But he didn't say anything about it.

We ended up at a delicatessen, a small place tucked in among larger concerns along Pine Street. McConnell had a late breakfast, and I had coffee.

Once his order arrived and I was steadier, he said, "Any more fires?"

I nodded, suggesting I wasn't even surprised he'd guessed. But he hadn't been guessing. He was just making conversation, apparently. Egg dripped from a fork as he stopped halfway to his mouth. "You're kidding. Where?"

"A barn in rural Perry County. A family named Kline, who had some connection with Sheriff Picard. It was more an attempted fire, I guess. But Ingle was already looking for someone he thought might be involved about eight."

"Eight this morning?"

"Yes, of course." I started to add the arsonist couldn't have traveled from downtown St. Louis by eight o'clock last night. It was a flip answer, but the thought made me shiver. Darn, it wasn't like me to shiver drinking coffee at mid-morning in June.

"What is it, Julia?"

I shook my head to clear it, and that didn't work, so I sat very still for a moment. Then I smiled and tried to explain.

"I started to be sarcastic—can you imagine?—and say it couldn't be eight o'clock last night because our arsonist couldn't have made it to Perry County that fast." His eyes widened. I lowered my voice. "You don't suppose it was the same person, do you?"

"Damn," he said softly. So no one but me could be offended.

He pushed at his food for a minute. "I need to get down there. This is getting serious, and I need to continue our investigation. But, we need to be careful."

I knew what was coming: the next suggestion that I stay out of harm's way. Trouble was, I half agreed with him.

"You're going to say I shouldn't be involved anymore, aren't you?"

"Yes."

"And I'm not sure any of us should be involved. Ingle—or someone else—is going to be more wary of you and Carl than of me. I worry for the two of you."

He seemed to consider that, staring at me. Then he took a couple of bites. I drank a sip of the good coffee.

He put his fork down, balancing it on the plate edge.

"Julia, I've been in danger before. Sometimes, the only way you get close to the police is to go out with them, on the street. And once you do get in with them, the whole point is being there when there's action. It's why I carry a gun." He shook his head. "I'm willing to keep looking into this. It's potentially a big story, and it covers several police jurisdictions. I never did get to Perry County. But I have to get there today. Even if I don't make it back tonight, I have to phone a story in."

His eyebrows angled down a bit more, and I interpreted it to mean he was responding to my concerns. "So, I'll keep at it. I don't know if Carl needs to. The *Post* has other axes to grind, and I could feed him enough to keep his editors happy. And you do need to back out." He stopped. "How did you learn about the fire anyway?"

"David Picard called me. He was distressed because he hadn't found out anything about the wheel."

He groaned, and I nodded.

"I agree I don't need to be following you around. But I intend to go and talk to Mrs. Picard. David seems to know all sorts of things, and I imagine she does, too. I can get off the train at Ste. Gen, and you can go on to Perryville."

"I may need to stay the night."

"I can come back on my own." Of course, I didn't want to do that. "Or Mrs. Picard would keep me for the night. I did pack for it."

"You packed for a visit?"

"Well, I needed to make it look good. The note on my door says I'm off to Callaway County. I'm not about to sit around and have

Amelia Ingle smother me for a day or two. And I don't want to be here when Carl finds out you've gone without him." For that matter, I didn't want to answer to Carl as to why I'd go without talking to him.

"You're amazing," he muttered. I didn't know how to answer that, so I added the clincher.

"Besides, you said the train ride is getting monotonous."

McConnell laughed. "O.K. But will you please stay with Mrs. Picard until I'm ready to come back? I wouldn't mind your help thinking things through."

"Yes, of course," I agreed, trying for demure. I could tell from his raised eyebrow he wasn't fooled.

◆ ◆ ◆

I did not find the train-ride monotonous. We discussed the case and what he hoped to find out. And what I might find out from Mrs. Picard. And whether I should expect a visit from Deputy Ingle. William concluded that I was as safe with Mrs. Picard as anywhere. The worst outcome was that Ingle would be suspicious. I must've been dizzy enough that I didn't object to his protective tone—or maybe I didn't want to say out loud that it was justified.

And then we talked some more. By the time we alighted, I was comfortable with first names. William knew more about me, and I knew more about him. Families, backgrounds, likes and dislikes. He was going to Cardinals games. I tended to favor the Browns, being a sucker for lost causes. Not that the Cards were that good either.

Marjorie Picard was surprised to see us, of course, but rose to the occasion. I explained I had some information about the wheel that I hadn't been able to explain to David on the telephone. And I asked if I could stay with her while William went on to Perry County as soon as the next train came through.

David once again volunteered his services. He pointed out that he could drive William to Perryville and get there before the next train could make the trip. In fact, he'd be happy to drive to the Klines. William asked if he knew where that was. David went still for a moment and then nodded.

We saw the two men off in the Model-T and settled in to do woman talk. About the weather, my family, her family, a sabotaged wheel, and who would do such a thing. She stared out the window for several minutes at the news about the wheel. We moved to the dining room table with coffee.

"Mrs. Picard, I don't know much about such things. How did the beer business work?"

"Well, dear, Claude would've found a loaded wagon waiting behind the Anvil Saloon after an early dinner." She considered her coffee, and I knew this could take some time.

"He'd have met Ettie or Gus Kline—Ettie often drove the wagons—just over the bridge in Illinois but close to the Perry County line. I'm not too sure what would happen then, but I think the Klines stored part of the beer at their farm, which is nearby, and then they'd distribute the rest throughout the county."

"So the barn someone tried to burn likely held the beer Sheriff Picard had delivered to the Klines only days ago.

"Yes."

Amazing. This gracious, upstanding woman sat here telling the daughter of another sheriff how the law was broken. I was in another world, one where different rules held. I wanted very much to talk to my father.

"You understand, my dear, I haven't seen the wagon Claude was in that night." Mrs. Picard's eyebrows and the tilt of her chin said she was working on staying calm.

"It was your wagon, wasn't it?"

"It might have been ours or it might have been the Klines'. I suppose we'll know when we buy a new wheel and get the wagon back here."

I needed to backtrack. "Explain to me, please, why the wagon might have been the Klines'."

"Well, they would trade off, you see. If it was our wagon that carried the beer on one trip, Claude and Ettie would just change the horses, and our wagon would be in Perry County for a while. Claude would return with their wagon. On the next trip, we'd get our wagon back."

Well, of course. Silly me. I thought they'd move the beer from one wagon to another. Mrs. Picard was looking at me when I turned pink, so I had to explain. At least she smiled. I broke down and smiled, too. The team exchange was so obvious. And being embarrassed was refreshing in a way. I rarely admitted such intellectual lapses.

"So, whoever damaged those wheels did so in Perry County, right?"

"That's correct, my dear. The wagon Claude died in would've been in Perry County for the last two or three months."

"And whoever did it knew that Mrs. Kline would be the first driver."

"Yes." She was so sad it hurt me.

"They wouldn't know the empty wagon would break down with him, instead of her."

"No, I shouldn't think so." She went to the kitchen, to make more coffee, she said. It took a while.

I got up and wandered the downstairs, taking in the comfortable, overstuffed chairs and sofas, the late Victorian furnishings. The

Picards had not remodeled in the style of the day, but then, it required significant funds to toss all the frills and flourishes and refurnish in cleaner lines.

I imagined various scenarios involving the wagon. I tried to put myself in the head of the person with the saw. Eventually, I worked out some conclusions. But, at the moment, I had no one to share them with.

Back in the dining room, I stared out the large windows. Mrs. Picard had taken down the heavy velvet drapes and was welcoming summer breezes with light muslin panels, edged with fat little tassels she probably had made herself. There must have been a hundred of them. I shook my head. I refused to spend my life doing that kind of thing. And therefore, as I used to explain to my older sister, had no reason to learn how.

The porch looked inviting, and I headed out to enjoy the day. The man strolling down the street seemed to see me just as I saw him. I would not have given him a second glance in St. Louis. Here, I would have smiled and nodded and then not given him another glance. The problem was that he jerked to a stop and stared at me as if he knew me. So, I spared the extra glance.

Medium height, thin, a workman to judge by the rather shabby dress. His pants were baggy, and he wore no vest between an ill-fitting coat and an off-white shirt. He turned toward me and stopped about half way up the path.

"Hello, Miss. Are you visiting from St. Louis?" He smiled, and I had two thoughts. People were even more aggressively friendly here than in Fulton. And, his teeth were so bad, I could see dark gaps from here.

From this safe distance, I was willing to say, "I'm visiting Mrs. Picard—and I do live in St. Louis. How did you know?"

"Your clothes, Miss." He smiled, showing more gaps. "Do you know Miss Ingle?"

Whoa. He knew Amelia? I debated a second and decided to be cautious.

"I know an Amelia Ingle."

"Yes, Miss. That's her. The pretty one. She's visited here as well." His voice carried the excitement of speaking about her.

"How nice." I didn't want to fish for more. Obviously, Amelia had been to Ste. Genevieve with Henry. And made an impression on this man—who smiled and nodded as if "nice" were the appropriate response.

"Yes, Miss. You have a good visit, Miss." He touched the brim of his hat. As he turned away, I could see that his hair straggled down his neck from under the battered golf cap. He returned to the sidewalk and crossed the street toward the middle of town. I didn't have to reply.

I shrugged. It was a small town, and everyone would know if there were visitors. They might know, somehow, that David had taken the reporter from the City and headed off to Perry County. Maybe this was why Dad had said he couldn't ask more questions. We couldn't be subtle about it.

I ventured into the kitchen to see if Mrs. Picard was O.K. She'd been crying.

I accepted another cup of coffee and asked her again about the money, but she had no idea. The Klines usually paid the Sheriff at the exchange, she said, and he brought cash home, a decent amount.

"And I'd put it away. David starts college in the fall. We were saving for Samuel."

O.K. I didn't know how I felt about a law officer bootlegging beer. But I wouldn't throw any stones in this particular case. Marjorie

Picard seemed secure in acknowledging the situation, and I did admire that kind of serenity in the face of her loss.

As bedtime neared, we reassured each other that the drive and the questions in Perry County could well take this long. Neither of us mentioned that the Model-T might decide on its own to rest along the way. Nor that whoever had tried to fire the Klines' barn could still be wandering about Perry County.

16

The evening banquet was superb. The Ambassador greeted Carl with enthusiasm. He was even gracious when Carl asked the nasty question about Kaiser Wilhelm's naval ambitions. The reporters writing for the English-language papers had to ask Carl about the occasional remarks in German between the Mayor and the Ambassador. It should have been a most gratifying evening.

Carl was miserable.

Every few minutes, he'd reach into the pocket of his good summer coat and finger the note that had appeared on his desk just after the luncheon. William was in Ste. Gen. Or maybe Perryville. Wrote to let Carl know something was happening there. Hoped to call something in to the *Globe* tonight but would have more Wednesday. And he'd see Carl then.

Carl couldn't have been anywhere but where he was. That's what he kept telling himself. But he was irritated beyond rationality that William was investigating without him. Why? Because Julia would be impressed if William found something? Ridiculous. Carl had let it be known yesterday that he'd found out the location of the wheels the hard way—by doing his research. William knew about the wheels only because that prohibition deputy had told him. Julia had seemed impressed with Carl's efforts. And it wasn't a contest. Not really.

Carl felt himself smile across the table at the wife of one of the Ambassador's staff members. He couldn't remember the man's name—and therefore he didn't know the name of Frau Whoever. Carl was simply making good small talk, sometimes in English, sometimes in German. Although the woman did have very nice hair, dipping down over her forehead in graceful brown waves. And she was looking at him with some interest.

And that was worrisome as well. Not the woman across the table. Julia. She hadn't been at work when Carl carved out a minute to read police reports. The Chief had sent her home to recover. And then when he found time to call the boarding house, just before the banquet, Fran had reported that Julia was off to see her father. To say what? That William McConnell would have the matter solved soon?

Carl told himself to stop it: stop worrying about William, stop fretting over Julia. Tonight he would write a story worthy of today's events. Tomorrow he would see the Ambassador off and then find William and sort out Julia's trip home. Maybe in a different order.

17

*From the **St. Louis Globe-Democrat**, Wednesday, June 12, 1910*

> *Special Dispatch from Perryville, Mo. – Mr. Gus Kline and his wife, Mrs. Ettie Kline, have been arrested after Sheriff Paul Carrey discovered a store of beer in a barn on their property in rural Perry County. The Sheriff was called to the scene to investigate a report of someone trying to burn the barn early Tuesday morning.*

I fell asleep thinking that Carl might well be right. The whole affair was about the beer, and someone was willing to risk the safety of one driver or the other to make his point. I woke up wanting to discuss my conclusions with William.

He and David arrived at about nine o'clock, looking damp and tired from a night spent in the Model-T. I was irritated when William wanted to eat breakfast before sharing his story.

I drummed a fork on the kitchen table across from him before he gave up and said, "All will be revealed, Julia. I believe Sheriff Carrey is having breakfast in Ste. Genevieve. He's going to collect Deputy Ingle and join us here, if that's acceptable." He turned to Mrs. Picard, who was frying her third skillet of bacon.

"Wait 'til you hear all this, Mama," David put in, his mouth just empty enough to be understood.

She studied her son. "I should make more coffee," was all she said.

I turned back to William. "Do you mean you know who sabotaged the wagon?"

"Not for sure, but there's a suspect. Ingle showed up in Perryville, and we talked to the Klines—they're in jail, by the way."

Mrs. Picard turned with a dripping fork, leaving spots on the tile floor. "The Klines are in jail?"

"Yes." William gave her a gentle smile. "They saw someone running from their barn and, a moment later, saw flames. They got close enough to recognize the man—or they think they did, at least. The fire wasn't much. But they sent a son riding off to get Sheriff Carrey. When the sheriff arrived, he saw enough spirits that he couldn't avoid arresting the Klines for possessing alcohol in a dry county."

"Both of them? Ettie and Gus both?"

William smiled. "It seems Mrs. Kline insisted. She told me personally it was her operation. Her husband just lifted the heavy stuff."

William leaned into his plate and added, "You'd like Ettie Kline, Julia.

Maybe. I had to admit I was curious about her timing. "You mean they called the Sheriff knowing they had enough beer around to get arrested."

William swallowed and nodded. "Mrs. Kline said the important thing was finding out who was around their barn. Figured whoever set the fire was involved in Sheriff Picard's death." He shook his head. "Carrey told me in private that they'd pay their fine tomorrow and be on their way home. But he confiscated the beer."

O.K. I did like Ettie Kline.

William finished a good swallow of coffee and turned to Marjorie

Picard. "I need to ask you a serious question, Mrs. Picard, before Carrey and Ingle arrive. Do you trust James Ingle?"

"Trust him? You mean about the wheel?" Mrs. Picard looked up from wiping bacon grease off the floor. David stared at William, toast neglected in his hand.

"I mean even more than that. Do you suspect him in regard to your husband's death?"

Marjorie Picard grabbed a quick breath, and her eyes widened. "Oh, no, Mr. McConnell. Why would he be involved? I never thought that . . . he wouldn't do . . . anything. Claude liked him."

William nodded and turned to David.

But David beat William to the question. "Do you trust him?"

"No," William said, but hurried to add, "Of course, that doesn't count for too much. I don't trust anyone."

"That must be . . . wearying, Mr. McConnell," Marjorie Picard said.

"It's my job, Mrs. Picard. Politicians, promoters, even police, have a lot to gain from getting in good with reporters. You learn early not to let yourself trust anyone—even the people you'd like to trust."

"That sounds lonely," I said.

"It is, sometimes. Often, as a matter of fact." He considered me for a second and moved on. "But we need to think about James Ingle. We may have to decide what to say to him."

"What would he have to gain from hurting Claude?" Mrs. Picard asked again. "He is such a nice young man. We've known his wife's family for years. And the Ingles that live in St. Louis seem to be quite upstanding." She turned to her son. "Don't you agree, David?"

David was thinking about it. His high forehead was developing wrinkles, aging him fast.

"I've been around the courthouse a lot, and the jail, when I'd take food over. I think James is sincere. I see now that he wanted to know about the wheel, not get it fixed. But that doesn't mean he was trying to hide anything."

"Did he ever talk about prohibition?" William asked.

"Yes. He was opposed to people drinking, he said. We argued some—not argued, you know, sort of . . . sparred. I'd say there was nothing wrong with a beer or a glass of wine, and he'd say that's true if that's all people ever had, but some people drank more than that and hurt other people. You know, the usual arguments."

Oh, I knew. James sounded downright moderate compared to his cousin Amelia. For that matter, Henry was moderate compared to his sister. I took a piece of toast from the holder and began to butter it, even though I wasn't hungry.

"But he knew what Claude did when he took the job," Mrs. Picard said.

"He did?" I said. A sheriff would admit he broke the law as a matter of routine?

"Well, yes, dear," she said. "It's a small town. The beer comes in and goes out from the saloon across from the jail. It's common knowledge in Ste. Genevieve. Everyone is comfortable with it."

"Everyone?" William said.

"I don't really know of anyone who would object. We all felt bad when Perry County went dry, but it did open up a financial opportunity."

William raised one eyebrow in my direction as if I might want to comment. Odd that he would ask, and odd that I was speechless. He continued, "Did your husband pay James or any other deputy not to say anything?"

"Why, no. To whom would they say something?"

She had us there. The tilt of William's eyebrows registered doubt.

Samuel came in the house, wiping his smallish hands on a rag that didn't look clean enough to make a difference. He was maybe fifteen and would hopefully hit a growth spurt soon. He looked more like his mother, blue eyes, reddish brown hair, but he'd made that turn away from pretty features to coarser male brows and a more assertive bone structure. He was the last of five children. And the daughters all lived elsewhere, Marjorie had said.

"Are you expecting company, Mama?"

She smiled at him.

"I suppose I am, dear."

◆　◆　◆

We sat around the dining room table palming cups of coffee. Ingle was tense, unsmiling. Sheriff Paul Carrey seemed much happier. He might be happy a good deal of the time: plenty of laugh lines radiated from brown eyes in a tanned face. He was particularly attentive to Mrs. Picard.

But when everyone was seated, it was William who called the meeting to order. "We can put some pieces in place," he announced. He began with Ingle. "I assume you haven't had a chance to telephone Armbruster."

"Didn't need to phone Armbruster. He phoned me. About half an hour ago."

"Yes?" William said.

"He gave me his impression of what had happened to the wheel. I mentioned you were here, Miss Nye, and he said I should ask you for the whole story." Ingle was looking less happy by the minute.

Sheriff Carrey said, "Deputy Ingle tells me the rim on the left front wheel was partially sawn through."

I nodded and went on to describe opening the door and seeing the lanterns roll toward us. It seemed a long ways off, sitting here on a pleasant June morning in Ste. Genevieve, the breeze blowing past the bleached muslin. But I could conjure up the fear, the realization that someone was willing to set fire to a building knowing that at least one person was inside.

Ingle and Carrey had questions. How did we get out? How much damage was done? How did the fire brigades reach the place so quickly? Who called in the alarm? Was no one detected in the area? I answered some questions. William answered others.

"So a St. Louis police officer was on the scene, saw the flames, and called in the alarm." Carrey was actually taking notes. He looked from me to William. "That was convenient."

We both nodded.

"Where would he have seen the flames from, Miss Nye? Can you reconstruct the scene for me?" This guy Carrey was good.

"Anyone walking down either street that intersects Third might have glanced down the alleyway and seen flames. I guess that's what Detective Kelley was doing."

"Detective Kelley," Ingle broke in. "A St. Louis police detective was walking a beat? Why would he be there?"

Of course, that was my question. But Kelley certainly wouldn't tell me. William explained that he hadn't had time to ask.

"What does his report say?" Carrey asked.

I made a huffing sound just the proper side of unladylike. "He may not have filed a report yet."

"Why not?" Ingle asked.

So, I explained the new procedure and Kelley's refusal to cooperate and how bad his reports looked.

William stepped in before I said something embarrassing and

suggested I tell them—speaking of Kelley—about Mr. Armbruster's conversation with the good detective. I hoped the tone of his voice told the two men his opinion of Kelley. I wouldn't want them to think I was the only one who disliked the man.

I explained that Mr. Armbruster hadn't let Kelley in on anything.

"You mean he didn't want Kelley to know that he'd seen the wheel or formed an opinion?" Ingle was frowning and drumming a spoon on the table.

"That's right."

"Even though he was willing to tell you about it."

"Yes, Deputy." I paused. "He did hesitate at first. Then he seemed eager to tell me, as if he wanted someone else to know."

Ingle stilled the spoon and sat there for a moment. "That puts Mr. Armbruster's statement to me in a more ominous light."

"What statement?" William asked.

"He said he and his family were closing down the shop while it's being repaired, and that they'd be out of town."

"Out of town?" I said.

"Scary detective you've got there," Carrey said. Every one seemed to think about that for a moment.

Finally, Ingle said, "Speaking of the wheel, we wondered if anyone has been around your car shed, Mrs. Picard. If our man is setting fires at the Klines, he might be interested in the status of the wagon here, might not know it's over in the county barn."

Marjorie Picard was wide-eyed, and David watched her closely. "Let's go see," he said and jumped to his feet. "We'll give it a once-over." He squeezed her hand as he passed.

We all rose, even though David and William had just come from the shed. I assumed David wanted to leave his mother to herself for a bit.

As we neared the shed, Carrey turned to Ingle. "Do you know this Detective Kelley? Could he have some connection with our caller?"

"A caller? About what?" William asked. "When?"

"The call from St. Louis about the cargo," I said.

William turned to me. I had been negligent in not telling him that odd bit. Carrey stepped in to explain before William could say anything. "The night the Sheriff died, I got a call at my house, saying I should investigate St. Mary's road right away. The caller implied he'd heard about a load of alcohol being sold and transported into Perry County."

"But he didn't give his name?" William stopped and pulled the memo book from his breast pocket.

"Nope. Just said he'd heard it through his contacts with the St. Louis police. I asked why the police hadn't contacted me, and he rang off." Carrey shook his head.

"Paul." It was just the one word from James Ingle. I read into the name a warning and a plea. I suspected Ingle wouldn't have shared this much information with William or any other reporter.

Carrey stared at him a moment until a voice said, "That's odd. From St. Louis? I think we should find out what it means."

Marjorie Picard had followed us. She held Samuel's arm. "You didn't tell me about that, James."

"Sorry, ma'am," he said and turned toward the shed.

William smiled at Mrs. Picard and proceeded, asking if Carrey was sure the call came from St. Louis.

I supposed Carrey wasn't concerned about James' Ingle's opinion, because he nodded and continued. "The operator confirmed the call was from St, Louis, but that was all she knew, of course."

"And what did you do with the tip, Sheriff Carrey?" William asked.

"I decided it couldn't hurt to look, so I rode on out. Wagon tracks on the southern part of the road indicated something had passed, but I didn't come upon anyone in my county. I was curious, though. I rode on to the bridge." He nodded to Mrs. Picard.

William nodded to Mrs. Picard, too. It seemed no one wanted to mention her husband without the small ritual. "Did you connect the Sheriff's death with the call?"

"If you mean the obvious thought that he was involved in a sale, of course." Carrey was frowning now. "But I thought the caller meant to alert me about the cargo, not the accident."

We all started walking toward the shed again. I decided to air my conclusions—even if I risked embarrassing myself.

"If the caller thought the Sheriff and Mrs. Kline moved the beer from one wagon to the other—like I did—then he was telling you the wagon Ettie Kline was driving would break down, maybe right after it took on the heavy load."

The men stared at me.

"But if the caller understood the system, then it was a matter of the wagon being rigged to injure one driver or the other."

David appeared in the door of the shed and stared at me.

"What do you mean, Julia?" William asked. I couldn't decide if the negative tilt of his eyebrows was aimed at me or at my conclusion.

So I explained what I assumed they knew. Turned out none of them had thought about the matter of the wagon exchange.

We were all quiet, wondering now if the person who'd damaged the wheel intended murder or embarrassment.

David said, "Sheriff Carrey thinks it might be that handyman, Caruthers."

Marjorie Picard drew a sharp breath. "Tom Caruthers? What does he have to do with it? I can't imagine Tom would want to hurt

Claude."

Paul Carrey jumped in. "We're not sure. We need to find him and ask some hard questions. But the Klines said the man they saw running from the barn looked like him. He's got folks in Clearyville, not far away. I went there, of course, but they say they haven't seen him."

"But Tom Caruthers was here yesterday," Mrs. Picard said.

Ingle and Carrey turned toward her so quickly she started.

"Where?" Ingle asked.

"When was he here?" Carrey asked the more important question.

David was at his mother's side. "Was he near the shed?"

"Why no," Mrs. Picard said. "He was walking down the street, not like he was headed anywhere in a hurry. It was in the afternoon sometime. I looked out the window when I heard him say hello to Julia."

18

The Ambassador was gone, thank God. Carl made a beeline for the boarding house to see if Julia had returned from Fulton. It was unlikely he'd embarrass himself. If she weren't there, resting, no one would be. New women worked during the day.

Carl knocked and fidgeted. He took off his hat and smoothed his hair. He slapped the hat back on and pulled out his father's watch. His father would have been proud of his work the last two days, although he might not have said so to Carl's face.

Footsteps surprised Carl. He yanked the hat back off and smoothed his hair again. He was smiling when the door opened. Smiling at Amelia Ingle.

There was a brief moment of surprise, and then both spoke at once, along the lines of, "What are you doing here?"

Carl didn't wait for Amelia to explain her absence from work. He wanted to talk to her as little as possible. So, he went right to the point. "Is Julia home?"

Amelia almost answered and then caught herself. "Why would you come looking for Julia? She'll be back at work when she's able."

"And she's not able. I'm trying to find out if she's O.K. today."

"Well, she's not here. She said she went to see her father in Fulton."

"She said she went? Do you think she didn't go there?"

"The note on her door said she was off to Fulton."

Carl stared at Amelia, trying to figure out what she was implying. She stared back.

"Fine." Carl put his hat on. "I'll go phone her father in Fulton and find out how she's doing." He turned to leave, tossing a "good-day" over his shoulder.

He was almost down the steps, thinking how rude Amelia Ingle could be, when she said, "Wait, Mr. Schroeder. You can phone from here."

Use the women's telephone for a long distance toll? Even stranger, Amelia was inviting him in when no other women were in the house? Carl turned to stare again, and Amelia's response to his silent questions was a blush. Strange, strange woman.

Amelia lifted her chin and turned on her heel. Carl felt himself blush as he made his way inside. Amelia indicated the phone on its table next to a ragged green velour chair against the wall. Then she retreated a safe distance toward the kitchen and watched.

Carl stared at the phone, and it was almost as bad as staring at Amelia Ingle. What he pictured was an angry Sheriff John Nye on the other end, no doubt questioning how Julia's friend had allowed her to get hurt doing a man's investigative work. He hoped William was right about the Sheriff knowing his daughter better than they did.

"Are you sure you wouldn't like to make this call, Miss Ingle? After all, you're a member of her household."

"And you're the friend who came to our house during the day to inquire after her, Mr. Schroeder. Be my guest."

Maybe he didn't want to call from here. But he did want to find Julia as quickly as possible, maybe talk to her. Carl grabbed the phone and asked the operator to make the connection to the Sheriff's Office in Callaway County. He paced the small distance the cord allowed, clicking his fingers on the body of the telephone in time with the noises coming from the earpiece.

Carl figured the Sheriff might be home with Julia if she were feeling poorly—but that seemed unlike Julia. More likely, she'd be at home by herself, lost in one of her Westerns or at the courthouse with her dad. He wondered if the Sheriff himself would answer.

He did. Carl thought he sounded alert to trouble, no doubt because the operator had identified the call as coming in from St. Louis.

"Yes, sir, this is Carl Schroeder, Julia's friend from St. Louis. We met last week."

"Of course, Mr. Schroeder. How are things in St. Louis?"

In St. Louis? Wouldn't Julia have told him what had happened?

John Nye heard the hesitation and went right to the point. "Has something happened to Julia, Mr. Schroeder?"

"Well, nothing serious, sir. But she left a note on her door saying she was heading home for a few days."

"Why would she do that? And what do you mean by 'nothing serious'? What's going on there, Schroeder?"

Carl hadn't considered the consequences of the call if Julia weren't there. Good Lord, Julia would be furious. He cleared his throat to give himself another second to think and started in.

"Well, sir, she was asking after the wagon wheel for Mrs. Picard"—not for her co-investigators, sir—"and she managed to get a small cut on her head. It's not serious, but I believe Chief Wright thought she should take a day or so away from work. I was asking after her to see if she was feeling better, and her housemates tell me she indicated she was headed your way."

There, that was honest. And Carl had managed it well enough. Now he was free to start worrying about where she was, along with the Sheriff.

"How did she get a cut on her head asking after a wagon wheel? It must've been pretty bad for Micah to send her home."

Darn. Carl started pacing his short circuit. "I'm sure she thought it was a simple matter, to ask about the wheel and when it might be repaired. But as she and the proprietor stepped into the back of the shop to look at the thing, someone threw a couple of lanterns in the workroom. They think a bottle of varnish or some such thing must have exploded and a piece of glass hit Julia. The police got her to a doctor, and he stitched it up. She seemed fine, afterwards, sir, but she must have lost more blood than we'd thought."

"Well, damn. I told her not to get involved in this thing."

"Yes, sir, we suggested that as well."

John Nye gave a short laugh. "And where do you suppose she is now, Mr. Schroeder? Because she certainly isn't in Fulton. If she's gone off investigating—"

Carl didn't want to hear the end of that one. "No, sir, I can't think there's more she could be doing. Now, Mr. McConnell has gone to Ste. Genevieve to look into . . ."

Carl paused and took a breath, as it became all too obvious where Miss Nye might be doing her investigating. Darn it. No. Damn it.

"Uh-huh," the Sheriff sighed. "I think you've got it, Mr. Schroeder." He muttered something else, and all Carl caught was "honest to God."

"I think I need to put in a call to Micah Wright, maybe to Marjorie Picard. I thank you for bringing Julia's little adventures to my attention, Mr. Schroeder. And I trust she'll be back in St. Louis soon."

Carl felt as if he'd tattled on a schoolmate. Even if he said his only excuse for calling her father was his concern for her, he had a feeling that wouldn't go over so well with Julia. At the same time, he wanted to march on Ste. Genevieve and give both William and Julia a piece of his mind. And he didn't want to be dismissed by Sheriff Nye.

"I can do that, sir—call Mrs. Picard, that is. If there's something new brewing in Ste. Genevieve, I need to get down there. I've been busy here covering the German Ambassador, but he's freshly left, and I'm ready to get back on the murder story."

There was silence on the other end. Carl spent a moment kicking himself for putting it that way.

"Murder. Is that what you said, Mr. Schroeder?"

"Yes sir, that's what Mr. McConnell and I think."

After another pause, the Sheriff said, "Very well, Mr. Schroeder, I'll phone Micah Wright and you phone Mrs. Picard. Please let me know if Julia isn't there—or isn't on her way back."

The goodbyes were quick and perfunctory. Carl replaced the earpiece and sat the telephone down gently. This called for some serious pacing. And another long distance toll. Carl headed for the door and remembered at the last minute to thank Amelia Ingle for the extravagant use of her toll service.

The expression on her face brought him up short. The remains of the blush were obvious, and her eyes were sparkling in her pink face. For a moment, Carl was caught up in admiring the effect. The thought that she might, in turn, be admiring him in the empty house surprised him.

"Did someone murder that Sheriff?"

Carl sighed and thought it was relief. He'd play it low-key, as William always did. Just another news story.

"That's what we suspect. Your prohibition business may have gotten out of hand. Good-day."

"What do you mean, my prohibition business? And who thinks it's murder? Where is Mr. McConnell? You don't think Julia's gone with him?"

Irritating woman. Which question was he supposed to answer? Why should he answer any? Well, because he had answers and she didn't.

"Mr. McConnell and I think it's murder, and that's why he's in Ste. Genevieve County, investigating, and I imagine Julia is indeed with him. Your prohibition advocates have gone too far this time, Miss Ingle. Or should I say your family has gone too far?"

Amelia's eyes went even bigger, and her small mouth was open wider than Carl could have imagined, and she looked a lot like her just-maligned brother. Carl expected all sorts of denials and arguments, and he wasn't hanging about for them. He almost made it to the door this time.

"Wait, Carl. You said you'd call Mrs. Picard, no?" She hesitated before the name, as if she didn't want to acknowledge the sheriff's wife, but then she hurried on. "I'm so concerned if Julia has wandered off with that man. I want to know when she's coming back, if she's O.K."

Such sweet concern. Carl put his hands on his hips and shook his head. "I'm going to telephone as soon as I get to my office, Miss Ingle."

"Oh no, please call from here. I'm so concerned. I don't want to wait to find out how she is."

"This is going to be expensive. Can you ladies afford the long distance tolls?"

"Please don't worry about that, Mr. Schroeder. Just contact the woman and find out where Julia is."

Carl considered her a moment. Really, she'd be very attractive in a nicely plump way if she could be sweet all the time. Carl usually turned his attention to Julia, but he could see why men were drawn to

Amelia Ingle. He shook his head and took up the telephone again. More clicks, a wait—during which he tried to avoid looking at Amelia—a brief conversation with a surprised Marjorie Picard, and Carl hung up the phone again. Not so gently.

"What? What's happened?"

"News has happened, I suspect. But dear Julia's headed home— with William McConnell. You don't need to be concerned, Miss Ingle."

Carl dug a half dollar out of his pocket and dropped it on the table next to the phone. He strode out, working on his opening lines for Miss Nye and Mr. McConnell. To think he was worried about her. Really. What were the two of them up to without him?

19

It was afternoon by the time we left Ste. Gen. William had questions about Tom Caruthers, but I had very few answers. I was looking out a window and went silent, picturing the odd man. When I turned back, William had settled down to work. It was almost an hour into the trip when he handed me several sheets of paper.

The story began, "Law officers in two counties are investigating the possibility of foul play in the death a week ago of Ste. Genevieve County Sheriff Claude Picard. As reported Monday in the *Globe-Democrat*, the Sheriff was involved in transporting a wagonload of beer to be sold in dry parts of neighboring Perry County. In addition, arsons in St. Louis City and rural Perry County have been linked to the incident."

Well, that ought to be the buzz of St. Louis for several days. Prohibition and foul play. What could be better?

The story went on to detail most of what William and I knew. He would tell his readers the wagon wheel had been destroyed in the St. Louis fire, but not before it was discovered that it had been tampered with. He didn't identify Armbruster as having made that discovery, in case additional danger awaited the man.

Another complication lay in the fact the money from the exchange was missing. All the lawmen involved were considering the possibility of robbery. And he detailed the incident at the Klines'.

I'd always figured newsmen only wrote about events, but William was pushing this story into being, as well as reporting it. I gave the papers back to him with a smile meant to tell him how impressed I was.

He smiled in turn. "Now," he said, "what questions does that raise in your mind?"

Hmm. "I'd want to know if there was really any connection with the St. Louis Police—because of the first message."

"Good." He could have been quizzing a cub reporter. "All I can do on that one is get a quote from Chief Wright. He'll say he has no knowledge of any police connection. And he'll say he suspects it was a matter of a criminal using the department's name to confuse matters."

That sounded like the Chief.

"And he will, of course, start thinking if someone on the force could be involved. Tomorrow, I'll find time to ask him in private if he's thought of anyone."

I smiled. I loved being on the inside.

"What other questions does the story raise?"

"How do we account for the robbery of Sheriff Picard?"

"Yes," William agreed. "Readers should wonder. What's your theory?"

"O.K. Someone wanted the beer found so it wouldn't be sold. That smacks of someone who cares about prohibition. But maybe, knowing where each of them would be, and that they'd be alone and carrying money . . ."

"That would make sense if it had been Mrs. Kline, but I wouldn't want to attack Claude Picard by myself. And the wagon apparently did skid out of control because of the damaged rim. How would anyone know where that was going to happen?"

William was leaning forward, elbow on knee, chin on palm,

staring out the window. We were once again in a private compartment. The *Globe* was paying, and I could see why it was worth it to them. Tomorrow, everyone in St. Louis would be waving copies of the *Globe* and William's story.

"The robbery is the strange part, isn't it?" I asked.

William nodded, without answering. After a few minutes, he leaned back and said, "And sometimes it's the element that doesn't add up that's the key to the whole thing."

"You sound like a detective."

He nodded and grinned. "It's why I like this beat. I get to play police without the danger, the hours, or the low pay."

"I can't imagine a job like yours. The freedom to go where the story is, to be your own boss in some ways." I sighed. "I have to get hurt to get a day off, and I won't get paid."

He stopped smiling. "I hadn't thought of that." He hesitated. "I suppose you live on a tight budget."

"You could say that. Still, I'm glad to have a position and an interesting one at that."

"Do you think getting the vote will get you more money?"

I laughed, and it came out bitter. "Maybe my daughter—or my granddaughter."

He smiled. "I'm trying to picture you with children, leading a conventional life, being a grandmother."

"I imagine I can have children without becoming conventional, Mr. McConnell."

William folded the story, tucked it in the back of his memo book, and stowed both in an inside chest pocket. "I imagine you can do whatever you want, Miss Nye."

He considered me a minute. "Mrs. Picard said no one was bothered by the Sheriff's bootlegging. I think you're bothered. And I understand your father was bothered."

"Why do you say that? Have you talked to my father?"

"No. James Ingle tells me Picard and your father had a rather serious disagreement about three weeks ago."

"I know Dad visited the Sheriff a couple of weeks before the accident. But what did Ingle say?"

"That your father and Picard had a heated discussion about bootlegging. Ingle overheard."

"Why did Ingle tell you that? Was he accusing my father of something?"

William's eyebrows rose a fraction. "The context was that some people didn't approve of what Claude Picard was doing. He didn't accuse your father of anything. And, if we think about it, Carrey or Ingle himself would have as much motive for simple embarrassment."

"What exactly are you saying, Mr. McConnell?"

If he noticed my use of his family name, banter aside, or the fact I was rigid on the edge of the seat, he didn't show it. He leaned forward. "I'm saying there were several people with motive to embarrass, not hurt, Ettie Kline. She was breaking the law in Carrey's county, and his fellow sheriff was cooperating. Maybe arresting her was politically awkward. Maybe Ingle hoped embarrassment would stop his boss from conspiring to break the law. A wagon breaking under the weight of the beer wouldn't have to hurt the driver, after all."

I twisted on the seat in frustration. "But that would mean they conspired to break the law themselves. I refuse to consider that lawmen don't believe in the law."

William leaned back. "It is indeed a flaw in my theory that lawmen would stoop to that kind of demonstration. Maybe it was someone else. Or, maybe someone we don't know understood that Picard would be driving the damaged wagon, and the whole thing had nothing to do with the beer."

It was a truce. My anger drained and sadness replaced it. It was several minutes later when I continued the conversation. "They were old friends. And Dad asked us to investigate."

"That's what Ingle concluded, as well."

◆ ◆ ◆

By late afternoon, we'd made our way under the elegant and modern tin-and-glass dome of the train shed and were pushing through the crowd in the Midway at Union Station. Travelers rushed toward the streetcars or bustled in and out of the arches that connected the Midway and the waiting room. Some gathered at the shops or visited the lunchroom. Others rested on plush, red upholstery. I had mellowed as we traveled, and we headed toward the large staircase that led to the Terminal Hotel, having decided to pause for a lemonade in the vaulted spaces upstairs.

I had William's arm so we could stay together in the crowd as we went toward the waiting area. He'd said something trivial that left me laughing. We must have looked as if we'd had a two-day holiday instead of spending our time investigating a murder. At least that's the way I interpreted the scowl on Carl's face.

And to add to my embarrassment, the Chief was standing next to him.

William was cool as usual. I started to pull away, but he tightened his arm to keep my hand on it. He guided us toward the two men, who were standing near one of the marble pillars.

Carl took his hands off his hips and strode toward us. The Chief looked less upset but far from happy.

Carl glared at William and pulled me away from him. I wasn't bleeding this time, and he didn't hesitate to shake my arm for emphasis.

"Why can't you tell someone where you're going? Why did you say you were going to your father's? Do you know how concerned he was?"

I twisted away from him, put a hand on his chest, and shoved, hard. "I don't have to tell you where I'm going. And what do you mean, my father was concerned? Did you talk to him?"

Carl recovered. I batted away his hand when he reached for me again, not caring if I embarrassed either of us.

"We phoned to see if you'd made it there safely." He was angry enough that it came out as a hiss.

"We? Who's 'we'?"

"Amelia Ingle and I. She was in a panic when it was obvious you hadn't even thought about going to Callaway County."

"You don't know I hadn't thought of going there. Something came up, something important. I spent the night with Mrs. Picard."

"Mrs. Picard." Carl glared at William, who finally said something.

"Mrs. Picard, Carl."

Carl stepped closer to William. "Do you think before you drag her into these situations? Do you know how this looks?"

"Julia spent the night with Marjorie Picard and found out information that's helping us investigate a possible murder. I spent the night tramping through Perry County, putting together more information on the latest arson. I trust it looks as if I'm doing my job and Miss Nye is helping—as she may as well do when she can't be at work, anyway. That's all it looks like, Carl." He tilted his head toward Carl. "And since when are you so concerned about appearances?

That's not very progressive of you."

Carl sputtered, and the Chief took over. "We know you were at the Picards'—now. Schroeder phoned there a little while ago. And I managed to calm your father. We were just concerned about you, my dear."

Called my father. Lordy. This conversation with Carl was not finished, and I did not want to even think about the conversation I'd have to have with Dad. Or Amelia Ingle.

William turned to the Chief and said, "I have a question for you, sir." It was no doubt the one about the St. Louis police connection. I wanted to hear the answer, so I stopped glaring at Carl for the moment and moved toward the Chief.

Instead I heard the crack of a fired gun. I don't know if I screamed before or after I heard William gasp.

Carl moved to catch him as he fell to his knees. I moved to screen Carl's back and scan the crowd on the stairs—which was now moving in panic, some up and some down. The Chief must have thought the shot came from there as well, because that's where he aimed his gun. But through all the screaming and running, I could have sworn I heard William call my name.

My hand was already in the satchel, but I dropped the revolver I'd just located and drew the shawl instead. I was on my knees and pressing it against William's arm before I thought about it. I was saying his name as well, although I couldn't imagine I was breathing well enough to make him hear it.

The blood was soaking through the entire sleeve of William's light wool jacket. I pressed harder, and he ducked his head and squeezed his eyes shut.

William was trying to say something to me. I worked to keep the same pressure on the wound and put my ear closer to his mouth. The noise around us was deafening. Or, maybe I wasn't hearing too well over the pulse hammering away in my head.

What I heard, in pieces, with dwindling volume, was, "Get the story out of my pocket." A groan. "Before the blood soaks it." A desperate breath. "See it to the *Globe*." I tried to say the paper was safe, and I would see that it got to his editor after we took care of his arm.

Someone was giving orders: "Into the store." I started to put an arm around William, to protect him from this stranger, when the man's words got through to me. "I'm a doctor. You," he jabbed a finger at Carl, "help me carry him. We're moving out of the open." His next order was for me. "Keep pressing on that wound. Do it while we move him."

Somehow we all made it into the sundries store next to the Station's post office. The doctor swept items, mostly tobacco from the smell, off the wooden table in the middle of the room. I managed to keep hold of William's arm while we moved. He wasn't making much noise, but I could hear his sharp breaths and stifled grunts, and I hated it.

The doctor wanted me to hold the now-blood-soaked shawl in place while he cut through the jacket and William's shirt. William was panting, "Julia, the story." The doctor responded by telling him to calm down, and I thought how ironic it was that anyone would tell William McConnell to be calm.

Hot water appeared. The doctor started to push against the shawl, and I was ready to let him deal with it, but he said, "No, keep pressing. Here, work this over the wound and drop the shawl." He handed me a clean cloth from his bag, and I did what he said. I focused on the wound and on the doctor's hands. I couldn't have handled Carl's job.

Carl was holding William's right hand and at the same time pressing his arm on William's chest, probably to hold him still. I could feel William's left leg behind me, bent so he could push against the surface. The wound was just below the elbow, so I was in effect holding his left arm still.

The doctor pushed the cloth and my hand back, said, "Hold on," and misted the wound with some kind of solution from his bag. He was talking to me, I realized, when William tried to rise off the table. I had the devil of a time holding on.

When the doctor moved the cloth and my hand back over the wound, I was panting, and so was Carl. So was William, but much more shallowly than before.

The doctor had a threaded needle, and I didn't want him using it on William any more than I'd wanted Dr. Patterson to sew up my little cut. Furthermore, I couldn't figure out how he could sew through the blood. I'd never been bothered by blood, but there was so much of it I had to breathe deeply and concentrate to keep my grip.

It got worse when he said, "Here, hold the skin together like this." The skin was ragged from the bullet's entry and holding it together was difficult.

I barely had the breath to ask the doctor, "Is the bullet still in there?"

"Yes," he replied. "But it's in the back. I felt it against the skin. We'll get it in a minute."

Damn. I hoped William hadn't heard him.

The doctor fell into a pattern: wipe at the blood, stitch, repeat the process. The blood flow was lessening. I stole a glance at William. He was white, and his eyes were closed, but he was mouthing my name. When I could get enough breath together, I said, "It's O.K., William. We've got time to get the story in."

"O.K.," the doctor said. "Can you hold his arm steady?" I didn't know what he meant, but it didn't matter because the doctor was bending William's arm at the elbow and motioning me to change places with him. I took a firm grasp, trying to hold his whole arm steady while the doctor cut a slit on the outside.

William's grip wasn't very strong, and the next glance I dared told me why. He could pass out any moment. He'd stopped saying my name. I would have panicked if the doctor hadn't been saying, "That's good. Hold it still," and expecting me to do it.

The bullet wasn't deep on this side. From what I could see, it bulged against the skin. There wasn't even much blood when the doctor made the cut, and the stitches on this side would be minor, probably not many more than I had in my head at the moment.

I held William's hand tighter, and then I kissed his knuckles. I had no idea why. I couldn't tell if the weak squeeze I felt was a response to my action or the first start as the doctor began cleansing the outside of the wound. I'm sure William forgot about the kiss immediately. I barely held onto his hand. Carl barely kept him from rolling off the bloody table.

The doctor tied a clean cloth around William's arm, bandaging both sides of his arm at once, pulling the cloth tight above and below the wound. Finally, he nodded me off. I staggered back against a taller display case and watched William. If he was close to passing out again after the cleaning, he didn't do it. He was breathing in shallow, short pants again and seemed to be hearing Carl, who was speaking close to William's face.

The Chief entered, growling back over his shoulder to two officers trailing him.

I glanced behind him, and he understood what I was asking. "No, whoever it was got away. We think someone ran on up the stairs through the arch and made it out onto Market."

I sagged against the counter. I felt trapped inside the shop, the smells of cigars and cigarettes and pipe tobaccos suffocating me.

The Chief was saying he had a phalanx of men ready so that we could all move out to a waiting ambulance and one of the department's automobiles. William was trying to get the Chief's attention and, when Chief Wright realized it, he hurried over to him.

When I looked at William, I could feel my pulse pound in my head, in my own tiny scratch, and in my own arms. I heard my name, and the Chief and Carl were both looking at me. I made my way across maybe four feet of floor space, scrubbing my hands on my skirt, and it took forever to get there.

"Mac says we need to get you and something—a paper?—to the *Globe* office. Is that right?" the Chief asked me.

I nodded and bent over William. He was watching me, still panting, and I was terrified for him. I pulled the lapel of his jacket toward me and took the memo book out of his inside pocket. The blood had splattered to his coat and soaked down it. Had he put the memo book in the outside pocket, it would have absorbed at least some blood. But the memo book was clean, as I had known it would be. At least it was until I clutched it to me. I realized my blouse was almost as bloody as William's coat. I looked at him in panic.

"It's O.K." He managed a brief smile. "Get the story to my editor . . . Jack Forrest. Answer any questions . . . you know all this as well as . . . I do." And then he was frowning, about more than the pain I thought. He turned to the Chief. "I needed to talk . . . get a comment."

He paused because he was losing breath. It was getting harder to hear him.

"Julia," he whispered, "ask him."

I wanted him to stop talking, because it hurt to hear him try. "I know, I know, I'll ask, and I'll tell Mr. Forrest, and the story will run. I'll take care of it, William. Please rest, I'll take care of it."

He looked at me and was calm again. He must have believed me. He seemed to say, "Thank you, Julia." I was reading his lips. He closed his eyes, and that did it. I was even more scared, and I clutched his bare shoulder with my free hand. Without opening his eyes, he whispered again, "I'm O.K., Julia."

I backed off and let strangers lift him to maneuver a stretcher beneath him. He shut his eyes tighter and gripped Carl's hand as they moved off. I could only stand there, holding onto the memo book for dear life.

The Chief appeared in front of me and said, "I was going to get you an escort home, but I guess you need to go downtown. That's an important story you're carrying, right?"

I looked at him, and everything came into focus for the first time since the shot had been fired.

"It's about murder," I said.

20

The Chief sat beside me in the back of the department's Darby auto while an officer maneuvered between the buggies and the electric streetcar cars and the pedestrians of early evening. I still couldn't breathe well, but I was thinking more clearly. Someone had to know William was returning to St. Louis with a story that would, as it played out, point a finger.

If that someone didn't know William had already written the story, it might explain trying to kill him—or distract him from the story. If the shooter thought I knew what William knew, then I would be a target as well, at least until the story came out tomorrow. Even then, how would someone know if I had more information that hadn't been in the story—or if William did?

We were pulling up to the *Globe* office when I got the breath together to ask the Chief to have a police officer stay near William's room at the hospital. The Chief smiled and patted my hand.

"I've taken care of it, my dear." He looked at his own hand and added, "Perhaps we can find someplace to get you cleaned up before you meet Mr. Forrest."

No way I was delaying, bloody or not. Getting this story to William's editor was my top priority. Maybe, if I got rid of the papers, I could start breathing right again. It was as if William would know, somehow, when the story was launched on its way to morning, and then we could both rest.

In the city room, desks overflowing with old newspapers and other debris sat in no particular pattern. I stared at one desk that stood like a ship in a sea of wadded paper. I could imagine the reporter yanking sheets with errors from the machine hard enough to make the platen spin and then balling the paper up and tossing it.

I had a general impression of a dirty room, but that didn't surprise me. The process of melting down lead type every day forced dirty yellow smoke into the rest of the building. This newsroom also had a cloud of cigar and pipe smoke floating about, covering some, but not enough, of the metal smell—and the human smells. Unlike offices I was used to, the men all seemed to be working in shirtsleeves and waistcoats.

I wondered which desk was William's.

A nasal voice with a slight English accent interrupted my thinking.

"Now that's what I call a bloody woman."

"Forrest," Chief Wright said by way of greeting.

Jack Forrest rose from behind a huge desk—two large desks now that I looked again, butted together and piled with papers around the edges. There was a clear spot in the center where he was laying out tomorrow's paper. He might have to rearrange things soon.

Jack Forrest was my height and several times my girth, even in my full skirt. His hair was white and wispy. I could barely see that his eyes were blue through the squint. I couldn't see his mouth at all behind the white mustache.

He snorted at whatever he read on my face and dismissed me. He turned to Chief Wright, and said, "I suppose this is a police matter."

The man had irritated the heck out of me with all of two sentences. I dropped the satchel to the floor and put my hands on my hips to get his attention. "It is a police matter, Mr. Forrest, that I am covered with William McConnell's blood. It's a matter of his sense of duty to this paper and to you that I have the story that led to his shooting. Do you want it?"

"McConnell?" He looked me up and down, then looked at the Chief. "Mac was shot?"

He paced clumsily behind his desk, maybe to get momentum for asking his questions. It was distracting.

"When? Is he alive? Where is he?" The volume kept rising. "What story?" He ended up asking the Chief, I think.

I stood my ground and tried to take a deep breath. I got enough air to speak. "He was shot in the arm as we were returning from Ste. Genevieve County. You know what he was working on." I pulled the story from my pocket and almost hated to give it up. On an impulse, I held out the papers William had written on but kept the memo book.

"William is at City Hospital. He wanted me to get this story to you. He wrote it on the train this afternoon."

Forrest took the story from me. There were bloody streaks on it, but it wasn't wet. Forrest looked at it, then up at me.

"Who the hell are you?"

"My name is Julia Nye." His wild eyebrows went up, and I knew he had just confirmed my political persuasion. Most women identified themselves—and their status—with Miss or Mrs.

"What's your part in this?" He didn't wait for an answer. He turned to Chief Wright. "Who the hell is she?"

"Watch your language, Mr. Forrest. Miss Nye is a liberated lady, but she's had a tough day."

The Chief put his hands on his hips then, and we all must have looked so belligerent that one part of me couldn't help but be amused. "She's my employee, she's the daughter of Sheriff John Nye of Callaway County, and she's been working with McConnell on this story about the death of Sheriff Picard."

"Your employee? The City of St. Louis is hiring female detectives?"

The Chief wasn't amused. William would have been. I clutched his memo book tighter.

"No, Forrest. She types for me."

I had no patience for this. "Why don't you read the story, Mr. Forrest? William wants me to make sure it includes a statement from Chief Wright, and we haven't had time to talk about that yet."

I sat down, and the two, gentlemen that they were, followed suit. Forrest spread the papers out on his desk, glancing from one page to another.

When he looked up, I said, "The question for Chief Wright is about his thoughts on the caller who suggested a St. Louis police source."

The Chief muttered under his breath. I explained to Forrest about the caller who had alerted Paul Carrey to look for smuggled beer.

The Chief sighed and might have answered. But Forrest wasn't ready to ask, yet.

"I still don't understand what this has to do with you. How do I know that William wrote this?"

The Chief huffed, and I leaned over the edge of the desk onto my elbows. "Is that a British accent I hear in your speech, Mr. Forrest? Is it some English thing about suffrage or do you just not trust women? You know William was in Ste. Gen and Perry Counties working on these stories. We stopped by here and left the message yesterday morning. The Chief knows what we've been doing. Or you can telephone James Ingle. You can telephone Paul Carrey. You can go by the hospital and ask William, but that would irritate him." *If he could answer you* flitted through my mind.

"And," Chief Wright added, "you can ask Miss Nye herself about the fire at Armbruster's. She was there and escaped the building— with a scratch." He gestured at my head.

"You ran that story, remember?" I was hoping to irritate him. But I didn't, at least not that I could recognize. He picked a pen up from his desk and said, "O.K., Chief. What's your comment?" Maybe he knew ignoring me would annoy me even more.

He took down the Chief's words, which were close to William's prediction. But then, what else would the Chief say?

Forrest leaned back in his chair and straightened the papers. "O.K. That's one big story. Second story is my ace police reporter gets himself shot in Union Station. Is there a police report to be had?"

The Chief groaned. "No, there's no report yet, Forrest. I was standing maybe five feet from McConnell, and we were talking. Miss Nye was standing next to him. I went after the shooter, and Miss Nye kept Mac from bleeding to death, along with some help from Potter, the doctor that works the Station. I imagine we could answer a few questions for you." He paused. "Of course, you might have another police reporter, and he can put together a story from some hand-written reports that will appear around eleven, midnight, when this shift ends. Or you can ask Schroeder over at the German *Post*. He was there, too, and might be willing to share the story. He stood. "Come to think of it, you do that. I need to get Miss Nye home."

Forrest turned and barked at someone to come and take down the answers to the questions he began asking about the scene at Union Station.

I answered what I could. The Chief did most of the talking while I clenched my jaw. I dreaded seeing Amelia. I desperately wanted to see William and was afraid to. I stood abruptly and said I needed to go so I could repair my wardrobe, that I was losing clothing fast working on this story.

And at the same time, I didn't much want to walk out of the building. I looked down at the blood on my white blouse. A perfect target.

◆ ◆ ◆

The Chief and I argued about my coming into work tomorrow. He said it wasn't safe for me to be out gallivanting around. I told him I had no intention of gallivanting. And if I weren't safe at Police Headquarters, sitting fifteen feet from his door, then I certainly wouldn't be safe in an empty boarding house all day. By the time we'd arrived at Miller's, he'd agreed to send an officer to escort me to work at mid-morning.

Miller's Boardinghouse was on Laclede Street just west of downtown St. Louis. It had once been a fashionable family neighborhood, but the fashionable families had moved farther west, and the large houses had been converted to flats. Mr. Miller was pleased to let this house out to a new working middle class, a group of "new women."

The Chief considered the boarding house while I let him hand me out of the auto. But then he held onto my hand and tried one more time. "My dear, two of you have gotten hurt now. This is not a game, you know, nothing like sorting out a theft in Fulton with your father. Once that story runs, you are not safe. Leave it to us."

I don't know what he could see on my face, but he changed the subject as if he wanted to take the sting out of his words. "How many ladies live here?"

"There are eight rooms on the second and third floors. We have seven women right now."

"Will anyone else be home?"

To tell the truth, I'd lost track of the time, but I said, "Yes. Some of us get home by five or so." Of course, I was hoping I'd beaten Amelia home.

No such luck. She was at the door. She ran with less grace than usual down the steps. "Julia!" The eyes were sparkling, and I sensed more wolf than fox. "Chief Wright, I assume you're Chief Wright, you found her! What's happened? Where have you been?" As usual, the questions poured out, and the Chief had no chance to confirm what the badge on his coat lapel announced.

"Well, miss, I'm sure Miss Nye will tell you all about it. If you'll excuse me, ladies. . ." He seemed happy to be escaping. "I'll see you tomorrow, my dear."

Amelia started to put a proprietary arm around me, and I ducked away from her. When I sprinted up the steps, I lost her for the moment.

Once inside, though, three other concerned women trapped me. Mary, Elizabeth, and Fran oohed over my blouse. The plaid skirt slowed them for a moment, but then they realized it was bloody as well. The questions were so much noise, and I tried to wave my friends away like gnats.

Amelia was a hornet. She was beside herself. And that was curious. A nasty thought occurred to me. She'd known William and I were headed home from Ste. Gen, according to Carl. Whom had she told?

A moment before I was dodging her concern. Now, I waited out her lecture to go on the offensive. I perched on the edge of a straight back chair in the parlor, being careful to keep my bloody skirt from spilling onto the fabric seat. As I did so, I felt William's memo book in my pocket. I pulled it out and, with it, the memory of William calmly listening to Amelia on the front porch. I looked up at her with a small smile, as she continued to fume.

"I have never known a woman so irresponsible. You get yourself hurt by poking into something that wasn't your business and, then, instead of letting us take care of you, you head off into more trouble. And you lied to us, telling us you were going to your father's. Why, I telephoned the poor man and worried the goodness out of him. How could you worry—"

"How do you know what I was doing Monday night?"

Amelia didn't like being interrupted. She stared at me a moment. Then she moved the attack up a notch and began walking a tight path back and forth in front of me.

"You're embarrassing us, Julia." She gestured around the room.

The women didn't look embarrassed. They looked as if they were glad it wasn't them getting a lecture from Amelia. "You're embarrassing the movement. Carl said you were in Ste. Genevieve County with that reporter from the *Globe*, overnight. Overnight, Julia? You know how careful we have to be to avoid the charge of being loose women. And you go off with a man, and one you hardly know, overnight? What are you thinking, Julia?"

"I'm wondering what you know about Monday night, Amelia."

Amelia stopped pacing and was almost pleasant for a moment. "I know what Carl Schroeder told me. That you were someplace downtown snooping around, and there was a fire. Something about looking for wagon wheels. Why do you care about wheels, Julia?"

She was willing to stop talking now and let me do the answering. I almost laughed. She'd stalled until she came up with the answer. And I couldn't argue with it. Maybe Carl had told her. I couldn't know for sure without asking him.

"You know, Amelia, it's none of your business if I'm looking for wagon wheels, or if I'm in Callaway County or Ste. Genevieve County."

She opened her mouth, but I had another question.

"Tell me Amelia, was it Carl who told you I might be in Ste. Genevieve County?" I tried to think when Carl would have figured out I was there.

"I thought you were going to your father's home. That's what you said."

O.K., she wasn't thinking all that fast. "How did you know I was in Ste. Genevieve? Did you call there?" I decided I could ask nasty questions, as well.

"Well, of course, Carl told me. He's so angry. You know he cares about you, Julia, and you go off with this perfect stranger. And you leave me worried and your father and Chief Wright. How can you just up and leave work, Julia? You are out of control." She fluttered her hands in demonstration. "And you haven't told us what happened. Whose blood is that, Julia?"

I decided the question and answers were at an end. Amelia kept asking who was hurt, but I headed upstairs to find something clean. I would bathe and maybe eat something. I needed to know if James had alerted Amelia—and if Henry was involved. But I would ignore Amelia Ingle the rest of the night and be all over her tomorrow. That was my plan.

As it turned out, Fran was cooking and the smell from the kitchen was bread to go with the spaghetti. The helpful thing was that Mary had slipped upstairs and was filling the third floor bathtub with hot water. It looked wonderful. It sounded wonderful, pouring into the tub.

Mary was almost Amelia's age. Unlike Amelia, she never played big sister, and I appreciated that. She was also tiny, under five feet tall and less than a hundred pounds. More than any of the smaller women, she made me feel awkwardly tall. She didn't smile often because her teeth were small and crooked. What a shame. I was enjoying her smile very much at the moment.

She gestured toward the tub, and I hurried to take advantage of the heat.

It seemed she was going to wait around in the bathroom, maybe to keep Amelia from cornering me while I was in the tub.

I slid under the surface to wet my hair and came up searching for the shampoo.

Mary fidgeted a few moments and then asked, "So, who did get hurt, Julia?"

"Mr. McConnell, the reporter from the *Globe*—who Amelia unfairly maligned."

It would be in the papers in the morning, along with the Picard story. "He was shot as we were walking through the Station."

"Shot? Oh, Julia, shot? Is he . . . ?"

"No, he isn't dead." I was in the mood for bluntness. "But he was shot in the arm, and it bled a lot. I was next to him, so I helped the doctor. William's in City Hospital now."

Mary made a sympathetic sound and examined the towel. "I hope you don't feel bad about what Amelia said. You know she has no room to talk about you seeing someone if you want to."

I was wide-eyed—if not open-mouthed. I ignored the part about me seeing someone. "What in the world do you mean?"

"I mean her room is next to mine, silly goose. I hear them."

"You're saying Amelia Ingle has a man come to her room?"

Mary nodded. "It used to be just once a week, but lately—maybe the last ten days—it's been almost every night."

21

There was a black space on the stairs above us. I don't know how I knew something hid in the darkness, but I did.

William didn't see what I saw. He kept walking. I tried to stay between him and the menace in the dark, to block the shot I knew was coming. I couldn't see him hurt again, although I couldn't really say he'd been hurt a first time. I was somehow behind William when the gunfire erupted from the blackness, and I caught him as he fell. He lay in my lap and called my name, over and over, and every time, it got softer. I tried to say his name more and more loudly, hoping to even out the volume of our combined cries and keep him strong.

He seemed to shrink, although he never shriveled. The whole, bleeding, beautiful man got smaller until he was a size I could have slipped into my pocket. So, I did. I put the tiny man in my pocket and drew my gun and fired and fired into the blackness as it came closer. Even over my firing I could still hear William calling my name. And I was calling his name when the gun in the darkness went off again.

I was lying very still, feeling the cut on my head throb with my heartbeat. And the room was still around me except for the doorknob, which was moving, jiggling. I jerked upright, feeling for a pocket that wasn't in my gown, whispering, "William, where are you?"

The keyhole answered. "Julia, wake up."

I moved toward the door and into reality and knew it was Mary. She pulled me into her room. We were as quiet as the darkness that had stalked me in my nightmare as we sat on her bed, against the wall she shared with Amelia, and listened.

When I was fully awake, I realized I wasn't sure how I felt about this. Eavesdropping on another woman's intimacy was not acceptable. But Amelia's suggestion about William and me wasn't acceptable either—on William's behalf. I tried to understand the words from next door as a distraction. I didn't want to think how William was faring tonight.

Neither Amelia nor her visitor obliged us by speaking in normal voices. I really couldn't identify Amelia from the whispers. And then the talking stopped.

Mary and I could see each other dimly. One of her windows opened south. Moonlight made a distorted rectangle on the floor. Her eyebrows went up as if she wanted to know if I knew what was going on. I did. I'd heard people be intimate before, happened to have heard pleasure and affection and passion from my brother and his new wife.

That was not what I was hearing now. Unless someone else was using Amelia's bedroom, this was a whole different side of her personality. The side that wasn't in control. I might be hearing passion, but I wasn't too sure about affection. She was gasping, just short of panic it seemed.

I leaned close to Mary and asked what was probably a stupid question. "Do you think she's O.K.?"

Mary took me seriously. "This is what I always hear."

I wouldn't want to hear this every night. If I'd awakened to this without Mary to reassure me, I might have worked out a quick excuse and knocked on Amelia's door.

Thankfully, it wasn't long before the putative lovemaking was over. There was more movement, sounds of walking about, and

Amelia was whispering again as though nothing untoward had happened.

Sure enough, in less than half an hour, Mary and I heard a window go up. Lord, it must have been hot in there without a window open. But come to think of it, we would have heard more if Amelia's east window had been open. Mary's window on that side was all the way up.

The fire escape on the third floor circled one side and the back of the building. One window of my corner back room opened onto it, as did both of Mary's windows. Amelia's room was on the front corner, so she had a side window that opened onto the metal walkway, near the steps.

Footsteps hesitated on the metal grill. Mary pulled on my arm, and I lay down beside her. I supposed if the man looked in and saw us, we would say Mary had invited me to sleep with her because of my nightmare. As opposed to eavesdropping and learning Amelia's secret.

The man moved past Mary's east window, hesitating between steps as if he was trying to walk on the metal without waking us. I thought he might look in and then leave. But he continued around the corner and glanced in Mary's other window. He was less likely to see us from there, because the moonlight on the floor would have made our shadow darker.

He continued on to my room, judging from the footsteps. My window was open, and moonlight would be spilling across my bed. I had no idea why that should concern me. Our story would hold, if he returned to tell Amelia. But I was bothered. Why would Amelia's lover come looking in my room or Mary's? I needed to know who the man was, even though I hadn't particularly wanted to know a few minutes ago.

I hadn't figured out a way to see his face, though, by the time he came back along the metal walkway. We heard him near Amelia's window, saying something. It sounded like, "I'll take care of it," or maybe it was "I'll take care of you." That would have been romantic, and nothing had sounded romantic to me yet. Maybe I didn't have Amelia's sophisticated tastes.

The man headed down the fire escape. We could hear a different, fading, creak of the metal steps. The window closed. I was surprised when an additional glow in Mary's window indicated a lamp going on in Amelia's room. The sound that came through the wall was so unexpected that I sat up and gasped—and smothered a laugh.

Amelia was typing.

I knew from experience that it was noisy sitting over a typewriter. It was also hot, I'd bet, from a combination of the electric light and the closed window.

Amelia wasn't that good a typist. There were small pauses between strokes and longer pauses that might have allowed time for erasing. I imagined her bent over the machine in less than good light, her spiky hair more disheveled than usual, sweaty from the summer night—and the sex.

Now Mary had both hands over her mouth, watching me. I assumed she was laughing at my reaction.

I smothered my laughter down enough to lean into Mary and ask if she'd ever heard Amelia type before.

"Most nights."

"Nights when the man visits?"

"Almost always when he visits. Even if they don't share the bed—which is rare."

Oh, beautiful, Amelia. Unpleasant relations and then you get up and start typing in the middle of the night. I collapsed back on the bed and pulled Mary's pillow over my face.

I quickly lost the laughter and fell asleep going over my list for tomorrow: find out if Amelia had known when we would return from Ste. Gen and who she might have told, discover the identity of the lover just in case he might be involved, check on William. The last would be both the easiest and hardest.

22

From the **St. Louis Globe-Democrat**, *Thursday, June 13, 1910*

Staff reporter William McConnell, of the Globe-Democrat, was shot in the arm Wednesday afternoon at Union Station, as he was returning from Ste. Genevieve County. He had been there covering the continuing investigation of the death of Sheriff Claude Picard. (See the story on the investigation above.)

Mr. McConnell was crossing the Station waiting room in the company of Miss Julia Nye, an employee of the St. Louis Police Department, when the shot was fired. St. Louis Police Chief Micah Wright was nearby. Mr. McConnell was taken to City Hospital and his condition is not known at this time

Mr. McConnell has been a reporter for the Globe-Democrat for ten years.

The kitchen smelled of bacon and toast, but the food was long gone by the time I made it downstairs the next morning. Amelia appeared, although I was sure she should be leaving for work by now. I offered a sour grin and moved around her, going for the oatmeal jar. She grabbed a newspaper off the table and blocked me at the same time.

"Julia! What is this? Why wouldn't you tell me about that man being shot? Did you know the *Globe* was going to use your name?"

I grabbed the paper. Below William's Picard article was a shorter article about the shooting at Union Station.

Amelia was trying to tell me how bad this looked and so on, and I was in no mood for it. I pushed her away, not roughly, just away, and tossed the paper on the big round table. As I shoved pans around looking for a small one, she kept talking.

I thumped the pot on the burner, slopping oatmeal and milk over the side. "Leave it be, Amelia. Go to work, and I'm going to do the same."

"You're going to work? When? And why don't you just go home to your father? You're hurt, aren't you?"

I was tired of the multiple questions, but at least these were easy. "I am all right. I am not running home to my father. And I arranged to go into work mid-morning."

Amelia glared at me. "All right, Julia, if you feel you must. I think it's a mistake, but you obviously don't care what I think." She bustled off, slamming the door.

Chief Wright was sending an officer to get me at ten. I cleaned up my mess and wondered if I could make it to the hospital and back. Silly thing to do. The whole idea of having an officer escort me to work hinged on the notion that I might be in danger. Besides I wasn't sure I could face William. I told myself first thing this morning that I'd think later about visiting. But, of course, I knew I would think about it all day.

My gut said I was responsible for the shooting. Frankly, I couldn't even make myself pick up the newspaper. I had to know why it had happened. Leaving the question to the Chief's men wouldn't begin to take care of my conscience.

The only place I knew to start was with Carl's suspicions about the Ingles. If Amelia were involved, somehow, I could check out her room. Lover-boy's "I'll take care of it" echoed in my head. I wanted to know who he was. Maybe there would be a picture or letter with his name.

I left the oatmeal cooling and was up the two flights with breath to spare now that I had a purpose. I tried Amelia's door and, of course, it was locked. I unlocked my south window. I normally would have left it open but the man's snooping last night had made me nervous.

It wasn't easy to climb out a window in a long skirt and petticoats, and I wondered for the hundredth time if I would live to see the day I could wear something sensible.

I started to push against Amelia's window glass, hoping to raise it that way, and stopped at the last minute. I raised my skirt, showing lots of thin petticoat if anyone had been looking, and pressed my hands against the glass through the fabric. I didn't want my handprints on the window, although I did note in passing that someone else hadn't been so careful.

Thank goodness Amelia had left her window unlocked. In case someone wanted in while she wasn't there?

The window sucked free at the bottom, and then I could put one hand under the lower edge and push up. I sat on the sill and swung my legs in.

The typewriter was on a tottery desk right beside the window, as if Amelia valued what air might seep in at night. So I hadn't gone far when I saw what I needed to see. I could have turned and scooted back out immediately. But I was stunned.

I not only recognized the form beside the typewriter, I recognized the subject matter and the typewriter's distinctive signature: uneven strokes, some keys that barely made contact.

Amelia hadn't finished last night. She'd have another night of typing to finish Detective Terence Kelley's report on the arson at Armbruster's Wheels.

Lordy. When I had shaken my head sufficiently for all the good that was going to do, I glanced around the room for pictures or such. Nothing. And I wanted out. I had to exit the way I'd come in, and everything was an obstacle. I couldn't get my skirts to cooperate. The window didn't just close. It fell so hard I was surprised the glass didn't break. I tripped in the metal grid. I all but fell into my own room.

And froze. Footsteps, too heavy for any of my housemates, were coming up the stairs fast. I lunged for the Hopkins & Allen. Then I stepped behind my sofa bed, thinking I should have closed the door to my room before I ventured out on the fire escape.

I saw him on the stairs and began to relax as Carl stepped into my doorway.

"Julia." Not a question, or even a verbal challenge. Just my name as if it were a welcome fact. The way you'd look out the door and say, "Rain," in a dry season.

I sighed, put the gun in my pocket, and went toward him. Carl followed the motion of the gun and whispered, "Christ, Julia."

Then he hugged me, gently. I don't know why I let him, really, but it was a warm and comforting thing, and I leaned against his chest for a moment.

"How did you get in?"

"Your front door was unlocked. And I glimpsed someone on the fire escape up here, turning toward the back." Carl gestured at the window I hadn't closed yet. "Was that you?"

"Yes. Checking things."

I pushed away, concerned that someone would see us, which was silly.

There were lots of things I wanted to know and things I needed to tell him, but I asked the obvious first. "How's William?"

He stood very still for several seconds, and I gasped.

"No, no, he was breathing better when I left him last night. He was as good as he could be. Aware enough to insist I get on over to the *Post* and get what stories I could in." He stared at me another few seconds. "Are you going to the hospital?"

I swallowed. "Maybe this evening. I've got to get to work, and I promised Chief Wright I wouldn't go out without an escort. He's sending an officer around any minute."

"I know. I went to Headquarters looking for you." He snorted lightly. "I'm glad you're finally going to be careful."

He said it like an indictment, charging that William wouldn't have been hurt if I'd been careful in the first place. Maybe I read too much into his statement, but guilt will do that for you.

"I'll be careful today, but I've got to know why . . . that happened. Carl, who knew that William and I were coming back from Ste. Gen with information on Picard?"

He rubbed his forehead, hard. "Amelia Ingle." He glanced at the door.

I shook my head. "She's gone."

"I called your father and Marjorie Picard from here. She overheard every word of my end of the conversations." If Carl felt guilty about that, he let it go. I could see him warming to his suspicions. "Do you think she called Henry? Or"—his tone shifted, and I would have laughed at the melodrama if it weren't so serious and personal—"maybe James called her earlier. She seemed to be saying she didn't really think you'd gone home."

"And James told her to arrange an assassination attempt?" I huffed. I was recalling that Amelia said she'd called my father: a lie, apparently

Carl started to say, "It could be . . ."

"Wait a minute. You called from here? And Amelia was home from work? When was this?"

"Early . . . middle . . . afternoon."

Why in the world Amelia hadn't been at work?

"And why were you here?"

"Looking after you, of course. I figured either you'd be here or no one would."

A knock on the door downstairs and a call of "Miss Nye?" got my attention. Lordy, Carl had left the front door unlocked just as Amelia had. I yelled back, "Coming!"

"I've got to talk to you about Amelia," I said as I turned to close and lock my window. "For now, explain to whoever's down there that we're checking the fire escape because there may have been an intruder last night." I gathered up the satchel that was now a purse.

"An intruder? Tell me."

"Go." I got a glare from him, but he ran down the stairs as I worked on locking the door to my room.

In the parlor, I found Officer Jamison, the young patrolman from the fire scene. Carl was indeed explaining that the ladies were concerned about the fire escape.

I jumped in to explain that we were wondering if someone could get into our rooms at night via the fire escape because we had heard noises last night.

Patrolman Jamison shut his mouth, maybe to hide his shock that Carl had just come down from our rooms. He recovered and said, "Yes, ma'am. Let's look around outside, and we'll be on our way."

Carl's glance seemed to confirm it wasn't only my paranoia that had made me greet him with a gun. Or that the gun was in my pocket, not in my bag.

I locked our front door, checked it, and said, "The fire escape starts right here beside the house." I led the way and could almost hear Carl behind me trying to put it together.

We rounded a dirt space that'd once held flowers and shrubs, no doubt, a space outlined by dirty red bricks. We kept cans for collecting trash here, near the foot of the fire escape.

Like most fire escapes, this one stopped something like six feet from the ground, high enough that it was something of a chore to get on it. It occurred to me that you could upend a trashcan and be about the right height to at least pull yourself up to the bottom step—if you were strong enough. Carl thought of that, too, and suggested it.

Jamison walked around the cans, while I thought out loud. "The cans would work fine except that we keep them rather full. It could get messy if a lid came off." Smelly, too, judging from what I could tell with the lid closed.

"I don't think anyone would need to do that, ma'am," Jamison said. He wrestled out a large, round, wooden cylinder, with a step built into it. If you glanced casually, it looked like another can, but it wouldn't have gotten our attention because it was pushed back behind a scraggly bush and had been lying on its side. You could see the dirt after Jamison set it upright.

"This would make it easy to get up on the step if you were tall enough." He was eyeballing the distance.

"Oh my, yes." I tried to sound distressed. I didn't know if it was to our advantage or disadvantage if lover-boy—and I was still dealing with the idea that it might be Terence Kelley—couldn't get in tonight. On the whole, I thought it wouldn't hurt to interrupt the loving for one evening. "Do you think we should leave it here?"

Carl was practically hopping. "Someone could use this to get into any of the rooms on the second or third floor. You can't leave it there."

"We don't have room for it, and I'm not sure I have the right to take it in." Jamison thought a minute and made his decision. "Let's ask the Chief—or a detective."

I nearly choked, not knowing which detective he'd find first. But it was reasonable. He only had a buggy, and there was no room.

"Besides," he said, "I don't think anyone would crawl up here in broad daylight."

I might as well agree with him. "You're right. I'd like to get to my nice, safe desk."

Carl rolled his eyes at me and said, "Why don't I bring lunch in so you won't have to go out?"

"Excellent idea," I agreed, with great, faked enthusiasm. He waved good-bye and hurried off down the street. Jamison watched him a moment and then looked back at me. I feared he was drawing conclusions about my relationship with Mr. Schroeder. That would have been funny except for a voice in my head that said, "Oh, good, Julia, you could get him shot, too."

23

By the time we got to Headquarters, I'd convinced Jamison we could step into the Chief's office and ask him about the worrisome fake-barrel. We did, and the Chief told Jamison to take a wagon and bring the thing in.

The Chief didn't ask after William or comment on the *Globe* story. He asked after me, and I said I was fine, maybe a bit nervous. He humphed as if he doubted that, and I decided to take his doubt as a compliment.

But the kid glove treatment ended there. Cops stopped by to say they knew I was dangerous, but they'd forgotten to warn Mac. Or that would teach William to go strolling with a "bachelor girl" in public. I detected some concern—for William, of course—in their teasing. He was popular with the cops, and they eagerly awaited word of his condition. Probably not as eagerly as I did.

Carl appeared just after noon, more jittery than usual and frowning. But he had what I needed: a good sandwich, an eagerness to hear my . . . gossip . . . and word of William, due to a quick stop at the hospital.

We wandered around with sandwiches and department coffee in hand, looking for a private place to sit. Carl fielded all the clever comments about the danger of being anywhere near me. We finally ended up on the back steps. Anyone could have come out the back door, which opened into a courtyard where wagons faced the street.

But we'd hear anyone who came out and could change topic. The only ones who could hear us unseen were the horses, and they were busy with lunch as well.

Part of me wanted to hear about William, and part of me was scared to know. So, I went to the investigative question. "Do you really think Amelia Ingle is in on . . . the shooting?"

"It's possible. Only a handful of people knew you and Will would be at the train station yesterday, and Amelia Ingle was one of them. Until we get this sorted, I think you should be careful what you say to her."

"Well, then. Wait 'til you hear this."

I started with saying that Amelia had given me a hard time about how bad it looked that I was with William. Carl hooted softly. He'd been willing to say the same thing, loudly and publicly, yesterday afternoon. I narrowed my eyes at him to let him know what I thought of such unsophisticated statements and told him about Mary's attempts to console me, in both telling me about Amelia's lover and inviting me to listen.

"You listened? Good God, Julia, you are . . ." He stopped. I raised an eyebrow and waited.

He shook his head and finally said, "That's so . . . rude."

I burst out laughing. "Carl, what is wrong with you? This is the family you've been accusing of everything from fanaticism to murder."

"I know, but it's such a . . . catty . . . female thing to do. How would that guy feel if he knew?"

"The guy? That's who you're worried about?"

"Well, yes." He risked a glance at me and hurried to finish his sandwich. "I mean, I can't imagine having a couple of women listening and giggling and . . ."

I sighed in impatience. "For one thing, we weren't giggling. There was nothing funny about it."

Carl's eyes widened. To get him off that track, I said, "And if you want to know how he feels about the whole building listening to his exploits, ask him."

"Are you saying I know him? You recognized the voice? Or saw him?"

"I couldn't, didn't. But I went back up to Amelia's room this morning to see what she was typing."

"Typing? How does typing come into this?"

I couldn't keep the grin off my face.

"What?"

So I explained that the typing seemed to follow the relations, rather regularly. I could hardly believe I was having this discussion with a man, but it was rather liberating. Very modern. Carl was shaking with the laughter he was trying to control. Finally, he wheezed and asked, "Who?"

"As I said, I went up there today to see what she was typing. I didn't suppose it would tell me who her lover is." I paused and looked around, expecting to find Terence Kelley on the step behind me. He wasn't there, of course, but I leaned in close to Carl, just in case.

"You know Detective Kelley doesn't let me type his reports."

Carl's eyes widened again.

"He says he'd rather do them himself than depend on some woman to get it right."

Carl's mouth fell open.

"But, he does depend on a woman, a bad typist with a worse typewriter. Of course," I tried to smile, "I suppose there are compensations."

Carl shook his head for several seconds and then jumped to his

159

favored conclusion.

"So, we have the detective who just happened to be at Armbruster's when you arrived to look at the wheel connected to the Ingle family. Maybe Henry Ingle set it all up. I can't imagine that Terence Kelley would have anything to do with Amelia or anyone in your household otherwise."

"Why do you say that?"

"He goes on all the time about how 'new women' are a curse. You irritate him just by being in the office. And then you open your mouth, and he's furious. You should hear what he says when he comes back into the squad room."

I swallowed hard. "So, why would he be seeing Amelia? He has to know her political convictions."

Carl fiddled with the paper from his sandwich, and I was sure he was working through the politics.

I tried again. "We don't know that Kelley had anything to do with this. He could just be a cad that gets his girlfriend to do his typing."

"Right. But we know he is a cad. He tells everyone women should stay in their place. Of course, he doesn't like reporters, either. Me, in particular, and I'm wondering if that's a temperance thing, too. It's certain he never goes out drinking with the guys." Carl wadded the paper wrapper. "That's it. He's temperance."

Carl started pacing. "Did Kelley get in using the fire escape?"

"I assume so. That's how he left. I think the barrel-thing had to be his."

"Then he'd have access to your room. I don't think you should sleep there, Julia." He'd developed a frown, but I didn't wait to hear more. I was off on another tangent.

"What if it isn't Kelley? What if it's some other police officer, who has assured Kelley his girlfriend will do the typing for him?" I hated it when I complicated my life like that. "Maybe Kelley doesn't even know who does the typing."

"I guess that's possible. So, you watch out for Kelley this evening. Find out what you can, but be careful. And I'll find out what Henry knows."

"When do we go?"

"Me, not you."

"You'll just provoke him, Carl. I at least need to be there to watch his reaction."

"It's too dangerous, Julia. I'll go by myself."

"Armed? Will you go armed, Carl, and by yourself?" Carl didn't carry a gun. Guns were a country habit he didn't share with William— or me.

"Could you shoot someone, Julia? Really?"

I looked at him and thought about yesterday. If I'd seen anybody identifiable as the shooter on that landing, I'd have drawn my revolver instead of a shawl. If I'd had a clear shot, I'd have taken it. The odds were good I'd have hit my target. Carl surely had no idea I was more than competent with a gun. John Nye's daughter was the best shot in Callaway County. Maybe beyond.

And what would have happened to William if I hadn't stopped the bleeding?

Carl was still waiting for my answer to the gun question when I asked, "Do you think he's going to be O.K.?"

He had to know what I meant, but he hesitated over his answer. "Well. You and the doctor stopped the blood loss. Unless there was something dirty on that shawl of yours, it shouldn't go bad."

I groaned.

"There's nothing else you can do, Julia. Just let him be. Being angry may be good medicine for him."

"Angry?"

"Well, it's hard to cover the story from a hospital bed. If he's able to stew about anything, he's going to be aggravated, trust me.

Aggravated with me, most likely. I would certainly go with Carl to the Ingles' house tonight. Maybe I could protect Carl, but, as importantly, it would be my excuse for not going to the hospital.

24

We agreed Carl would escort me out of the office at five, and we'd visit Henry Ingle. I headed upstairs and, as I opened the doors, Terence Kelley was coming around from behind my desk. With a particularly unpleasant smirk on his face.

"I saw you and Carl Schroeder in the courtyard, flirting." It was an announcement on his part, not a question. And, of course, it probably had looked like that.

I narrowed my eyes at him as I moved around the desk to my chair. "Mr. Schroeder is a friend, as you well know, Detective. He came over to tell me how Mr. McConnell is doing."

"So, you're involved with both of them?"

"I'm not involved with either of them in the sense you mean, Detective Kelley. And if I were . . . it's not your concern."

He put his hands on my desk and leaned toward me. "The fact that we have hired a nosy, pushy whore to work in this office is a concern to all of us."

I'd had the occasional heckler refer to me, to us, as whores while my friends and I lectured in public. But I'd never had an individual get close and accuse me. I bit back comment after comment, most of them involving Amelia. I didn't dare until I was sure.

And maybe he wasn't involved—with either Amelia or the whole Picard matter. He surely wouldn't go out of his way to irritate me if he wanted me not to consider his appearance and behavior at the wheel shop. Or maybe he was just arrogant.

I calmly picked up a report before I answered, "Well, I'm not a whore, and I'm sorry you feel that way, Detective."

I had started keeping a small vase with flowers, nothing special, only the flowers they sell down at the market, on the left front corner of my desk. I heard Kelley curse and looked up to see him start with the vase, spilling water as he swept his forearm all the way across the six-foot wide desk. Papers, supplies and a small ceramic dog crashed across the desk. Water sprayed over me and the papers in my typewriter.

I was on my feet before everything crashed to the floor. Terence Kelley and I stared at each other, and the looks flared into a competition to see who was angrier, who was more determined, who would say something nasty, something they'd regret, first.

"Terry!" I knew the voice was George St. Martin. The way he said the name—and who else would call Kelley 'Terry'—told me he hadn't appeared coincidentally. He'd seen enough of the exchange to be shocked by what Kelley had done.

The Chief barreled out of his office and yelled, "Kelley" as well. He came around behind me to examine the mess on the floor. "What is this?"

"A day's worth of reports," I replied. George grabbed Kelley's shoulder and tried to pull the taller man backwards. Kelley shrugged him off.

The Chief did manage to pull me backwards, behind him almost. "I don't know what this is about, Kelley, but I will find out, and we will discuss it later. Right now, you get out on the street and do your job."

Kelley still glared at me over the Chief's shoulder.

"Go!" Chief Wright yelled with enough force that I could hear an immediate decrease in the murmur of voices from the squad room doorway.

Kelley mouthed, "Bitch," and backed out the door. The Chief grunted as he read Kelley's lips.

The Chief and George stared at the double doorway for a moment. There was a shout, as Kelley must have run into someone going down the stairs. Both the Chief and George St. Martin swiveled to consider me.

"What was that about?" the Chief asked. I smiled at him, a sour smile that must have suggested I wasn't going to say much, and knelt to pick up the papers. He turned to George.

"Did you see what this was all about?"

I glanced up to see that George's eyes were green and wide, his dark brown hair spikier than usual, as if the scene had scared him. He clearly did not want to answer the question.

"Well, I'm not sure. I think they were having an argument."

"I could hear that. About what? What are a detective and our typist arguing about?" The Chief stooped to help me pick up the papers. "What did you say to him, Julia?"

To my surprise, George answered the Chief's question. "Truth is, Chief, Terence said something to her, and she didn't respond. So he got her attention with . . . this." He gestured to the mess.

The Chief jerked to his feet, dripping papers in his hand. I took them from him and dropped them in the trash basket beside my desk. He followed their motion as if he couldn't believe I wasn't angry about the wasted day's work. Then he looked at me a second time and drew back.

Maybe he understood that I was angry about Marjorie Picard's grief and about William's pain. And somehow, that was linked to whatever had passed between Terence Kelley and me.

He turned to George. "What did he say?"

George took a deep breath. "He called her a nosy, pushy whore."

And now enough of the crew crowding the doorway had heard that it was going to be an issue.

I used one of the drier pieces of paper to sweep pieces of ceramic into a pile. The dog's head stared at me. I stared back for a moment, wondering if there was enough of the dog left to glue him back together. Maybe. I could pick up the pieces and take them home to sort out. I glanced at my oversized bag, thinking I could put the pieces in it.

Then I looked at it again. It was upside down. Could I have done that when I jumped to my feet? No. I might have kicked it to one side, but not turned it upside down. Did Kelley want me to think I'd upset it as I jumped to my feet? I pictured him standing slightly behind my desk as I came in the room.

I crawled toward it and picked up the bottom of the bag. A comb and a handkerchief were on the floor underneath it, and as I raised it, an apple rolled out.

I held it there a minute while the Chief stared at me. Abruptly, he turned to his office and ordered both George and me to join him. "Bring the satchel," he added.

I left the three items on the floor and carried the empty bag upside down into the Chief's office. The murmur from the small crowd of officers rose as they watched us walk away.

The Chief sat down hard in his chair as soon as George had closed the door behind us. "Tell me, Julia, what's going on."

I put the bag into one of the barrel-back chairs and rested my hands on the back of it, considering him, hoping to communicate that I wasn't going to say everything I knew in front of George.

"I didn't knock this over. I haven't looked at it since I came back from lunch. I didn't take it with me to lunch." I glanced at George. "Someone was into it."

"Are you linking this to Terence, Julia?" George asked. "Because if you are, I think you're wrong."

"Why do you say that, Detective St. Martin?" the Chief asked.

"He's got a bad temper, but he wouldn't go digging around in a lady's bag." George was quiet and earnest, defending his friend.

"Julia," the Chief turned to me, "What would someone have been looking for?" While I hesitated, he added, "And did they find it?"

How much to say. How much to say in front of George.

"Well, the bag was nearly empty. I took it to Ste. Genevieve and emptied it out last night. All it had in it today was what you saw out there, a comb and a handkerchief. An apple I picked up this morning." I thought a minute. "Maybe a hair ribbon. I usually carry a spare." I dug in the bag, and the white ribbon was there. I pulled it out and showed the Chief. "My keys should be in an inside pocket." I dug those out with relief. But I was stalling. I couldn't find the little bag that held an extra cylinder-worth of ammunition. I couldn't remember at the moment if I'd put it back in the bag.

And, of course, the important things that might have been there, weren't. The Hopkins & Allen was in one pocket of my skirt, William's memo book in the other. I didn't care to mention any of that in front of George.

I was glad the Chief asked the next question because George wouldn't have answered me. "Do you know where Terence Kelley was during lunch, George?"

"No. I'm working on the McConnell shooting. I've been interviewing witnesses and came back after lunch." He glanced at me. "When were you away from your desk?"

"From just after noon until ten, fifteen, minutes ago. I ate in the courtyard with Carl Schroeder."

George sighed. Honestly.

The Chief said, "O.K. Someone upturned your bag looking for something they didn't find. Lock it up next time. And be even more careful than that, Julia. You get an escort home tonight, and I want you to stay there."

He stood up, and George and I were dismissed. As we went out the door, George added his admonition. He leaned close and said, "Please do be careful, Julia. I worry about you."

"I intend to, Detective St. Martin." I kept walking toward my desk, dropped the bag in my chair and veered off toward the custodian's closet to get a broom. George hesitated and then left. Perhaps to interview more witnesses to the McConnell shooting.

I wondered when he would get around to interviewing me.

25

The Chief and I had a brief confrontation over the matter of who would escort me home. Jamison was standing by, but Carl arrived right at five and volunteered. After several minutes of debate, we agreed that both would escort me. The Chief mentioned the satchel incident, and Carl had to hear about that. I could tell he was getting anxious. I'd never seen him frown so much.

At the streetcar stop, I said, "Look, Officer Jamison, we're just a couple of blocks away. Go on home or back to work." I tried to seem sympathetic. "We can walk from here."

But Jamison was too good for that. He did stop short of going in the boarding house again. Assassination attempts were one thing. Three suffragists on the front porch was another. I thanked him and hoped he knew I meant it. He reminded me that someone would be by at six in the morning.

Carl and I stood around and chatted with the girls. Under normal circumstances, Carl would have enjoyed a mild flirtation with Fran, even though I was pretty sure he didn't think Fran was as special as she thought he was. Now, even Fran was frowning. Carl's conviviality level was slipping.

"Well," I sighed, "Carl and I have an errand to run. I should be back in time for leftovers."

They all started to protest, even though I'm not sure they understood the situation. Amelia would have been difficult, but she hadn't appeared, maybe wasn't home yet.

We made our escape, walking fast toward the streetcar stop. I thought I heard someone, Mary maybe, calling my name. But I knew if we turned around, it would be a lot harder getting away a second time. So, I pretended Carl and I were in such exuberant conversation that I couldn't hear.

It took a while to get out to the University City neighborhood where the Ingles lived. We tried to talk about what we would say to Henry, about what had happened at the office. As people would move away from us, we'd managed to share our latest thoughts. But we were traveling in the same direction as the people who worked in the city and lived in the new homes springing up west of downtown, west even from Forest Park. The streetcar was crowded.

Henry Ingle lived with his parents. He had no obvious political compulsion to live elsewhere or romantic requirements, either. We thought he'd be home because he was the early shift at the bank where he worked.

Sure enough, Henry answered the door. His eyebrows rose, and he tilted his head at us.

In the background, his mother asked who it was. Before Henry responded, he whispered, "Is Amelia O.K.?"

I whispered back, "Fine, last time I saw her."

"Some friends of mine, Mother," he called back.

"Oh," Mrs. Ingle bustled into sight before we could make a move to sit on the front porch. "Oh, Julia, isn't it?"

I'd met Mrs. Ingle and her husband once before, when they'd paid a Sunday afternoon call to the boarding house. They'd seemed curious about the women their daughter was living with at that point, some of them being a bit transient. I'd only been there a couple of months myself. I was surprised she remembered me, although I certainly remembered her well enough. She was so much like Amelia. She was plumper, maybe even prettier. Her cheeks dimpled and her eyes sparkled when she smiled at me, and then she turned the smile on Carl. It didn't work.

Henry dutifully did the introductions. He didn't have the women's dimples, and his eyes weren't sparkling. He said he and Carl needed to discuss a matter and would do so on the front porch. Mrs. Ingle frowned. I hoped she didn't intend to listen in. So, when she asked if I'd like to rest inside while the men had their talk, I decided to take her up on it. I glanced at Carl, and he nodded, as much in surprise as in approval. I hoped there was only talk out here.

Inside, I readily agreed that it was going to commence getting hot any day now. That exhausted the weather topic, and I complimented Mrs. Ingle on her décor. It really was nice, the new prairie style, all smooth wood surfaces and straight lines and sturdiness. The new house had simplicity built in, unlike Marjorie Picard's, and Susan Ingle had the new furniture to match.

I walked over to a cabinet that drew my eye. The glass between its flat, lustrous oak panels was opaque and leaded. One door was slightly open, on purpose, to suggest its contents, books below, and on the top shelf, a stack of ribbons, blue ribbons, from what I could see. Contest ribbons.

"Oh my, someone has been winning at something." The thought running through my head was that Amelia did indeed debate competitively.

Mrs. Ingle seemed glad to have something to talk about. She joined me at the cabinet and said, "Yes, these are Henry's, for the most part."

She pulled out an open-top case that had stacks of ribbons. The blue ones were on top with others beneath. Still, it was a nice collection . . . honoring something. I tried to pick one up and got a handful that were pinned together. The one on top read, "First place. Handguns Competition. St. Louis Shooting Society. Spring 1905."

Mrs. Ingle turned her head to read with me and said, "This would be one of the last years that Henry competed."

Years? "Well." I looked over the number of ribbons, all blue, in this group. "He must have been good."

She laughed, maybe at my tone. "It's our family hobby, my dear. Henry's been shooting since he was young. His father insisted it was good discipline, but the truth is, they enjoyed the shooting and the time they all spent together." She paused and looked fondly toward the porch. "Henry can enjoy the competition without letting it consume him. I think that's a very good trait, don't you?"

I hadn't thought about it, but now I focused on the contrast between Henry and his older sister. Amelia let her interests consume her. I wondered if that's what Mrs. Ingle was talking about.

"Yes, now that you point it out, that is a good trait. Of course, some causes require dedication, like the suffragist movement."

"Oh, indeed, yes, my dear. But it is a gift, I think, to be passionate about a cause—as Henry is about prohibition as well as suffrage—and not become obsessive."

She looked me in the eye and smiled, something of a sad smile. Maybe we were thinking along the same lines: Amelia overdid a good thing. I smiled back and tried to think of how to broach the subject when we heard a noise from the porch, like someone or something hitting the wall in the next room. I said, "Goodness, I hope nothing is broken. Carl and Henry should be through talking. Let's see if something has fallen." Right. I led the way to the door.

26

Carl had thought in detail about how to proceed at the Ingles's. He'd decided on being to the point and insistent. Julia's presence would have been nice if the matter went smoothly, but that was unlikely. He was glad she'd gone inside. There'd be time for airing a victory on their way home.

Henry's frown deepened as they moved away from the door. He seemed resentful already. And was about to get more resentful if Carl could manage it. Henry led the way to the end of the porch, away from the open windows of the parlor.

He turned abruptly. "It's an unusual time to call, Mr. Schroeder. How can I help you?"

"I want to know what you know about a murder in Ste. Genevieve and an attempted murder here."

Henry's blue eyes got brighter and bigger, and his chin went up. He seemed to calm himself with an effort and sat back against the brick knee wall of the porch. He seemed not to want to raise his voice, so he hissed. "Are you accusing me of complicity in those events?"

Amusing. Henry's hissing would have been more effective if he hadn't been half a foot shorter and sitting.

Henry tried again. "Are you saying I went to Ste. Genevieve County and murdered a man I scarcely knew but by reputation? And then walked into Union Station and took a shot at a man I do know, if slightly? Are you suggesting, Mr. Schroeder, that I would be mad enough to do that?"

"I'm saying you and your cousin and your sister have had the opportunity to be involved. And the motivation."

Henry's fine eyebrows rose. Carl had to admit that the outrage in his eyes seemed genuine. He was glad Julia wasn't there to see it.

"The motivation? What possible motivation?"

"Oh, come now, Ingle. You and your cousin are prohibition. You got rid of a man who was bootlegging liquor. You tried to stop the story that William was bringing back. We know how strongly you feel about prohibition. But you've gone too far."

"Feel about prohibition?" Henry stood as if he wanted to start pacing but didn't dare get his mother's attention. He turned away and then turned back. Carl rocked forward, leaving him little room to do more.

"We favor prohibition because alcohol kills people. We don't kill people to advance the cause of prohibition."

Carl chose to ignore the sense in his words.

Henry threw up a hand. "If you suspect us because we're prohibitionists, you have a long list of people to choose from, Schroeder."

Thank goodness Carl had an answer for that. "You had that wheel delivered to Armbruster's, right? Only you and James knew it was there. And then someone told David Picard. As soon as Julia goes to ask after it, someone sets the shop on fire. James knew William was headed back here with the story and could have called you. For that matter, Amelia knew and could have called you. It would have been convenient if that story hadn't run. And your cousin stands to be sheriff in Picard's place, to take over his job—minus the beer trade. That's a lot of motivation. Or a lot of coincidence."

"Well, Schroeder, you're just wrong." Henry had started shaking his head during Carl's recitation. "I don't know who else knew about the wheel. And perhaps other people knew that Miss Nye and McConnell were headed back from Ste. Genevieve together. But I didn't." Ingle snorted. "And James would never commit or condone murder. He is a law officer, and he upholds the law. He may not have approved of Picard breaking the law, but that wouldn't tempt him to do likewise. You really know neither me nor James to make such allegations."

"Suggest someone else." Carl leaned closer.

To his credit, Henry didn't back up. "I'd like to know who's firing at people in Union Station as much as you do. I'm quite concerned for Mr. McConnell. If you think it's your job to solve these cases, go look for a real lead, Schroeder. Meanwhile, get off our porch."

He turned away, with a bitter glance, but Carl didn't give way.

"I may leave, but I'll be watching you. If you make a move to get rid of me or Julia—that would be a mistake."

Henry's fair complexion started to turn red. Of course, Carl could imagine that he was pink himself. "I do not engage in violence, Mr. Schroeder, not even when I'm provoked by the likes of you and your drinking buddies. And I certainly would not harm or threaten Miss Nye. I suggest in turn that you leave me—and my sister, should you be inclined to follow this ridiculous obsession with my family—strictly alone."

"Your sister is just as crazed as you are, Ingle. Staying out of her way is one of my priorities."

Henry took a quick breath and, as he exhaled, shoved Carl against the wall of the house. A small wicker table stood behind Carl, and he all but sat on it—and on the vase of pansies. The vase didn't crash to the floor, but it did fall over, and the moisture soaked one leg of his trousers.

In the time it took Carl to stand, Henry was at the front door, opening it for Julia, who seemed to be rushing to the rescue.

She stopped and put her hands on her hips and didn't seem to regard the situation with any degree of seriousness. Behind her, Mrs. Ingle bustled out and said, "Oh my, Mr. Schroeder, are you hurt?"

Henry took his mother's arm and pulled her inside. "He's fine, Mother. Let's let him and Miss Nye be on their way."

Embarrassment and irritation washed over Carl. Clearly, he couldn't go after Ingle with the man's mother on the porch. From the look on Julia's face, he wasn't even sure he could get past her. She took his arm and turned back to say, "Yes, we do need to hurry on. I enjoyed your home, Mrs. Ingle. Henry."

"Miss Nye. Please be careful in whatever you're about." Henry's voice was tight.

Julia stopped. "We will be careful, Henry. Thank you."

27

We rode the almost empty streetcar back into the City without talking—now that we could. I judged that Henry Ingle was innocent. Dad would groan about the weight I put on my first assessment of people's character, but Henry Ingle simply didn't seem the type for murder or arson. O.K., he didn't seem the type for shooting competitions either, but the ribbons said otherwise.

I sighed. "I should tell you what I found out while you were shoving each other about." Carl turned a troubled face toward me. "Guess what the Ingle family hobby is?"

"Causing trouble?"

"Be serious, Carl. Their 'family hobby' is target shooting, according to Mrs. Ingle."

Carl looked ready to jump off the seat. "Guns? The Ingles have guns?" The two men standing on the platform glanced back inside.

"Be quiet, Carl. They do competition shooting. I saw some of Henry's blue ribbons. Of course they'd have guns."

Carl threw himself against the back of the seat. "I knew it," he shouted. I glanced toward the men at the back. *He's always right*, my smile tried to say.

"Carl. It could be coincidence." I spoke softly. "Lots of people shoot for a hobby."

"Nobody I know."

That wasn't strictly true. I certainly had used guns as a hobby, back in Fulton, although I'd never had much use for formal competitions. "Lots of people do," I repeated.

Carl seemed to think I was defending the enemy and turned in the seat to mutter about prohibition in general and the Ingles in particular.

"What are you going to do now?"

"Well, I'm going to get you home so you can spy out the evening activities of your favorite housemate. Then I'm going to see William. Maybe I'll make it to work."

"O.K. Maybe you can tell William I have a chore for the evening, spying on Amelia."

Carl turned. "Are you going to go see him sometime?"

That was a hard question. I tried not to let my guilt show through. Or even wonder why Carl was staring at me, as intense and unsmiling as he'd been about the Ingles.

"Of course. Sometime. It's hard with the escort and all. Maybe after all this is settled."

Carl was nodding. "Good idea. That you wait. Let's get you home safe for now."

I knew I was in trouble, though, when we were close enough to the house to see the front porch. Everyone seemed to be standing out front but not to enjoy the evening or the gathering clouds. We needed the rain. Amelia was in the middle of things. Speaking of storm clouds.

As soon as we were close enough, she was yelling. "You got a police escort home and then you left? Julia, what are you thinking?"

Before I could answer or make it clear that I wasn't going to answer, Mary spoke up. "Julia, your room's been vandalized!"

"What are you talking about?" Always a silly thing to say.

I ran up the steps, and Carl was behind me. Amelia was saying Carl couldn't go up to my room. She was closer to a lecture on men in our rooms than she could know.

The doorknob was broken. I used my elbow to push the door the rest of the way open. And then I stood there, observing. After a moment, Carl put his hands on my shoulders and patted them, awkwardly. I reached up and patted his hand, in turn, absently. My room was a square, about fifteen feet by fifteen. Wallpaper, not garish. Just enough flowers and leaves to remind me of outdoor things. Well-lit, with its south and west windows. A lot of furniture had to fit in to make it a home, but I kept it neat to compensate.

My first reaction was anger that someone had violated my neat, personal space. My next thought was that I knew what do.

My father had let me accompany him, probably to occupy me at first, when he was investigating crimes that involved this kind of thing. After the first couple of times, he'd decided I saw the room in a different way than he did. He'd come to value my opinion, which had made me work all the harder at the ill-defined skill.

Now I stepped just inside the door and tried to see the pattern. Among the ripped bed linen, tossed and walked-on clothing, dumped drawers, what was the pattern? I spent a full two or three minutes looking for the telling details. I squatted for another minute, studying from this angle. I heard Amelia ask what I was doing and say I shouldn't be alone. I heard Carl say that I was fine. And I was.

I closed my eyes to picture the scene and then opened them again to confirm my impressions.

It was not random violence, although someone was angry enough to go beyond a simple search. Someone wanted something they thought was in my room. The someone had dumped drawers on my bed, an elegant, curved couch, functional for sitting, and expandable to a regular size bed. Most evenings I sat on the couch, reading, with sheets and blankets beneath and around me, and then lay down and fell asleep in the same place.

So there wasn't much width to the bed, and items from the drawers had spilled on to the floor. When the desired item, whatever it was, didn't materialize, the vandal had cut up the blankets and sheets folded on the seat. It must've made someone feel better. With scissors. Not a knife.

The drawers in the cabinet of my Burdick sewing machine were pulled out and turned upside down. The vandal hadn't tipped the whole thing, for which I was grateful. The head could have been damaged. But it would have been a fine gesture. Either the person didn't have the strength or feared the noise. That much metal hitting an upper story floor would have alerted anyone below. Which made me wonder when it could have happened.

Clothing was lying on the floor. I had the impression someone had gone through it, probably through the pockets in the skirts, and then kicked it—or danced on it. One outfit was not tossed.

A slender pair of bloomers and the matching jacket was draped over the back of the sofa bed, still on hangers. I'd made the bloomers when I was a teener, back when they were the fashion. Except that most bloomers were designed frilly and feminine. My bloomers weren't much fuller than the short pants boys wore. The jacket was long enough to fall past the crotch. But the buttons stopped a good bit higher, so that I could walk with the greatest of ease. Or scramble over a fence. Or ride a horse.

I often wore it with the man's old lingerie shirt that was hung under the jacket, a pair of heavy stockings that balanced the lightweight wool, and a man's golf cap that happened to be a near match. The stockings and cap were out of the jacket pockets where I stored them, and arranged . . . so the vandal could consider the whole ensemble? Odd.

My two suitcases had been pulled from their spot in the bottom of the armoire and searched. They were lying open on top of some clothes, under others.

So, what did someone want? What would I have that was worth this? Surely it was related to the Picard case. And William's shooting.

The thought of William made me reach for his memo book, lodged in my left pocket, where it had been all day.

Maybe.

Maybe someone figured I had to have it and that it contained more details on Picard than what William had used. It might. Maybe there was something about the money belt. I hadn't read it. I was just protecting that little book, as if taking care of it were the only thing I could do for William.

I stepped back out. The room had offered all it could tell me. Now I needed to know who was home when.

"Who found this?"

"I did," Amelia said. Wouldn't you know. "I got home early and saw the door ajar. I went to investigate. When I rushed downstairs, you were just leaving with Mr. Schroeder. Where did you go?"

"What time did you get home?"

"About four. Business was slow, so Mr. Braden said I could come home early." Amelia worked in a millinery shop. Business could have been slow, but I'd never known her to come home early before. Except last week. The day Dad came to town to tell me about Claude Picard. "Answer my question. Where did you go? I'd have thought you'd want to stay safe at home."

"This is safe?" I gestured at the room.

Amelia pressed her hands hard on her hips. "You know, I think you should go to Fulton and your father. You could be endangering us all."

I ignored that, too—easier because it wasn't a question.

"Was anyone home when you got here?"

"Why, no."

"Was the front door broken in?"

"No," she said, with a frown. "It wasn't. What does that mean?"

"It means your vandal had a key," Carl said.

"Why, that's . . . we've got to do something. Whoever it is could come back!"

If Amelia was faking it, she was good. And then it occurred to me that if we changed the lock—and removed the fake barrel—her lover might have a hard time getting in. And I wanted him in. I needed to find out if it was Terence Kelley or someone else.

"Well, I don't think anyone would come back tonight. We'll phone Mr. Miller and tell him, and he can get a locksmith out here tomorrow. We'll have to ask for seven new keys." *And you'll have to get one made for lover-boy*, I added, to myself.

I turned to Carl. "We should call the police before I start picking up. They should see this."

No one moved. "I'll call the Chief. He's been concerned."

Amelia's eyes were enormous, and Carl was beginning to smile. As I pushed past them, I realized that the rest of the household was on the stairs, listening.

I wasn't too upset. I didn't see any permanent damage, and this whole thing needed to move off dead center. If nothing else had happened, I wasn't sure where we'd have looked next. Now, tonight, when I was alone in a room that had been vandalized, I might decide to worry. I might decide to be more careful than I'd been today. All in all, I might bed down in Mary's room again. The better to observe night visitors.

Yes, the Chief was glad I'd called him. He was still at work for whatever reason and was going to send a detective right out. I repeated back to him, "A detective."

"I think John Dougal is in the squad room."

"Oh, that would be great, Chief Wright. I'm pretty sure nothing is missing, but I don't think I can start picking up the mess until the police see it." Police other than Terence Kelley or George St. Martin.

It was his turn to be quiet. "Do you know if someone was looking for something, Julia? And were they looking today, in your bag?"

I wasn't about to answer that one with the audience that had gathered. "I'll see if I can think of anything by morning."

I returned the earpiece and said, "Police are on their way," almost gaily. "Do you want to stay, Carl? Is there extra food?" I glanced from Mary to Fran, both of whom nodded.

Carl sighed. "I need to get to the office." He looked at me a moment and couldn't seem to find anything to say with everyone watching him. He finally settled on, "Be careful," and headed out.

"Let's eat," I said.

We did. Detective Dougal came a little later, looked around, and left. I took a pillow into Mary's room for the night. As I dug through the mess to find clothes for tomorrow, I spied a small leather tobacco bag under the edge of my sofa bed. It held six rounds for the Hopkins & Allen. Its position suggested I had dropped it last night or this morning as I'd worried the satchel. Surely it would be in a more obvious spot if someone had taken it from my bag today and intended it as a calling card.

28

Despite my protests that no one was likely to break in tonight, Amelia and, for that matter, the rest of the house insisted on all but boarding up the front entrance.

They put a heavy buffet against the door and then filled the top surface with jelly glasses and other breakable items, everything that anyone was willing to donate to the cause. The idea was that if anyone even pushed against the door, it would make so much noise that we would all jump to our feet from a dead sleep, rush downstairs, wade through the broken glass, and capture the villain with our indignation. The ladies considered the back door secure. It didn't unlock from the outside.

Mary suggested we turn in early. Maybe I could get some sleep before the night visitor tried to figure out a way to get in.

She woke me in the wee hours. Amelia had started typing. Maybe Amelia always woke at this hour and was getting some work done before her man arrived. And then we heard a different noise. In the temporary light afforded by the moon, Mary and I looked at each other. The new noise could well be someone trying to get on the fire escape.

We'd left the south window open wide to get some air. The one on the east was only open a crack. That way it wasn't quite so inviting, but if anyone entered, I was shooting, regardless of which window they chose.

The light disappeared, as the dark clouds that moved ahead of the storm shifted over the moon. The breeze blowing Mary's curtains was gusty and damp. We would have to close the windows soon.

But for now, I heard sounds. Footsteps. Then it was obvious the window in Amelia's room was opening.

The voices were not as subdued as they had been last night. Amelia's visitor was angry about something. I bet he'd had to use a trashcan because of the missing step. If he was smart, he tied the lid on. And then I worried that he'd carry a rope with him.

But why was Amelia angry? I tensed as I heard furniture hit the wall. I certainly hoped he'd shoved at the furniture instead of shoving Amelia.

I'd brought a sturdy piece of paper big enough to roll and put up to the wall. I was more than dismayed to hear a whimper.

Amelia bounced back, maybe literally.

Through my paper roll, I could catch every few words. I heard, ". . . searched Julia's room . . ." and ". . . called Chief . . . "

The man had been better than Amelia at whispering until now. His response started with, "You're not serious," and then he throttled it down. I heard "who would do that?" And then just snatches: "looking in her room . . ." and "of course the police would . . ."

Hearing that much confused me. The man was indignant that someone had broken in? That made no sense if it were Kelley. He was certainly on my suspect list. There were two possibilities. Either the speaker wasn't Kelley and the man was angry for some reason I couldn't know, or it was Kelley and he hadn't been my vandal.

So I needed to figure out if it was Kelley who whispered harshly, yards away.

My plan for that was threefold. I'd taken Fran into my confidence just before bedtime, dropping Carl's name to great success. I'd asked her to be awake around two or three o'clock, to see if anyone was using the fire escape. Her room was just below Amelia's and near the fire escape stairs. I asked her to get the best description she could.

Secondly, I was willing to peek out Mary's east window if that was the way the man exited. I could hear the window go up and be hiding behind a curtain. If he came trying windows again . . . well, he would.

A third option was that he might go down the stairs and out the back door. I intended to be watching from Mary's keyhole.

Of course, it was possible he would say something close to the shared wall, and I would recognize the voice. But I knew that visual recognition was better—if I were trying to convince the Chief.

As it turned out, I was pretty sure I did recognize the voice. Neither of them was as careful as they'd been the night before. And if they were going to have relations, after this kind of arguing, I wasn't at all sure I wanted to be listening.

The hissing rose and fell. I heard the man say, "You are out of control," and the sentiment as well as the voice sounded like Terence Kelley. But it was odd anyone would say that to Amelia. As best I could make it out, she said, "You do something about this," and got a growl in return.

And then a chair overturned, I thought. There was another furniture sound, something scooting on the floor, maybe the desk or the bed. It was dark again, the moon having disappeared, but Mary reached out and squeezed my arm. She seemed concerned and, if she'd heard all of this before, she wouldn't have been.

To be sure, I leaned into her and whispered, "Is this normal? Do you think she's in danger?"

There was a thud, as if Amelia—or both of them—had hit the bed hard. And continued to thrash on it. I heard Amelia do more than whimper. Her cry was loud enough to be heard even if you weren't listening on purpose.

And that was my chance. If they were going to wake us, I could go to her door and make sure she was O.K. My concern for her was legitimate. After all, our building had been vandalized. It would be the smart thing to do to make sure we didn't have another intruder.

I whispered to Mary that I was going to Amelia's room. She whispered back that it wasn't safe. I said I had a gun, and that slowed her next response enough that I had jumped off the bed and was headed for her door before she could whisper anything else. She caught me, and I thought to say, "Keep this door open just a crack and see what you can see. Close it if you sense danger."

I confirmed the H&A in my pocket, ready to fire through the fabric of my robe if needed. I was at Amelia's door and ready to knock, when I heard voices again. The man, and now I was sure it was Kelley, said, "Just be careful, you hear me. I won't have you getting hurt." Amelia was saying something that started out, "You listen to me . . ." and the tone was so familiar I almost felt sorry for him.

The first footstep toward the door made me spin to find cover. It would be so much better if I didn't confront Terence Kelley at Amelia Ingle's door.

The door to the unused fourth bedroom might be open. I tried it and hit something inside the door hard enough to make a sound. I jumped but crowded into the room with a pile of unused suitcases. I managed to keep the door open no more than a quarter inch, by keeping my finger in it. The moonlight from the south end of the hallway was faint, but it was there.

As I withdrew the finger, Amelia's door flew inward. I had a clear view of Terence Kelley flinging it open, and it might have hit Amelia.

She gave a little shriek and, if I hadn't been hiding in the wrong room, I'd have stepped out in unpremeditated sympathy.

Kelley ran around the railing, which had its head outside Amelia's room, and went for the steps, which began next to Mary's door. He didn't seem to notice the cracked door from either room. He didn't stop to look at my room. He carried a large white envelope, and I was betting Amelia had finished the arson report.

He was gone before I had a chance to see more. My attention went to Amelia, who was standing at the railing outside her room, hissing again. "Terence, you bastard."

Then I saw her go straight and rigid and say, "No!" It would have been loud except that she seemed to lose breath. She began running down the stairs herself, trying to yell quietly. "Terry, Terry," she was saying in a strange, strangled, scream, "Stop, be careful, Terry!"

It was enough noise to wake me, had I been asleep. So, I tumbled out of hiding and ran for the stairs. Mary's door opened, and I gestured her to follow me. As I got to the second floor landing, Fran looked out her door, and I said, "This way."

But I doubt she heard me. Just then, there was a clatter of glass hitting the floor, and Amelia repeated, "Terry, be careful."

Before any of us gained the first floor, I heard the buffet scraping over wood amidst a flurry of voices. Kelley was cursing about insane women. Amelia was telling him he should have listened to her, although I suspected she'd forgotten our new furniture arrangement until he had started down the stairs.

The voices behind me said, "What is it? Who is it? What's happening?" The rest of the second floor emptied out.

The door slammed as we rounded the newel post. The street light on the corner gave me a last glimpse through sheer curtains of Kelley's running figure. I wondered if the other women had seen him.

A last glass fell from the buffet and rolled along the floor to clank against one of its mates. Mary thought to turn on a lamp, and we all squinted in the sudden glare.

Amelia turned, and she was furious. "There was an intruder," she would have been yelling again, but now she was truly out of breath. "You have got to get out of here, Julia."

I simply stood there. Everyone else was silent as well.

Amelia tried again. "See, Julia, it was a good thing we did this," she gestured to the buffet.

Mary spoke first. "But, Amelia, the man was inside and went out." I glanced at the other women, and heads were nodding. Ruth said, "I heard him, running down the stairs."

Amelia said, "Don't be silly. That was my running down the stairs. I heard someone at the door and came down to investigate."

"But it couldn't have been you I heard," Ruth said.

"Of course it was." Amelia had her hands on her hips now.

"But I heard boots on the stairs. I'm sure I did," Ruth insisted. "You're barefoot, Amelia. We all are." Amelia's eyes widened.

I had trouble hiding a smile.

Mary must have decided she'd had enough. "He was upstairs," she said.

All heads swiveled toward her. "I heard a door slam," she said, "and I was worried anyway. I went to look." She nodded to me, as if she were explaining why she had gotten out of the bed we were supposedly sharing.

"I saw a man running down the stairs, before he made the turn."

Amelia stared at Mary, then turned to me. "And what did you see, Julia?"

Decisions, decisions. I could lie now and go along with the story Mary was offering me. If it ever came to identifying Terence Kelley, of course, I'd have to backtrack. It might be worth it. I didn't want Amelia to know I knew about Kelley at this point. The two of them together was too suspicious.

"I wasn't sleeping well, so I woke up when Mary got out of bed." I'd leave it there.

It worked, because Claire, who was inclined to panic anyway, said, "Oh, my, if he was upstairs, he might have been looking for Julia. Could he have been in your room, Julia?" She turned to me, concern flickering in the big blue eyes.

"Well, I can go check, but how would he have gotten in?" I wasn't willing to let Amelia off the hook. "My window was closed and locked, since I wasn't going to sleep in there." Mary and I exchanged glances.

She said, "We should go up and look. If he didn't come in down here, he must have come in on the third floor—through somebody's window off the fire escape."

"We should look," Claire agreed, "and maybe we should call the police." She'd seemed interested in John Dougal. But perhaps I impugned her motives.

I said, "Why don't we make sure the back door's locked and then go upstairs." Several of the women headed for the back door, and Fran wisely headed for the front door to close and lock it.

Amelia headed for the stairs. She didn't look at me or say anything. The fact that she'd obviously lied about finding someone coming in hadn't been lost on anyone if I were correctly interpreting the small frowns aimed in her direction.

Mary and I fell in behind Amelia. She looked back at us and moved faster. But it wasn't as if she could lose us. In fact, she slowed by the time she reached the third floor, and we had a small parade, all six of us following Amelia to her room.

She acted surprised to see us when she got to her open door. She was glancing from one of us to the other, when Mary stepped around her and into her room.

"Oh, my, Amelia." Mary managed great solicitude. "Did our intruder come in through here? Look at this." She gestured to the rest of us in general. I stood back. I didn't want Amelia to know that I knew about the typing. But several women crowded into Amelia's room to cluck over whatever had overturned.

I went to the door of my room and pushed it in. Ruth called to me, "Is it O.K.?" I assured her it was.

Fran came out of Amelia's room, past Amelia herself who was staring at the people moving in and out. "You're sure no one came in through Mary's room?" Fran asked

Mary replied, "Neither Julia nor I were sleeping too well. I've been awake off and on."

Fran swiveled around slowly, enough to make her full, lacy gown flare. We could all be tailored in the daytime, but I'd noticed that nighttime wear was a lot more traditional. She considered the door to the vacant room and said, "Is this locked?"

Elizabeth said, "I put a hatbox in there a week or so ago. I wondered if it would be locked when I came up, but it wasn't."

Amelia moved across the hall and pushed the door open, even further than I had. More suitcases moved. From the light in the hall, we could see the suitcases on their sides, and even a hatbox sitting on top of a suitcase. Amelia turned with a light in her eyes and found me. "Maybe he came in through here."

Fran stuck her head in the room. "Not from the window—this one doesn't open onto the fire escape, does it?"

Amelia continued looking at me. I tilted my head and considered her, as if she just happened to be in front of me while I was thinking. "I wonder if the vandal could have opened this door first, before he got to mine."

Several heads nodded, and Fran said, "That would explain this little mess." She dismissed the room and pulled the door to. She turned back to Amelia. "So, he must have come in through your room."

"No, I couldn't have been sleeping that soundly," Amelia said, all innocence—horrified, really, that someone could have come in her window.

Mary took a deep breath and said, "I know, of course, that the man was in your room, Amelia. I hear him night after night."

Amelia's "No," had little volume. Then she just stood there looking from one to another. Fran considered her long enough for it to get awkward. Elizabeth and Claire were glancing from woman to woman. Ruth was staring at the floor.

Amelia looked at me, and I shrugged.

Mary turned toward her room. "I think it's O.K. if you have someone visit, Amelia, but to be safe—what with vandals and all—we need to know when he's going to be here."

She continued on to her room without waiting for a response. No one else seemed inclined to say anything. One by one they all filed past and down the stairs. I followed the last of them and turned to look back at Amelia from the door to Mary's room.

Her chin was up, and her eyes were sparkling, ready for whatever jab I might produce. I shook my head and shrugged and turned away. She said, "Julia!" as if there were a command coming, but I was closing the door. Sweet dreams, Amelia.

29

*From the **St. Louis Globe-Democrat**, Friday, June 14, 1910*

> *St. Louis Police say they have no leads yet on the shooting of Globe-Democrat police reporter William McConnell. Mr. McConnell was shot Wednesday in Union Station while returning from Ste. Genevieve and Perry Counties, where he was investigating the death of Sheriff Claude Picard.*

A huddle of cops watched Terence Kelley hand me his report the next morning. Everyone would have heard of our confrontation the day before, but Kelley must've said something in the squad room to get an audience like this. He laid the report, still in its white envelope, on my desk and glanced up as if he expected me to say something. Maybe he thought I would discuss his nighttime activities.

I said, "Thank you."

He rushed out the door, leaving his tracks on the floor. The rain had hit about four o'clock, just as I was getting to sleep. The streets had turned into the usual mire, from a combination of dirt and manure on the stones. I couldn't complain. My tracks were in front of me, too.

George St. Martin must have been waiting to see if Kelley survived the encounter with me.

"Now," he bustled in from the squad room. "Let's get this preliminary report done." The crowd was still behind him.

The "preliminary" part was rich. It could be his excuse for all sorts of shoddy work—including not interviewing the witness who was standing next to William McConnell when he was shot.

George sat down in front of my desk and started in, dictating to me. He must have been running late, not to have just written it and escaped.

I filled in the routine details, but even those made me nervous. When George read from his notes the beginning of the narrative, noting the time the victim, William McConnell, walked into the Station, having arrived by train from Ste. Genevieve, I was having trouble typing. George stopped. I assumed he was waiting for a response, but I got busy correcting an error. I rarely made errors, particularly taking dictation.

"I haven't put your name in yet."

"Oh, we can do that now. How about, 'McConnell was accompanied by Miss Julia Nye.' Is that an appropriate next sentence?"

George was quiet a minute, then he nodded.

I started typing, but he reached out and put his hand on my arm. "I can keep you out of this report."

I stared at him. "My name was in the paper, Detective. Everyone knows I was there."

"Yeah. McConnell's paper ran it. That's gratitude." His hand tightened on my arm, and I pulled away.

"Well, I might have wished they hadn't used it, but they did, and I was there. Nothing wrong with that."

George snorted. "Nothing wrong with that? How do I write this without it sounding as if you and McConnell had spent the night together down there?"

Thank goodness. I'd been sitting here afraid to breathe, afraid to hear George retell the shooting. Now I was angry enough that it was going to be a lot easier.

"Have you asked what we were doing, where we'd been?" I leaned forward, hoping I was quiet enough that the anger wouldn't be clear to the squad room.

"Where you were is your business, Julia. I'm trying to help here." He was being quiet, as well, but the entourage of cops stirred. I decided to stop whispering.

"Do you mean to tell me, Detective St. Martin, that there is no mention in here of where we'd been, what William was investigating?"

"Well, I can put that in later, you see. The important thing right now is to find out what the witnesses saw."

"And who the witnesses saw might have a whole lot to do with where we'd been." The murmur from the crowd at the door of the squad room rose.

He was getting angry in turn. "Do you really think someone would shoot McConnell just because he was coming back from . . . from whatever he was asking about in . . . wherever?"

I slammed both hands on the desk. George's eyes widened another notch. "Whatever? Wherever? Do you even know what he was writing about?"

"Of course," George said. "The death of that Sheriff. That's the whole deal with the wagon wheel. Of course, McConnell didn't inquire after that. He sent you to do it."

"He did not! And I'd bet this report," I poked at the white envelope Kelley had offered, "doesn't say that."

George got to his feet. "We are trying to protect you here, Julia. We are trying to protect your reputation." He was back to speaking intensely, wanting me to understand.

He likely was sincere. He was just wrong. "Let us get this straight, Detective St. Martin. I have done nothing to deserve a negative reputation. You can put this in your report: I spent the night in Ste. Genevieve with Marjorie Picard. William spent the night somewhere in rural Perry County." I didn't know if George's raised eyebrow was relief or disbelief.

"The point is that someone cared enough about what we were doing 'down there' to try to kill William. Maybe it would have been sufficient to kill me or to kill Carl Schroeder. Someone might have thought that would scare William off the story. If you haven't investigated that story, Detective, you haven't investigated this case."

He was turning red, and he didn't have a complexion that colored easily. "Are you telling me how to do my job?"

"I'm telling you that if you're ignoring a potential killer's motivation because you're worried about my reputation, you won't solve this case. And you may be leaving me in danger." I reached for the typewriter. "You may be putting Carl in danger. Maybe William, again." I glared up at him. "I don't want your protection. I want to know who shot William McConnell. So, what do you have, Detective?"

The murmur from the crowd died in a heartbeat, and I looked back to see Chief Wright standing in his doorway.

He nodded at George to continue.

Venting my spleen helped, as did thinking that the report might offer something positive to go tell William, something to take Carl's mind off Henry Ingle. The calm was short-lived.

George sat back down and offered his report in short bursts. He had been interviewing witnesses. He'd followed the Chief's lead that said the shooter was upstairs, firing downward. He'd even talked with Dr. Potter, confirming that the path of the bullet could be consistent with that notion. I swallowed hard and didn't look up.

The witnesses, meaning everyone George could find who was near the stairs, were confused, it seemed. The people he'd identified were mostly employees, people who had been moving about on breaks or running errands to other parts of the station. The employees had said there were lots of travelers among the crowd standing on the landing. People liked to come up while they were waiting for a departure or arrival, to study the milling crowd.

What everyone had said was that there was a man who seemed to have some authority—some said he acted like a police official out of uniform, others thought he might be one of the Station's own security employees—and that he had pushed his way up the stairs after the shot sounded. The man had reassured people, saying, "be calm," "let me through," and he had gone through the people on the landing, looking about, seeming to ask questions of a few people, although no one knew what was said for sure. Then the man disappeared out the Market Street exit, avoiding the true security officers. The man didn't have a gun in evidence, although in hindsight everyone seemed to think there was a bulge in his pocket, or, in one case, under his suit coat.

This was more than I had known before, and therefore good. The disappointing part was that no one could agree on the man's description. I had to admit I was anticipating a description of Terence Kelley.

But only one description even vaguely fit Kelley. Another account said the man was short and had red hair. Another agreed with short, but said he had dark hair.

It turned out that there were only four men who could offer a description at all, three employees and a traveler passing back through from Kansas City. The rest just said that there was such a man on the stair. Maybe. Great work.

I typed the last sentence and looked up. George settled back in the chair.

"That's it?"

"That's it. For now."

I settled back myself. I willed myself calm, in part because I was anything but calm, but also because I've noticed that it's the last thing men expect. They say they don't like hysterical women. Maybe they don't. But they're scared of a woman who won't get hysterical.

"That's it," I repeated. "There is no evidence that this man did the shooting. Right?"

George sighed. "I was hoping to find this man so I could see if he had some history with McConnell."

"Even though he was no more likely to have been the shooter than any of those other people on the landing."

George was getting unhappy. "It's a preliminary report, Julia. It takes time to do this, you know. I've been asking about this mysterious man. It's unusual to have someone impersonate a police officer."

"And how do you know he was impersonating one?"

"That's enough." George jumped to his feet again. "Of course, it wasn't an officer. And I don't have to sit here and explain my investigation to a typist." He looked to the Chief, who stirred himself from the doorframe.

"It is a preliminary report, Julia."

George's shoulders settled in relief.

"But, I'd take her questions seriously, George."

George went to downright agitated. He couldn't seem to stand still, and his notes shook in his hand. The Chief added, "Maybe someone had other motivation, George, but all this likely involves the

Ste. Genevieve incident. If you don't investigate that angle first, you may well be leaving Miss Nye and Mr. Schroeder in more danger than they would otherwise be in."

He nodded to me and to George. Then, the Chief glanced at the crowd at the squad room door. They scattered back to work. George escaped with them.

I pulled the report from the typewriter. There were three copies, sandwiching two pieces of carbon paper. I made two copies as a rule. A third one was invariably dim. One went in a file that was sorted by date, another in a file sorted by the name of the victim and the kind of crime. I put the first two in their proper places. And I folded the third into my little bag, borrowed from Claire.

Now I needed time to go talk to those three local witnesses. Not a careful thing to do. And, having identified Terence Kelley last night, I should be more careful, not less. But at the pace George was moving, the witnesses could forget. I needed to find out if they could identify Terence Kelley as well. What I would do then, I didn't know.

◆ ◆ ◆

I'd already filed Kelley's report when the Chief came out asking for it. When I retrieved it, he motioned me into his office.

I sat and tried to relax while he read.

This one did mention me. It also said Kelley happened to see the flames as he walked past. It said two lanterns were missing from their spot near the back door of the tool seller's shop. It seemed correct in every particular that I was aware of. What it didn't include was any hint of who had thrown the lanterns. Or why Detective Kelley was walking in the neighborhood in the first place.

Convenient. No holes in this report. An unsolvable crime.

The Chief shrugged, tossed it on his desk, and changed the subject. "George will come up with more, Julia. He's a good detective."

I shrugged in turn, and he sighed.

"So, was anything missing from your room?"

"No, nothing."

"Do you have any idea what someone could have been looking for?"

"Yes." Deep breath. "The more I think about it, I'm sure the satchel and the room incidents were the same thing. Someone is looking for William's memo book—although I have no idea why they would think I have it, instead of him."

"So? Do you have it?" He was leaning forward on his desk.

I patted my pocket.

The Chief leaned back and smiled. For a couple of seconds. Then he started frowning. "What could be in it?"

"I don't know. I think William put almost everything he knew into the story."

"Have you read it?"

"No." I hadn't. It seemed too personal. I only wanted to take care of it and get it back to William.

The Chief considered my answer for a moment. "O.K. So, someone must have seen you with it. Where? At the boarding house? At the Station?"

"Those are possibilities," I agreed, thinking. "The only other place is at the *Globe* office, when I gave Forrest the story. I took the story out of the book and then held onto the book."

"O.K. Let's check it."

I handed it over, reluctantly, and the Chief flipped through several pages. He took several minutes reading, nodding his head along the way.

"Nothing there that would help anyone, but, of course, that just means Mac didn't have anything incriminating. If there's a guilty party looking for the book, they don't know what is and isn't there."

The Chief returned the book, to my relief, and leaned forward. "Julia. Be careful. Let an officer take you home at quitting time, and then you stay there."

"I'm not sure home is all that safe," I said, trying to make it sound light. For a moment, I was tempted to tell the Chief about Amelia and Terence Kelley. But maybe he was innocent and I didn't want to be the one to damage either of their reputations. Carl would hoot at that.

I got up, and the Chief handed me the report. "We'll get it figured out, Julia."

I gave him a little salute with the papers in my hand and turned to the door. I was opening it when the telephone on the table behind my desk started ringing.

I jumped and asked the Chief if he was expecting a call on that line. He said no, so I hurried over, grabbed the earpiece, and said "Julia Nye." Usually I came up with something more professional.

"Miss Nye, just who I wanted to talk to! How are you, Miss Nye? This is Paul Carrey, sorry, you wouldn't recognize me. I'm glad to hear that you're O.K."

The man reminded me of Carl with all that energy.

"Sheriff Carrey, it's good to hear from you. Is everything O.K. in Perry County?"

"Well, I'd say we're doing a bit better than you city folk. I was more than distressed to hear about Mr. McConnell. How is he?"

"He's . . . safe in the hospital."

Carrey hesitated a moment, maybe wondering about my less than sure response.

"Is he able to hear about some of our news down here? I can't do much else for him, but I thought maybe I could pass a story on to him."

I gulped down my growing guilt at not visiting.

"I haven't been to see him, but I was planning to go today. I'm sure that if you've got news, he'll do his best."

"Well, maybe he can let someone at the *Globe* know about it, if he can't do it himself. 'Course, you may be right interested in this yourself."

I could hear the smile in his voice.

"What?"

"We've arrested Tom Caruthers."

I took a deep breath. "How did you find him?"

"He was talking to folks about how fitting it was that the Sheriff died smuggling beer. He paused. "Frankly, he doesn't seem like the prohibition type. Most of 'em are better educated. I couldn't name half a dozen such in Ste. Genevieve—or Perryville, for that matter. But it seems he did care."

Lordy. "Do you think he was after Sheriff Picard? Or the beer? Did he know about switching the team?"

"Well, the thing is, he isn't too bright. It doesn't take a city person to be ignorant."

I laughed. "O.K., Sheriff, you've got a point there. What about the fire at the Klines?"

"He's denying it, of course. But the Klines say he's the man. That's why we arrested him. We really don't have any evidence on damaging the wheel."

I was silent a moment, thinking. Paul Carrey seemed O.K. with that, as if he'd expect me to want to think.

"What about . . .?" I had to get over this difficulty of talking about the shooting. I'd never reacted like this to anything. To make things worse, the Chief was listening in.

"McConnell's shooting? We verified that, right away. Several people saw him in Ste. Genevieve after you all left that afternoon. Couldn't have been him, Miss Nye, couldn't have been."

"Oh." I really didn't think it would have been. Still, resolution would have been nice.

"Well, I do thank you, Sheriff. I'll pass all this on to William—and to Chief Wright. Do you want to talk to the Chief? He's standing right here."

"Well, why not? Now you tell Mr. McConnell I'll be in my office all afternoon if he wants to call or have someone else call. I'd imagine they'd want all this person to person, huh?"

"Yes, I'm sure they will. Sheriff Carrey . . . thank you for the good work. I imagine Marjorie Picard feels better knowing something, anything."

"That she does, Miss Nye, that she does. It's been good to talk to you." He ended our part of the conversation, and I was relieved. I needed to think. I handed off to the Chief, who went and stood by the telephone table while he heard the story firsthand.

I wanted to get to the hospital, right now. It would have been so convenient to have the shooting and the Ste. Genevieve events be related. It would have been such a relief to walk out of this office and stroll into William's room with good news—and without trying to watch my back as I got there. Instead, I needed to warn William as well as let him know about the story. And I was scared at the same time. Carl had seemed hesitant about my visiting. His attitude combined with my guilt to produce a knot in my gut every time I thought about going.

Could William call Carrey? Could I help him? Would he want to have anything to do with me after Wednesday?

O.K. I was going. Meaning I'd find out how he felt soon enough.

30

I smoothed my skirts and my hair and, less successfully, my pounding pulse and caught the streetcar to City Hospital instead of eating lunch. By the time we turned onto Lafayette, I had my opening line down.

Nurses watched me closely down the hall. That was good. They were suspicious of anyone going to see a patient who had at least one police officer outside his door. If they'd said I couldn't go down that hall, I'd have turned and left without question.

As I got to the door, I saw that there was only one officer there at the moment, and I knew him. Luke Arnold was one of the older officers to still walk a beat—and sometimes he got assignments like this one because of it. He was smart, if not ambitious, and I was glad to see him. He greeted me as if he were happy to see me. Maybe expecting me.

We were exchanging pleasantries, and I was readying myself to knock on the door, which was open a slit, when I heard William. Or to be more exact, I heard a groan that said he was in pain. It wasn't much, it wasn't loud, but it was pain, and I was back in Union Station, feeling all I had felt then: an overwhelming concern and the urge to run at the same time.

"It's O.K., Miss Nye," Luke Arnold assured me. Something was showing on my face. Or maybe it was that I was clutching at my skirt, for whatever good that did. "The nurse only went in to clean the wound."

"Uh, listen, Officer . . . Luke, I only came to give him a message. Why don't I just write this down for him?" I pulled the memo book from my pocket. "I need to leave this with him anyway."

I clawed at my bag and gave up. "Do you have a pencil?"

"I do, and you're surely welcome to use it, but you can go in any minute now."

"No, no, that's O.K." I moved down the hall and used one of the deep windowsills to scribble Paul Carrey's news. And I do mean scribble. My penmanship is adequate but I was shaking so hard I hoped William could read it.

I hesitated over a greeting and decided there was no doubt for whom the message was intended. I didn't have to decide between "William" or "Mr. McConnell." Or "Dear William." I wrote as fast as I could and then started sucking on my lower lip as I tried to end the message. "Sorry I missed you," sounded silly, since it wasn't as if I didn't know exactly where he was. "Forgive me," was a bit much since I didn't know if he blamed me for anything. Or maybe I didn't want to admit that he might. I settled on "I look forward to seeing you." That was bold, given that I was standing outside his room too scared to go in. But, I needed to get out of here. The hospital smells were closing in as the tobacco smells had earlier.

I turned to give the memo book to Patrolman Arnold and stopped short. A woman came out of the room, looking from Arnold to me.

She was pretty. Small but shapely. Dark blue eyes, light brown hair with wavy coils, showing because she wasn't wearing a hat. So, she wasn't a casual visitor. She dressed in a conventional style, in shades of brown. She was frowning at me a bit, but beyond the frown her normal expression was pleasant, calm, friendly. Of course. William wouldn't have mentioned a woman friend out of the blue. It simply hadn't come up in our train-ride conversations.

Arnold looked from one to the other.

"Hello," the woman said. "Were you coming to see William?"

"No," I tried to say, and the breathing problem made it hard to be heard. I cleared my throat. "I needed to get an important message to him . . . about a story." Clearing my throat hadn't helped.

To my surprise, she put her hands on her hips and shook her head. "He doesn't need to be working." I doubted that. If there were something he could be doing, I imagined he'd prefer it to lying around in a hospital room. Hurting. Was he so bad off he couldn't read the message? Who was this woman, darn it?

Arnold got up and might have been starting introductions. But I didn't want to know.

I turned to him and said, "This is important, Luke. It's a message from Sheriff Carrey. Please make sure Mr. McConnell gets it. Will you?" I glanced, at least twice during the little speech, at the pretty, frowning woman. When I mentioned Sheriff Carrey, she frowned more.

I handed Luke Arnold his pencil and the memo book. I hated to give it up. I smiled at him and at the woman and turned for the exit. Cowardice. I was trembling as I hurried away. But I still heard William's voice saying, "Who is it?" as if he'd sent the woman out to look. I was running down the long hallway when I actually heard William call out. "Julia!" echoed behind me. He wasn't delirious with fever. I couldn't judge if he was angry or in pain.

◆ ◆ ◆

I was disappointed in myself. No guts. And no one had ever noted a lack of sand on my part. This whole affair was changing me. I didn't bother to wait for a streetcar headed east on Lafayette. I took the first one I saw, headed west. I rode out past Tower Grove Park, knowing the car would turn around eventually and deliver me back downtown. Normally, I'd have enjoyed the greenery, but I had to figure out what was causing me to act like this.

I slowly admitted to myself that I worried about William beyond a conventional compassion. Because I was fond of him. Fond of a man I'd met less than a week ago. Fond of him in a different way than I was fond of Carl. I sighed. Not only was William very possibly angry with me because I'd gotten him involved, but he likely wouldn't return an affection I barely recognized in myself. I'd never felt anything quite like the fears that were rolling around in my gut. One of which involved his keeping company with the woman I'd just seen.

I was almost reluctant to get off the streetcar downtown. I hoped I'd be able to concentrate on typing instead of turning this newfound affection over in my mind. When I pushed through the doors, I realized I wouldn't do either for a while. Carl was sitting on the corner of my desk.

He jumped to his feet. "Aren't you supposed to have an escort? Did you go out to lunch without me?"

I swallowed. "I've been to the hospital to drop a message off for William."

His red eyebrows went up. "What's going on? Did you not see him?"

I wondered why he linked those two questions. "You don't really need lunch, do you? Do you want to talk in the police barn again?"

"I would like lunch. And I want to know what's going on. And I don't want to smell horses while I hear this."

"I need to get back to work. I have errands to run later."

"That sounds as if you're going to get in trouble. O.K., the barn, but the gossip will flow."

And he thought it mattered at this point?

We jumped the puddles in the courtyard from last night's rain and made it to the barn. The horses determined that we had no food and snorted in disapproval.

"What was your message for William? Why didn't you see him?"

"The message was from Paul Carrey, who was concerned William had gotten hurt and wanted to give him a story."

Carl's reporter instincts surfaced, and his eyes widened.

"He—or maybe he and James Ingle—have arrested a man for setting the fire."

"Who?"

"Tom Caruthers, a Ste. Genevieve handyman."

"Could he have shoot William? Does he fit any of the three or four descriptions St. Martin came up with?"

I shook my head. "You'd think anybody could fit one of those descriptions, wouldn't you? But the man was seen in Ste. Genevieve after we left that afternoon."

"Do they think he damaged the wheel?"

"Probably. But they can't prove it."

Carl paced away three or four steps. "I need to go down there."

"Today?"

"I'll get down there, phone in a story on the arrest, and talk to James Ingle in the process."

"As you did with Henry? That was helpful."

Carl turned. "Julia, it's got to be the Ingles. They're in the right places, and they have the motive. Well, the Ingles and Terence Kelley. Did you find out anything last night?"

I couldn't help smiling. The man might be dangerous, but the scene with the buffet was too good. I explained to Carl.

He was laughing by the time I'd finished. But then he returned to his conspiracy story.

"O.K. We've got the two of them together. Amelia knew about you being on the way back from Ste. Genevieve. She told Kelley. Kelley is our shooter, and St. Martin is covering up for him with all these odd descriptions of the same man. That's it. Unless Henry was the shooter. Either way."

"Maybe." I still had my doubts about James and Henry Ingle's involvement. I didn't have many doubts about Terence Kelley. I just didn't know about Amelia. And I didn't like the idea that George was involved. But it would explain that dreadful report.

"Maybe, nothing." Carl regarded me for a moment. "So, did you give this message to William in person?"

"No, the nurse was in with him when I got there, so I wrote out a message and left it with Luke Arnold. "

He nodded.

"Why? What is it, Carl?"

"It's only that he's . . . angry."

I swallowed hard.

Carl nodded and said, "I've got to go if I'm going to get back with a story. What is it you're doing tonight?"

I sighed. "I'm going to find George St. Martin's witnesses and get a clear description."

"And what will you do if St. Martin—and the Chief—find out?"

Yes, that was the risk. Or one risk. "I'll hope the Chief doesn't fire me."

Carl ran a hand through his hair. "I guess I hope so, too. Be careful." He turned back, took my hand and squeezed it, and said, "I mean it."

"You, too," I said.

On an impulse, I held onto his hand a moment to stop him.

"Carl, give me an estimate. When will you be back? I'm going to worry myself silly if I don't know when you'll be back."

He stared a moment. "Are you going to meet me in Union Station?"

"I don't know. I hadn't thought to. I only want to know when you'll be back." I let go of his hand. "Do you think you can make it back tonight?"

He looked at me another moment then sighed. "I probably can't. I'll be back tomorrow."

I watched him dodge puddles and leave. I would have liked to go with him, to try to protect him. I couldn't handle another man shot and hurting and blaming me. How would I stop this, if I wanted to? We were in danger if we continued the investigation or if we let it drag on.

31

The Chief directed a young officer—even younger than Jamison—to see me home tonight. It seemed no one had told Chief Wright that I'd been out on my own once today. But this youngster was no match for Jamison. Or me. I told him I had to visit the hospital, and that I'd get an escort home from there, and it worked. I made sure of his name, so I wouldn't forget it: Ruhl. I wouldn't trust this one with anything important. Like my safety.

I managed to get to Union Station in decent time, but it was still past five, and most of the offices were closing. I swallowed hard when I looked up the stairway, but I didn't have time for another disgraceful exhibition. I had to find at least one of George's witnesses.

I went into the hotel that that occupied the western end of the top floor and asked for Raymond McGee. I knew I'd located him when I saw a man's head jerk up and his eyes widen. He clearly didn't want to talk to me. He made a rush for it, trying to get out of the office door around me. I stepped in front of him.

"Mr. McGee." I was as polite as I could get. "I'm pleased to have caught you. I work for the Police Department, and I need to ask you a quick little question."

He stopped to stare, and that was his undoing. I moved forward, and he shuffled back into the office space. "You don't work for the Police Department. You're not in uniform." He apparently realized how silly that sounded. "I mean to say, they don't have women at the Police Department."

"Actually, Mr. McGee, I'm a typist there. And I'm trying to clear up some confusion for Detective St. Martin, the one you talked to yesterday. You said the man you saw was short and had dark hair and was telling people to be calm. Is that the right description?" He didn't respond. "Because Detective St. Martin wouldn't want the description to be wrong in this report. And I want to get it right before I type it up."

"You type the police reports?" McGee wasn't easy.

"That's it, sir. And I want to get this description down right. Is short and dark-haired correct?"

"We have a woman who types here."

Lordy. "Is that right, sir? Well, I'm sure she works hard at getting the details correct, as well. It wouldn't do to have a mistake, would it?"

"You know, you could come back tomorrow and talk to Gertrude. She was talking yesterday about how that man was acting."

Gertrude? George hadn't mentioned any Gertrude.

"Oh, my, Mr. McGee, that's an excellent idea. What is Gertrude's last name? I'll ask for her."

"It's Gertrude Vezjak, Miss Vezjak, that is. She can tell you what she saw."

"Excellent. When is Miss Vezjak in?"

"Oh, I think she gets in quite early, around six. She leaves at five. You just missed her." McGee was happy to tell me to talk to a woman.

"And does she go to lunch? I'd hate to come back during the day and miss her."

"No, miss, she doesn't ever go to lunch. Eats right there at her desk. Not very professional the boss says, what with all the places to eat and Harvey's right here. She goes out for breaks, but not far. You can find her here."

"Well, that is very helpful, Mr. McGee. I'll tell the Chief I found such a helpful gentleman." Of course. "Oh, but, I do need to tell Detective St. Martin I confirmed your description. That was short and dark-headed, right?"

"I've really got to be going, miss. Got to get home to the wife, you know."

I moved as he did. "Short and dark-haired, Mr. McGee?"

"No, no," he said as he went into a sideways shuffle. "Tall and dark-haired, I said. Can't you women get anything right?"

I hesitated a split second, in anger, and he was gone around me. I stood there with my hands on my hips and watched him scurry away through the marble halls into the throngs. When I turned, a negro cleaning woman, by appearances, was watching me. There was a spark of humor in her eyes that made me throttle the anger down a few notches. I was holding up her cleaning—as well as Mr. McGee's dinner.

"Sorry," I said, and smiled at her. "I'll go and correct my mistake."

She laughed out loud, and said, "You do that, miss."

♦ ♦ ♦

The supper hour was in full swing in Union Station. Travelers and locals were enjoying restaurant food in Harvey's and casual treats elsewhere. The smells of coffee and more substantial fare filled the air.

I'd rushed down the stairs from the hotel office without looking around, and now I sighed and leaned against a wall. It was not peaceful in the usual sense, because of the evening bustle, but it almost felt safe. I was anonymous standing back under the staircase, out of the way of the crowd but protected by it, out of the way of bullets.

But not, it seemed, out of the way of the city's finest.

I don't know what even led me to see them. The crowd was thick, but Terence Kelley was tall. I could see a bit over the crowd myself, and there they were: Terence Kelley and George St. Martin. My breath swelled up my throat and caught there. The two were heading toward the stair, and there was an intensity about them that was scary. Scarier, of course, was the thought that they would, one or the other, look my way any moment. Reason told me that I was well hidden in my shadow, but fear told me to get out of Union Station right now.

That was silly. This was an opportunity to watch them, consider why they were here together, learn something about my prime suspect and the man who should be investigating him.

George switched between watching Kelley and glancing upstairs. The conversation seemed to die a moment, and then George must have said something about the stairs. Kelley turned on him. They stopped in the middle of the traffic, and it had to flow around them. Kelley was yelling in his friend's face and waving his arms. He might intend to hit George. I craned to watch them. I would have loved to have heard them, but there was no way I was getting closer.

The anger seemed to recede, and they both relaxed a bit. Kelley must have given in to something by the look that passed between them. They started off toward Harvey's restaurant. I lost my angle on them, and they disappeared in the crowd.

How fortunate I came down stairs when I did. Five minutes later, and I would have been looking down at Terence Kelley. And then

George St. Martin might have wanted to know why I was there, and if he had asked around, he would have found out I was asking for his witnesses.

And, of course, there might have been another scenario. Maybe Kelley thought Carl could be coming back through here tonight. And how would he know Carl was working on a story in counties south? I wiped at what felt like sweat forming on my forehead and ran a hand over my stitched skin.

So, it was no surprise that I jumped and would have screamed had I had the breath when a voice said, near my ear, "We have sidestepped him, thank God."

I whirled about, reached for the H&A in my bag, and looked down at Mr. Armbruster. He was smiling, but the sweat beaded his receding hairline and concern crinkled the edges of his eyes.

"How are you, Miss Nye? I am so sorry to have frightened you just now."

I took several breaths and let go of the gun before I answered.

"I'm quite O.K., Mr. Armbruster. You did surprise me, but I agree with your sentiment." I glanced back toward the foot of the stairs. No sign of either man, although the crowd was heavy enough to make that uncertain.

"Are you concerned about Detective Kelley seeing you, Miss Nye?" He was whispering, just loud enough for me to hear by leaning close. "I saw him as he came in and made my way to a less traveled area . . . as you have, perhaps?"

I didn't know why I trusted him, except, of course, that he had trusted me so much on the matter of the wheel. "Well, I don't like the man too much, and I wouldn't want to engage him in conversation unless it was necessary."

Mr. Armbruster smiled, enough to show uneven teeth, and said,

"Are you coming or going?"

"I'm headed home. I need to make my way to a streetcar. I was resting here after running an errand. But what are you doing here, Mr. Armbruster? I'd heard you'd decided to leave the city for a while."

"Yes, I have been in Kansas City. It seems wise now, does it not, with the unfortunate accident to Mr. McConnell?"

He used the word accident as a euphemism, the kind of thing you say so the people around you don't overhear you use a stronger word.

"I am back in the City to see to some business affairs. As a matter of fact, the accident"—the word was softer than the ones around it— "convinced us to stay away for as long as it takes to clear up the matter."

"Well, that may be smart."

Mr. Armbruster frowned. "You must be careful yourself, young lady. I have time to see you to a streetcar before my train, and then I think you must stay safe at home." His German accent was coming through, as it had when he'd been concerned about me at the shop. When he'd refused to tell Terence Kelley the truth. That seemed even more important now.

"I'm sure you're right, Mr. Armbruster. But before I go, I've wanted to ask you something."

"Yes?"

"Why did you tell Detective Kelley you hadn't seen the wheel? You were right, you know. I heard from Sheriff Carrey in Perry County today. They've arrested someone they think may have damaged the wheel."

He smiled, and his face went a bit red, as if he were trying to be modest and not succeeding. "Well, you know, miss, wheels and such don't fall apart of their own accord. If you know the wood, the workmanship, the dumb objects will tell you the story."

"You're obviously very good at reading it, Mr. Armbruster. I'm glad James Ingle knew of you. And I'm also glad you opened them when you did."

"Oh, he did sound quite worried when he telephoned me. He said the wagon might have been thought to be carrying a heavy cargo, beer, he said." He paused again, maybe wondering how much I knew. "Of course, he also made it clear that this particular wagon was not carrying such a cargo when the accident occurred."

"I see. But then, why were you suspicious of Detective Kelley?"

"Well, you see, if alcohol were involved in the matter, Detective Kelley would not be the man you would want to, how did you say it, 'engage in conversation'."

Whoa. "I didn't know that Detective Kelley has been vocal one way or another on the prohibition issue. Is that what you mean?"

"Indeed." Mr. Armbruster actually stopped and glanced around, although he would be able to see even less than I could, being several inches shorter. "I had met, well, seen, Detective Kelley only once before. At least I had not noticed him at any of the other demonstrations I had attended."

He ducked his head in shyness. "I do not approve of these laws forbidding us to use beer. It is un-American, I do think. So, I sometimes go to the public gatherings where such things are debated. I do not say much myself." He offered a small smile. "But it is important to have many people there, you see?"

I smiled at his explanation. I did indeed understand the politics of public demonstrations.

"At one such demonstration, this spring, the group involved was the Women's Christian Temperance Union. I must tell you, Miss Nye, that the women scare me more than the men, on this matter. I know you, well, I would guess, from your dress . . . and . . . I can imagine, that you favor the vote for women, and I must say that scares me because I would not want these . . . these . . . fiery women, voting on whether my family can drink at a beer garden."

He stopped a moment, maybe to see if I was about to turn fiery. But I could surprise him. "I do support suffrage, Mr. Armbruster, but not all women who want the vote would vote for prohibition. I wouldn't."

"Oh. That is good to hear, Miss Nye." He was willing to keep talking. "At any rate, our Detective Kelley was patrolling the demonstration. Although he was not in uniform, he did wear a badge so that everyone would know his authority. One of our group was arguing with the woman on the platform, interrupting to say things like, 'But that's not true, ma'am.' Mind you," he shook his head, "none of us was disrespectful—although it is hard not to argue with such nonsense from these women." An image of Amelia Ingle on a platform popped into my head.

Of course. It could have been Amelia. That would explain Kelley's presence in the crowd. Because the St. Louis Police Department did not send detectives out to keep the peace at temperance rallies.

I wanted to ask Mr. Armbruster who was speaking, what she looked like, but he frowned and moved on with his story.

"I guess Detective Kelley thought my friend was being rude, too rude by Kelley's standard. It did not seem so to me, or to any others of us. But Kelley waded into our group and pulled my friend away. Some of us tried to follow, to protest Kelley's actions, but several uniformed officers appeared and told us to keep it peaceful." He frowned at me, as if my association with the police made me responsible, as well.

"We were not suggesting violence, Miss Nye. We were concerned about our friend. And we should have been."

Mr. Armbruster looked away from me. I had to lean into him to hear. "Detective Kelley must have a bad temper, Miss Nye. He pulled our friend back into a nearby alley and began to hit him. My friend is small and has no skills in fighting. Although I should not think he would have fought a police officer in any case. Mr. Kelley hurt him, broke his nose, and left him with bruises and cuts. Left him there, and walked off."

Lordy. How much of an insult to Amelia would it take for Kelley to have beaten the man?

He turned back to me. "He did not arrest him, did not charge him with anything. My friend said Kelley called him a drunkard and insulted his German name. Detective Kelley may not support prohibition in public, Miss Nye, but in an alleyway, when he can use his authority and his fists to his advantage, he . . . he makes his allegiance clear."

32

Carl rushed through Union Station. After leaving Julia, he'd had to convince his editor he could come up with more than the arrest of a country bumpkin setting a fire, convince his mother she should hurry and pack a night's worth of clothing, convince his older sister he wasn't aiming to get shot in Union Station.

Carl hated traveling—not seeing new places, but getting there. Seeing new places appealed to his sense of adventure. Sitting on a train drove him crazy. Sometimes he drove other passengers crazy by striding up and down the aisles. Today, he intended to sit still long enough to write down all he knew and suspected about the case. Not that that would take two hours.

An hour and a half and several excursions through the aisles later, Carl had his list but he couldn't think of a way to confront James Ingle that wouldn't be futile, if not dangerous. He considered option after option and then decided to go on to Perry County and talk to a sheriff more likely to share his concerns. Even if it meant riding through another county. Carl sighed loudly, getting a laugh from a couple of teener girls who'd been watching him. He'd have to change trains at Ste. Gen, but it wasn't likely James Ingle would be patrolling the depot.

It was a short wait, the train schedule for the Perryville line being designed to match that of the larger rail. Carl used the men's toilet, timed his turn back toward the platform, and headed for the steps, looking straight ahead. He noticed an unusual movement to his right and stopped with a hand on the rail, a foot on the first tread.

The movement was a sudden lack of movement. Henry Ingle looked to be frozen in mid motion, no doubt because he saw Carl.

There was a lot he could have said, but Carl decided that a confrontation here in enemy territory was not wise.

"Hello, Ingle." Carl tried to mimic the kind of cool response William McConnell would have achieved without effort. "Coming or going?"

Henry seemed to worry that question. "Just arrived," he said. Carl realized he hadn't covered all the cars during his constitutional.

The conductor moved down the platform busily, the "all aboard" meant for him, Carl assumed.

Henry glanced at the man and said, "I take it you're headed south. On assignment, perhaps?"

"Tracking your crime spree, Ingle." Maybe that wasn't the smartest thing to say, but Carl felt safe as he swung up the steps and left Henry on the platform. As he moved down the car, he didn't bother to look out the windows in Henry's direction. He took a vacant seat at the far end of the car, so he could angle back in the corner and watch both doors.

The train headed south without incident and, after a while, Carl relaxed and straightened in the seat. He worked through the questions he wanted to ask Paul Carrey and wondered about the reception he'd get. Somewhere along the way he fell asleep to worrisome dreams.

The conductor woke him. Carl thanked the man before he was quite awake and then sat wondering if the conductor had been part of the dream. He checked to see that the depot approaching the train said Perryville on its sidewall.

It was getting dark, although Carl could see three men chatting at the door of the Depot. They were the only people in sight except for an elderly man who seemed to be dozing on a bench at the other end of the platform. Carl shook his head hard, to finish waking up, and clapped his hat on.

One of the men disengaged from the cluster and came toward Carl, smiling. Carl hoped the smile was as friendly as it seemed. He was getting better at this investigative work. An answering smile without suspicion would have been his usual reaction.

As it was, Carl sat his bag down, smoothed his coat, and waited for the man to approach, with no particular reaction. There was no place to run, after all.

"Mr. Schroeder, I assume." The man offered a hand. "Paul Carrey, Sheriff of this county."

Carl stuck out his hand without thinking, his mind busy trying to make sense of Carrey's presence. Someone had been on the telephone or telegraph announcing Carl's arrival. At least no one had pulled a gun yet. Carl decided to act pleased to see the man he had indeed been seeking.

"Sheriff Carrey. And how might you have identified me, sir?"

"Hair," Carrey replied. "I was told to look for a tall redhead on this train."

Carl nodded, picked up his bag, and headed into the Depot beside Carrey.

"And who told you that, Sheriff?"

"James Ingle."

Carl stopped in the middle of the small space and turned slowly, testing the area. When he turned back to the smiling Sheriff, Carrey said, "Don't worry, Mr. Schroeder, you're with the law."

"And William McConnell was with the Chief of Police of St. Louis

City, sir."

Carrey got serious. "You're right, of course. Do you think someone's after you as well?"

"It's possible. If James Ingle wanted it to be so."

"James Ingle?" Carl thought Carrey's shock was real and didn't know whether that was a good sign or not. But it seemed Carrey was taking him seriously. He nodded and said, "Well, let's head for my office, Mr. Schroeder, and we'll sort this out in relative safety."

Carl had noticed gaslights as the train pulled in, but now it was several degrees darker, and he could see that electricity hadn't made it to Perryville. As he and Carrey hurried up the slope to the town square, he caught himself thinking William would enjoy the old-fashioned town: no electricity, no pavement, maybe no autos. The other thing Carl noticed was four saloons, and he hadn't even seen the opposite side of the courthouse square.

Carrey led the way to his office. It was well-used, piled with papers, comfortable with little touches that said his wife visited, a couple of plants and embroidery work. He gestured to a seat in front of the desk, rounded behind it, and smiled. "Sorry I can't offer you a drink. It's legal in town but not smart here in my office."

Carl laughed and relaxed—a bit.

"What else can I offer you, Schroeder? A character reference for James Ingle?"

"I might like to hear that. As it is, I'm very suspicious of the entire Ingle family. And their associates."

"Well, if you'll tell me why that is, I'll see if I share your concerns—or can lay some to rest."

"Fine. Either James, Henry, or Amelia Ingle could have been involved in every incident including Picard's accident, the arsons, William McConnell's shooting, and the latest—although minor—

thing, a ransacking of Julia Nye's room."

Carrey jerked his head up a notch. "That's an impressive list, Schroeder."

Carl moved on. "As for associates, there's Amelia Ingle's lover." Carrey raised an eyebrow. "A St. Louis police detective, yet."

"Not the man named Kelley." Carrey leaned forward. Carl thought he could see the man making connections. Good.

"The same. You've heard of him?"

"Only from Miss Nye and Mr. McConnell in talking about the arson at the wheel shop. Did they ever figure out why he was there?"

"No. He's not talking. In fact, he's spending his time harassing Julia."

"How's that?"

"He went through her bag at work, tried to distract her by knocking things off her desk, insulted her. He's at the top of my list for the damage to her room."

"What would he have been looking for?"

"I'm not sure, although Julia has some idea." Carl didn't add that she hadn't bothered to share it with him. "I left before I could talk to her about it."

"It sounds as if she might be in danger. Does she live alone?"

Carl considered the man. Maybe it hadn't come up. "No, Sheriff. She lives in a boarding house with . . . like-minded . . . women. One of whom is Amelia Ingle."

Carrey leaned back in his chair. "Aha. And that's how she knows about Kelley."

Carl nodded.

"Now," Carrey said.

Carl tilted his head.

"She didn't mention the connection before, when she was here with McConnell."

This man was good. "Well, sir, she didn't know it then. It seems that Amelia has been acting . . . odd . . . and one of the roommates decided to confide in Julia. Turns out Kelley has been sneaking into the house. And having Amelia Ingle type his police reports. Julia happened to see one."

Carrey leaned backward in his chair, chuckling. Carl frowned.

"And Kelley is the detective who doesn't let Miss Nye type his reports and instead turns in . . . something that doesn't meet Miss Nye's standards. Right?" At Carl's raised eyebrow, he said, "That's how she described Kelley to me."

Carl got the picture and nodded, smiling himself.

"You're fond of her," Carrey pronounced.

Carl couldn't have been more surprised. "Julia?"

Carrey smiled.

"Well, we're friends. I support the suffrage cause, and I know a lot of the women in the movement."

Carrey kept smiling.

Carl didn't know why he'd hesitated. "I am quite fond of her. Right now, I'm concerned about her. And William McConnell. He's my friend as well. Maybe my best friend."

Carrey sobered up and leaned forward.

"I see the connection with Miss Ingle and Detective Kelley. What else makes you suspicious about the Ingles?"

"Prohibition. Prohibition and fanaticism. They've had the opportunity and the motive. Isn't that what you look for?"

Carrey nodded and invited Carl to be specific. Carl was glad he'd laid out the details for himself on the train as he went through a possible Ingle connection in hiring the handyman and having Kelley make the call to Carrey, the Ingle connection in getting the wheel to

St. Louis—and possibly having Kelley on the scene when Julia went to ask about it—and the possible Ingle connection in William's shooting.

"It could be James Ingle called Henry because he knew William was headed back with a story—if he knew that. Or," and Carl hesitated because he couldn't hide his carelessness, "I could have alerted Amelia Ingle when I went looking for Julia and then phoned Marjorie Picard. Amelia might have called Henry based on what she heard me say."

Carrey considered Carl closely and said, "James did know what McConnell was likely to print. As I did. Both of us gave him information pretty freely when he was here. James wasn't happy with it, but he didn't really hesitate. What else do you have?"

"Well, James Ingle is acting Sheriff. That's a good entry to getting elected Sheriff for a full term, I'd think."

"That's how I did it," Carrey responded, looking out the window at more gaslights flickering on in downtown Perryville.

He continued staring a few moments and then turned back to Carl. "This would all make sense, Schroeder, except for two things. One, I don't think James Ingle is involved. I know him. The man favors prohibition, but I've never heard anything approaching fanaticism. The same can be said of his family. His wife, his cousin Henry, they seem like decent people, Mr. Schroeder. Do you know the St. Louis Ingles?"

"I know Amelia Ingle. I don't doubt her willingness to be involved. She's fanatic about her causes. Henry Ingle . . ."

Carl thought the Sheriff had been honest with him. What did he want to say about Henry Ingle—to be honest?

He tried again. "Henry Ingle and I have had our differences, discussing prohibition. And we know that he's a crack shot, capable of the shooting in Union Station."

The two studied each other. Carl asked, "What's the second thing that makes you doubt my story?

"Well." Carrey paused. "I was going to say that when James Ingle phoned to alert me to your possible visit, he seemed eager to talk to you. Said he was trying to put some pieces together. I find it hard to believe that a sheriff would want a reporter's help piecing together a murder investigation if he was the killer."

Carl nodded, trying and failing to think of a counterargument.

They sat in silence for a few seconds, and then Carrey stood. "I think my first objection still stands, but tomorrow, I go with you to Ste. Gen. I'll think about what we should say to James."

"How about we talk to Caruthers? Maybe James Ingle hasn't asked the right questions."

Carrey nodded, a slight frown crinkling his forehead. Must be rare. Carrey had smile lines, not frown lines.

Carl stood as well, and Carrey suggested that he might want to try the Hotel Perry on the east side of the square. "Or there's the White House. It's a bit on the rowdy side. Serves a lot of beer."

The man was irrepressible. You couldn't help but like him. Whether you should or not. Carl made a note to himself to discount that as he tried tonight to sort out Paul Carrey's arguments on behalf of James Ingle.

33

Home offered an unusual surprise. Any number of odd—and unpleasant—things could have been afoot, but the large dress box and the hatbox next to it, were not anything I'd have guessed.

Amelia had her complaint ready. "Julia, is some man sending you clothing?"

"What do you mean?"

"The delivery man said it's compliments of Mr. Forrest. He was instructed to tell you that."

Mr. Forrest? William's editor-Jack Forrest? Couldn't be. I opened the dress box to find what looked to be, without picking it up, a very nice three-piece outfit, skirt, waist, and jacket. But I only had eyes for the folded note inside.

The card said the *Globe-Democrat* appreciated my efforts in getting Mr. McConnell's story to the City Editor, particularly given the difficult situation surrounding Mr. McConnell's accident. Huh. In particular, Mr. Forrest regretted the damage to my attire, and the newspaper would like to recompense me by providing the enclosed outfit. And they did hope it suited my taste. And many thanks again for my help.

As I read it to myself, Amelia tried again. "Really, Julia. I have to protest. This is unseemly."

That was too much. I lowered the note and turned to her. "You are calling anything I've done unseemly? I do not have a male visitor in my room every night, Amelia. Anything I've done pales in comparison."

Just like that, she was breathing fast and her blue eyes were flashing and she started toward me. I thought she intended to grab the note from my hand, and I put it behind me. She took my shoulders and started to shake me. With one hand, I shoved her away, hard.

Amelia backpedaled and landed ten feet or so from me, scooting one of the overstuffed chairs back half a foot. She scrambled to her feet with no grace at all. "You hussy," she screamed. "How dare you accuse me of having a man in my room? You go with men you don't know and get involved in all kinds of sordid affairs and keep company with that German drunkard and you insult me?"

Behind her, the other women had gathered.

Instead of coming toward me again, she turned and bumped an end table and ran toward the stairs. "You are done here," she shrieked back over her shoulder.

I watched her to the first landing and turned to my housemates, Mary with her dish towel in hand, Claire with a bowl and spoon, frozen in the motion of stirring when the excitement started.

I wanted to know if they were blaming me for something, or if they also thought Amelia's behavior bizarre. Surely they'd all gotten Mary's message from last night.

I looked from one to another, and they started looking at each other as well, instead of staring at me. Elizabeth craned to see up the stairs, maybe wanting to see if Amelia was going to reappear.

Elizabeth was always the one who said the most obvious things. I didn't think she was dull, although she certainly wasn't quick. She simply thought out loud.

Her light blue eyes were squinty, and there was a line between her brows as she said, "Doesn't she realize that we know about the man who ran out last night? Why did she say that Julia shouldn't accuse her of having a man in her room?"

Fran patted Elizabeth on the arm. "Amelia is . . . Amelia. She has to be right, and she has to be the leader."

Fran's been here a while.

"Which reminds me," she said, "you'll be pleased to know that Mr. Miller sent a locksmith and your room is secure, Julia. Here's your keys."

I tucked them in a pocket.

Mary was wiping her hands on the towel—her usual prop. We teased her about putting it down before she went to bed. She was frowning, and her hair was straggling into her face. "What I don't understand, Julia, is why he didn't leave from the fire escape as he usually does."

"You mean Amelia's man? You've seen him here before?" Claire asked.

"Heard him," Mary reminded her, still wiping. "I hear him—or someone—in her room, but he always comes and goes through the window onto the fire escape."

"Well, that's sort of funny, actually," I said. I took the box and plopped in the nearest chair. "The morning after the shooting, a police officer came to escort me to work. But I'd heard the man—his name is Kelley—the night before. So, I told the officer we were worried about security. And I was. Kelley had glanced in my window and Mary's, the night before, and I didn't like that."

Claire and Elizabeth started making their jittery noises.

"We found a barrel behind the garbage cans that looked like some old trash piece lying under the fire escape. But when the officer picked it up, it had two steps built into it."

All five of them were staring at me. "You mean he left a step for getting up on the fire escape right there underneath it?" Mary's brown eyes glittered, and she was doing damage to the towel. "Anyone could have gotten into our rooms on a warm night."

"Well, not anymore. The officer had it taken into the police station as a precaution."

Fran was thoughtful. "That would explain the mess around the trash can."

Mary turned to her. "What do you mean?"

"When I emptied the waste basket from the second floor this morning, one of the garbage cans was overturned, and there was trash all over the place. I picked it up. And I don't mind saying I was irritated. But I figured it was some street urchin, making mischief."

Elizabeth was breathing fast and thinking out loud again. "So this Kelley used the trash can to get on the fire escape, but he tipped it over and didn't want to jump down into the trash."

Mary and I nodded.

Elizabeth looked back up the stairs, and Claire followed her gaze. They didn't seem too happy with their senior suffragist. Which was O.K. with me.

I decided to go back to Forrest's card while Mary went on about men and fire escapes. I decided that Forrest himself hadn't actually written it. I didn't think he could muster this much courtesy, given what I'd seen of him.

I tried to read between the lines. I had indeed complained about my clothing. Still, the paper didn't owe me anything. Not for bringing in a story that I cared about. Not for doing what I felt I owed William.

In my head, I recalled my name echoing down the hall today. Was he really angry? Had he suggested to someone from the paper that they spend the money to make sure that he and Forrest owed me nothing?

I heard a throat clear and looked up to see Ruth watching me. "Are you O.K., Julia? You seem . . . wistful, maybe." She considered the card. "Who is Jack Forrest? Someone you haven't introduced us to?"

I laughed and broke away from thoughts of William. "Oh, no, no." I read the note to the room at large.

"Oh, how exciting," Elizabeth said.

"Let's see it then," Claire said.

"O.K." I pulled the outfit from the box and got about as excited as Elizabeth. I stood to see its length.

The suit was packaged so that the waist was inside the jacket, and the whole outfit was pinned together. When I picked the jacket up by the lightly padded shoulders, the outfit unfolded as if I had plucked it from a catalog page. Except that suits like this weren't found in your standard Sears catalog.

It seemed my obvious political persuasion had caused Jack Forrest to send someone out to buy an expensive but, more importantly, edge-of-fashion outfit. The jacket would blouse instead of being cinched in to follow the line of a corset. It was simple in its tailoring. The waist was a wonderful silk and tailored, too: tucks, but no frills. And the skirt was the latest fashion, a hobble skirt with a kicky little insert so you could walk. It would hang straight, I knew, with no room for and no need for petticoats.

The suit was a shantung silk, a gray-green one moment and green-gray the next, matched with a fine gray silk for the waist.

Claire bobbed in excitement. "Julia, try it on!"

I was taken aback. I dressed in styles that certainly weren't conventional, but one couldn't say they were fashionable. I had never had an outfit that was daring in the way this one was.

A voice in my head said new women didn't take gifts like this—not because it came from a man and was unseemly, but because we didn't let men dictate fashion. Of course, it was inconceivable that Jack Forrest had personally picked this outfit. He would snort if he ever saw me in it.

I considered the women in my progressive household and said, "I don't know. Do you think I should keep it?"

They all, even Mary, looked at me for about a heartbeat and said, "Yes!" in unison. We had not come as far as we thought we had.

So the part of me that was interested in such unprogressive notions as how I looked in an outfit decided to try it on. If I looked just terrible in it—as I did in a traditionally fashionable dress that required a better endowment of hips and bust—then I could get on my high horse.

I took in Claire's bright eyes and said, "Help me," because I knew she would enjoy it so much. Then I dragged the whole thing into the back room. As I moved away, something fell from the chair. It was a dainty silk handbag that matched the suit perfectly.

I slipped into the unusual garment. It felt strange not to need even the one petticoat I wore. Claire patted and fussed and oohed. We had a mirror in the hall tree that sat near the door in the front room, and I headed for it.

Everyone was waiting when Claire and I emerged, and I wondered if dinner was burning. I hurried over and took the hat from the box. It was bigger than anything I ever wore, but not so big as to be ridiculous. It contained neither fruit nor birds, nor even an elaborate flower arrangement. It did have a couple of feathers along an elegant silk band. In fact, it was shaped rather like an exaggerated fedora. And the feathers weren't aigrette, so I had no qualms about the creatures that had donated them. I put it on my head at an angle that felt right and went to the mirror to adjust it.

The image in the mirror was incredible. This was the style I was built for. The skirt did indeed hang very straight, and I stood even taller than usual. But in this dress, tall was good. In this dress, thin was even good. Mary couldn't have worn this dress because she was too short. Amelia couldn't have worn it because she had too much in the way of hips.

I also didn't have Amelia's bust line and padding was a form of pandering to men's notions of how women should look, so I didn't use it. That meant most waists just hung there. But this waist and jacket were designed to hang.

My mother's voice was saying that I'd never look good in anything. And I had thought she meant I'd never be good at anything. After she died, my sister Betts took over and tried to convince me that a tomboy would come to no good—but it didn't matter because I'd never be womanly, she'd say in frustration.

Well, I had just achieved womanly. I turned and smiled at my friends. I don't know what they saw on my face, but each one hugged me in turn. Finally, Mary said, "I'd take that off before I eat, if I were you."

◆ ◆ ◆

Dinner that evening was the first relaxing meal I'd had in days, even though the topic was predictable. My housemates, with the exception of Amelia who had yet to come out of her room, questioned me relentlessly about the reason a newspaper editor would send me such a fine suit. I told them about the investigation, minus my speculations about Amelia. It felt good to get their impressions and talk about the case. By the time the meal was over, they were reassured about intruders. If there were danger, it was only for me—although they didn't seem to recognize even that.

I needed to do one more thing before bed. I needed to telephone Dad.

The green velour chair that sat next to the phone table wasn't our most comfortable, on purpose. I assured my housemates I'd put my best estimate on the toll in our common kitty. Then I settled in to the most comfortable position I could find. This could get contentious.

I wasn't disappointed.

"Well, Julia, have you returned from gallivanting around the countryside? Do you have other adventures planned I should be aware of?"

"The holiday was fine, thank you, Dad, except for the ending."

Several degrees of sarcasm evaporated. "How is Mr. McConnell?"

Dad usually read a St. Louis newspaper every day, which saved me from having to recount the story.

"I haven't heard he's in danger, so I guess he'll be O.K. The Chief doesn't want me gallivanting anymore, so I haven't actually visited." Well, that was the short version. "There's news from Ste. Gen," I added.

"That you know how?"

Honestly. "I know because Sheriff Carrey telephoned Headquarters while I was working this morning."

"Oh. O.K. About what?"

"They've arrested a man for the fire at the Klines—where the beer was stored. And they assume he's the one who damaged the wheel on the wagon Claude Picard was driving."

Silence. When Dad spoke I knew he'd moved beyond criticizing my behavior.

"Your friend Schroeder said he thought it was murder. Any explanation from the man they arrested?"

"Maybe it wasn't murder, Dad. The man might have thought the wheel would go when the cargo was loaded onto that wagon. A woman named Ettie Kline always met Sheriff Picard to take the beer to her place in Perry County. But they didn't shift the beer. They switched the teams."

Dad did this thing where he muttered under his breath, and I'd never figured out exactly what he said. I'd figured out the general context of irritation when I was ten. He was muttering.

I took it as my chance to ask him about the law enforcement issue that still bothered me.

"Dad, I'm confused. I'm sorry about Sheriff Picard, but I'm not sure how I should feel about what he was doing. Maybe it was Ettie Kline who was breaking the law. But he helped her. I don't want to criticize your friend. I've gotten to know Marjorie Picard, and I like her. You know, they were saving the money from the beer-running for college money for the two sons."

After a space, Dad said, "Well, Julie, Claude was always . . . entrepreneurial."

"Entrepreneurial?"

"Ste. Gen is an old-fashioned place, and Claude was an old-fashioned lawman. It was a good fit."

It was my turn to hesitate. Family lore alternately blamed and praised my mother for moving us back to Fulton. "Is Callaway County a good fit for you, Dad? Should you have stayed here?"

"It's a good fit, Julie." The affection was obvious in his voice. "I just couldn't send Verne to college."

Ah. I loved this man. And I was willing to keep teaching him.

"You couldn't send me to college either, Daddy."

He was still laughing when he told me to stay out of trouble.

I sat there after I'd rung off, staring at the dress draped over a straight chair, the hatbox in the seat, assuring myself Dad had said he wouldn't have done what Claude Picard had done.

I looked up to see Amelia staring at me. Then at the dress. Then at me. Before I could think what to say, she snorted and headed for the door. Bag on her wrist.

34

From the **St. Louis Globe-Democrat**, Saturday, June 15, 1910

> *Special Dispatch from Perryville, Mo. – A Ste.*
> *Genevieve man has been arrested for arson*
> *involving a barn in Perry County in which bootleg*
> *beer was stored.*
>
> *Perry County Sheriff Paul Carrey says Mr.*
> *Tom Caruthers, who works as a handyman in Ste.*
> *Genevieve, is also under investigation for*
> *damaging the wagon that was driven by Ste.*
> *Genevieve Sheriff Claude Picard the night of his*
> *death.*
>
> *Sheriff Carrey says he believes the damage led*
> *directly to the accident in which Sheriff Picard*
> *was killed. Sheriff Carrey and Acting Sheriff*
> *James Ingle of Ste. Genevieve County are*
> *cooperating on the investigation, and Mr.*
> *Caruthers is being held in the Ste. Genevieve jail.*

My trusty police escort appeared like an alarm clock at 6 a.m. and waited for me just outside the door. It was Ruhl again, and he was staring. I'd decided to wear the new dress. Why not? I never went anyplace special to wear such a thing, so I would wear it to work and get teased and wear it to a conversation with whomever I could find at Union Station on my lunch break. The silk handbag had the usual few items I carried. It was just large enough to include my revolver. A paper bag held a cheese sandwich. I would eat it on the streetcar on the way to do my detective duties.

Sure enough, the cops were in rare form. It was one comment after another, most along the lines of what I was doing after work. Even the Chief stared and then muttered, "Very nice, Julia."

When lunch finally came around, I slipped out ten minutes early as I had yesterday. Carl hadn't contacted me, but he probably wasn't back in town yet. I wondered if a story had made it into the *Westliche Post*, but I didn't have a copy and couldn't have read it if I did.

Once out of Headquarters, I couldn't stride in this dress as I often did. People looked at me. *Men* looked at me, a different look than my plain-and-simple bachelor-girl outfits got.

I figured out what it was. In my usual garb, people looked at my clothes and wondered how I could be so unaware of fashion. Now people were looking at fashion and wondering about me. Interesting. Maybe unnerving.

When I reached the offices of the hotel inside Union Station, Mr. McGee stared. I thanked him again for his help the day before—and asked for Gertrude Vezjak. He pointed rudely at a woman seated at a small typing table jammed against a wall. The modern need to produce typed rather than hand-written documents made the services of women like Gertrude—and me—important. It didn't make us important personally.

Gertrude was sipping soup. Probably a cold soup since I didn't know how she'd have warmed it. Yuck. I gave her my best smile. I was hoping she would leave with me if I offered to buy her coffee.

I introduced myself as I had to McGee, explaining that I was a typist for the Police Department. She stared at me, looking from the hat to my feet. Like most of my skirts, this one stopped at my ankles. I made my own skirts like that on purpose. This one was short because I'm pretty tall for ready-made. My shoes were what I always wore, but the hose were a gauze lisle. It was more ankle than anyone in the office saw outside the privacy of their homes. At least at work.

"A typist?" she said.

I nodded. "Mr. McGee said you might be able to tell me about the shooting this week. I understand there was a tall, dark-haired man involved, and that you saw him."

She was both wary and interested, I thought.

"The detective who came didn't want to bother any of the women who might have seen the man. He didn't want to distress you." Hah.

But she seemed to believe that. She nodded, her mouth open none too gracefully.

"So, we were wondering,"—'we' being the police department, I implied—'if you could tell me what you saw. Perhaps we could have a cup of coffee while I have a bite of lunch." I'd been too anxious to eat on the streetcar and lifted my own cold lunch.

Her eyes widened. They were brown and pretty. I smiled encouragement. "I'd be delighted to buy you a cup of coffee."

Gertrude obviously didn't do this sort of thing often. But I could imagine the curiosity surfacing, maybe the desire to have something interesting to tell her family and friends for the next couple of weeks. She nodded.

We went down the stairs that ended near the spot where William had been shot. I tried to breathe evenly. I made myself move normally.

The lunchroom was overflowing with people ordering, but I pulled Gertrude along and smiled and made inane small talk until we each had a cup in our hand. The benches back in the waiting room were all full, so we leaned against the end of one until two young men got up. They stood too close and watched us sit. Watched me sit. I was beginning to consider the dress a nuisance.

I offered Gertrude half the cheese sandwich, and she took it. I took one bite of my half and asked my question. "Ladies have such a good eye for detail, I think, much better than men, really. I know it was distressing, but could you tell me what you saw?"

Gertrude might have been hesitant at my unusual request, but I didn't think she was distressed talking about the event. She had found it all more than exciting, and the best part was the mysterious man.

"He was most handsome, ma'am," she insisted. And then she smiled at me in that way women do, overcoming all divides of class and age and politics. Great. Someone found Terence Kelley attractive. Two someones, if you counted Amelia.

"Really?" I tried to sound as if I'd like to hear about a handsome man. "What did he look like?"

"Oh, ma'am, he was tall and had glossy black hair, sort of long on top, so it was . . . flying . . . loose . . . a bit. I couldn't rightly say what color his eyes were, but there was this nice crinkle around them, I thought."

Could be. Kelley did wear his hair fairly long on top. Like William. "He wasn't wearing a hat?"

"No, he wasn't. It was in his hand. He might have lost it, dashing up the steps like crazy, you know, and grabbed it up before I saw him."

"He came up the steps? Which steps?"

"Why, those right there, ma'am."

She pointed to the steps that we thought the shooter must have used to fire down at William. I managed the briefest glance in that direction.

"Did he come up the steps before or after you heard a shot fired? You did hear a shot, right?" I should have asked her that first.

"Oh, yes, ma'am. It was fearsome loud, echoed up through the rafters. I thought the big window might break, but it didn't."

"And the man?"

"He was running up the stairs, as I said. Can you imagine? Someone had just fired a gun, right here in the Station, and he was running up those steps right toward him. I hope you can figure out who it was, you and the police, ma'am, because it one of the bravest things I've ever seen."

It was my turn to sit with my mouth open ungracefully.

First things first. "You saw the tall, handsome man running up the stairs just after the shot was fired, toward the shooter, right?"

Gertrude thought about it. She closed her eyes. Goodness, I was glad I'd found this woman.

"You know, I'm not sure. It could have been he caught my eye before the shot was fired. Sometimes, I take a break and watch people. I like to lean against that cool tile in the summer and watch the crowd." She paused. "He was so. . . I don't know . . . sort of scared, real intense-looking, you know. He caught my eye, and I watched him real close. I didn't even know someone had been shot downstairs for a long time." Gertrude was doing a great job. I was struggling to breathe, but she didn't notice, because she was picturing the scene, brown eyes wide now.

"Maybe I did see him first. He froze for a second, I mean just a second, and then he was running again, moving toward the place what the shot sounded like it came from. So, I guess I did see him first." She seemed pleased to have sorted it out.

I swallowed. "And did you look toward the shot?"

"I did . . . maybe not first thing. I watched the man. But I looked to where the man was headed—before he got there."

"And what did you see, Gertrude?"

"Nothing too clear, ma'am. There was someone with a bundle in his hand, I think. I mean I have this notion of someone holding something in front of them, not big, just a bundle. You know how people carry bundles of things when they travel, so maybe it was a traveler with a bundle." She shrugged.

"Can you describe the person?"

She sat for maybe a quarter minute, thinking about it.

"I'm not rightly sure, ma'am. I don't think he was tall like the handsome man, but not short either. Sort of heavy, but not fat, you know? I mean, I was looking down at the landing."

"Did the tall, handsome man have a gun?"

Gertrude turned to me with a snort that suggested I hadn't understood a word she'd said. "Really, Miss. The handsome man was headed toward the man on the landing. He wasn't shooting. He didn't have a gun. It was the man with the bundle what he was headed toward." She was smiling again. "And then he was helping, you know, telling people to be calm. I had stepped closer along the railing, and I heard him say that, but then it got right loud."

O.K. Time to back up. "Are you sure the person with the bundle was the one who fired the gun? Or was that who the handsome man was headed toward?"

She considered me several seconds. "I thought it was the same person, until you asked."

Darn. This was harder than I'd thought it would be.

"And what happened when the handsome man got to the man holding the bundle?"

"Well, I guess he didn't see the man who had fired, or who I thought had fired. He kept telling people to be calm and looking around, like he was looking for someone else. He directed a husband and wife with a child, and a woman who was by herself, and an elderly couple, out the door, out onto Market Street and went out that way himself. I moved down the railing to see where he went. I could see him looking around, and then he disappeared.

"I see." I glanced at her empty coffee cup. Mine was only down a couple of sips, my half of the sandwich still missing only the one bite. "When we go back up, can you show me where the man was on the stair, and where the other man was on the landing?"

"Oh, yes. That would be easy. I can picture it all."

How had George missed this woman?

We rose and put the coffee cups back on the counter. The lunch crowd was starting to thin, and I didn't want Gertrude to get in trouble. I might have more questions. Someone licensed to ask might have more questions.

So, we started up the stairs, and my stomach was tight. We paused on the first flight when she stopped and said, "He was right about here . . . looking right up there."

I followed her finger's trajectory. The location could have been under the doorway arch. A shooter could have stood in the arch, against the post, or against the frame, watched for us, aimed and fired, stuck the gun back in a bundle, and then stepped back. Terence Kelley could have been looking right at the person, from this point on the stair.

I was trembling but I remembered to ask Gertrude for any more details on the handsome man's appearance. She couldn't tell me more about features, but added that he was slender and looked very good in a dark gray suit. Kelley had a dark gray suit, but I hadn't seen him Wednesday and might not have remembered anyway. Terence Kelley enjoyed his clothes and had more suits than any other man I knew. Except William.

I thanked Gertrude. My voice had gone soft, and I don't know what she thought about that. But she seemed grateful, as if I had made her day more interesting. That was fair. She'd certainly made my day more interesting.

35

The Hotel Perry was quiet, but Carl couldn't rest. He was nervous signing in and nervous getting to bed, even though he'd tested the window and the door. It was hot in the closed-up room, but Carl didn't feel safe with a window that opened on a fire escape. Too much happening recently on fire escapes. So, Carl lay awake, sweating, debating whether he should or should not be scared, should or should not trust Paul Carrey, should or should not think about being fond of Julia.

Despite his worries, he fell asleep and woke drenched in the early morning hours. He struggled to his feet, washed as best he could, and opened the window for the breeze. It was cool, and it helped. He sat watch, anticipating daylight.

What if Carrey had contacted Ingle during the night, either to warn him, or more innocently, to try to answer some questions for himself? How safe would this day really be?

Dawn happened, and Carl had cooled down, physically. He felt a knot in his stomach, the kind he used to get when he performed, played or sang. But this settled a bit lower in his gut, less fluttery, more solid. He figured it might be with him all day.

Paul Carrey was waiting in the lobby when Carl appeared just before eight o'clock. The milk train had left early, this far out from the city. But another train was headed north, and the two shared a fairly easy silence. Carrey asked a couple more questions about Henry

Ingle, and Carl tried to be honest. Carl asked if they thought Caruthers would admit to damaging the wheel. And if the man had a connection to the Ingles. Carrey said the handyman sometimes worked for James.

In Ste. Gen, they both looked about and walked quickly up to the County Jail. Carl fidgeted as Carrey asked the jailer to give them access to Tom Caruthers. The knot in his stomach tightened when the jailer said he'd had word from Acting Sheriff Ingle to wait for him—in case anyone wanted to see the prisoner.

Carl turned at the sound of a step behind him, expecting James Ingle. Instead, he was looking down into the bluer eyes of Henry. James must have been the shadow behind him.

36

Maybe I had dressed up to get fired. Maybe I would get fired in front of my father, because he was standing right behind the Chief, who was angry. Dad was angry, too, but he took in the dress, and the frown softened up some.

The Chief stared at me, swiveling as I moved around him to get to Dad. I gave Dad a kiss and a smile, and he whispered, "Nice dress." He didn't compliment me often, at least on dresses. Sometimes on my shooting, but not on dresses.

The Chief was impatient. "Where have you been?"

I had no idea what to say. I couldn't lie to him. Not only would he find out, but I had to let him know what Gertrude Vezjak had said. I could think of no way but to admit what I had been up to, today, if not last night. Furthermore, I didn't care to discuss it in front of the few cops milling about. Anything I said would spread like crazy, and George would know I'd been retracing his work. That would be embarrassing or dangerous or both. I shrugged.

The Chief jerked his head toward his office. Dad followed us. Darn, I hated to have him hear this.

We all settled. I tucked my legs meekly back under the chair. Dad went first. "Julia, you have got to be more careful. In fact, I want you to come home."

"Home? Dad, no, I can't."

The Chief said, "Julia, it's too dangerous for you here. And you won't listen when we tell you to be careful, and you won't accept the police help I'm trying to give you."

I shook my head. "Dad, Chief Wright, I know that, but I can't leave. There's too much happening, and I'm too involved."

"I told you not to get involved, Julia." This was as stern as Dad got. "I told you to ask Schroeder and McConnell to do it, not to get involved yourself. Micah says your room has been ransacked. That is too involved—"

"But that's the problem, Dad. I did ask Carl and William to get involved and look what happened. I have to do what I can to find out who shot William. I owe him that."

Dad and the Chief exchanged looks that I interpreted to mean they'd expected this.

"The thing is, Dad, it's as if I'm the one . . . it sounds conceited . . . but I'm the one with all the pieces. I just haven't put them together yet."

"Well, your father has a new piece of the puzzle. Would you like to hear about it, Julia?"

When the Chief put it that way, I wasn't sure I did want to hear it.

"I got a note, delivered first thing this morning, from here," Dad said.

"From St. Louis?"

"Yes. The young man who delivered it said he'd brought it from St. Louis, and that was all he could tell me. Said he was supposed to go right back and was taking the spur north. Ran off immediately."

I wanted to know if Dad had really let him leave that easily. But I also wanted to know about the note. So I asked that question first.

Dad didn't pull the note out. He must have memorized it . . . or else it was short.

It was short. "Tell Julia and William McConnell and Carl

Schroeder to stop their investigation before another one gets hurt," he recited.

Now that was scary. I suddenly wondered where Carl was. I wished I'd asked before I came back to work.

I must have seemed agitated, because the Chief said, "Good. I hope you're scared."

Wrong thing to say. I didn't bother to hide my irritation. "I'm worried about Carl. I haven't heard from him since lunch yesterday. And he was going to Ste. Genevieve when he left here." I didn't care to add that the thought of him walking back into Union Station, near the stairs, near where I'd been thirty minutes ago, was making my stomach tighten.

Neither Dad nor the Chief said, "Damn" in front of me, but I could tell they were thinking it.

Dad said, "What about McConnell?" My stomach tightened some more.

But the Chief leaned back in his chair. "I think he's the one we worry about least. I have an officer outside his door—and he's not out running up and down the countryside, at least."

Which apparently reminded him. "Now, young lady, you know how dangerous it was that you went out without an escort today, although, in hindsight, it might not have done any good to have Schroeder with you." He leaned forward again, and this was the moment of truth. "Where were you? As you are quite the liberated lady, let me repeat that: Where the hell were you?"

I started to check to see if Dad was offended or amused, but it was only my own reaction that counted. If was going to lose my position over this, I might as well make a good stand of it.

"I was talking to a woman in Union Station, one who saw the shooter."

The Chief leaned back with a thud. Dad twisted away from me and groaned.

"Honest to God, Julia," the Chief muttered. "That's why the City of St. Louis pays detectives."

I leaned forward with my hands on the ends of the wooden arms, elbows canted outward. "The City of St. Louis isn't getting its money's worth."

Dad started in. "Julia—"

"Dad, the report doesn't say anything—except that it has at least three different descriptions of the same man. The detective who wrote it is best friends with the man who was likely on the scene, at the shooting and at the wheel shop."

Dad said, "Are you saying a St. Louis cop is involved?" just as the Chief said, "Are you accusing Kelley?"

At least I had their attention. I took a deep breath.

"I believe Kelley was on the scene both times. I don't think he was the shooter. Not according to the witness who seemed to have a good view of things."

"Oh," the Chief said. He took a moment to comb his mustache with his teeth, a sure sign he didn't like my conclusion. "Who did you talk to, Julia?"

"First, I talked to a man George had listed in his report, and I found a woman recommended by that witness. The man wouldn't have suggested George talk to a woman—and maybe the woman wouldn't have talked to George." They were both staring now. "But, over a cup of coffee, she gave me a lot of information." I tried for demure, but I doubt I achieved it. "Do you want to hear what she had to say?"

Dad rolled his eyes, and the Chief jumped in the chair. "Of course, I want to hear, Julia. I want to know everything you said to those people and everything they said to you." This was as close as he'd ever gotten to yelling at me. "Start from the top!"

I eased back into the chair. I told them about Mr. McGee's corrected description and Gertrude's impressions of the shooter and the brave man on the stairs.

"So," I concluded, "I still don't know who was shooting. But I think Terence Kelley was on the scene. I think he knows who the shooter was. I can't prove it."

They were both silent a moment. Then Dad asked the Chief, "And this Kelley was at the wheel shop?"

The Chief nodded. "Julia saw him there." He paused. "And, of course, he investigated, since he happened to be on the scene. All we have is his report and what Julia saw from inside the shop."

"Why was a detective on the scene?"

"I haven't asked him yet. But I will."

Dad considered that. "Does this Kelley have a connection with anyone else in the case?"

The Chief shook his head. I must have made some movement, because he said, "What, Julia?"

I sighed. "If Carl were here, he would say it's obvious Kelley's involved."

The Chief's eyebrows went up.

"Carl thinks the Ingles are involved, first off. James, you know, is the Chief Deputy in Ste. Genevieve. Henry and Amelia are his cousins. Henry was at the funeral and brought the wheel to St. Louis for James. I don't believe James and Henry are as radical on prohibition as Carl seems to think. I can't see them being involved for that reason. But Amelia is something else. She's really out-of-control over the issue. Just last night she referred to Carl as a German drunkard. I have never seen Carl drunk. I've never seen him have more than one or two beers." I stopped. I hated to close this particular circle.

"And Amelia and Kelley are seeing each other." I said it quietly, as if that made it less startling.

"What exactly do you mean by that, Julia?" Chief Wright said.

I sighed. "They . . . Kelley comes to her room at night. You recall the barrel Jamison brought in?" The Chief nodded and explained to Dad what we were talking about. "Well, that's how Kelley was getting on the fire escape. He was coming in Amelia's window."

Now Dad was on his mettle. "You mean a man is visiting one of the women in your house?"

Oops.

"I think the only one of us who even knew was Mary. Her room is next to Amelia's, and she can hear them. I didn't know until the other night. I stayed with Mary . . . after the shooting. And heard them."

I hesitated.

"What?" the Chief demanded.

"Well, you know how irritated I get that Kelley won't let me type his reports. And then he turns in these reports that look terrible. It's a matter of false pride on my part. I'm always afraid someone will think that's my work." I don't know why I was being so self-effacing. Maybe to soften what I was about to say. "Amelia types them."

They both frowned at me as if I couldn't be serious. The Chief said, "How do you know this?"

This was getting embarrassing. "She types at night in her room. After he visits. He must drop off work for her to do."

Dad was smiling again and trying to hide it. The Chief was combing his mustache furiously.

"Are you sure she's typing for him?" the Chief said, "Are you sure it's him that visits, Julia?"

I swallowed hard. "Well, I had to know who she was seeing. So, I went her in room when she was at work. I was coming in late, Thursday morning." I glanced from one to the other. "The report lying next to her machine was the one Kelley finally turned in yesterday about the fire at Armbruster's Wheel Shop."

The nice thing about that kind of statement was that the content almost made them overlook the fact that I'd been in Amelia's room by stealth.

Almost. Dad shook his head. The Chief seemed less concerned.

"The man in her room could have been someone who delivered Kelley's typing chores," the Chief said.

I offered a weak smile. "I know. I wanted to see who it was, for that very reason. And events conspired."

I described the buffet scene again, and they got the picture. The Chief was trying not to grin.

"I'm afraid I saw him clearly. It was Terence Kelley."

Dad got his grin under control. "And why does Schroeder think there's a connection?"

"Carl always sees things in a political light. He assumes if the Ingles are prohibition advocates, they'd be involved in anything." I looked to the Chief. "Do you know if Kelley is prohibition? I don't think I've ever heard him say. Carl thinks so, but Kelley and Carl don't get along." I didn't see the need to pass on Mr. Armbruster's interpretation.

The Chief sighed. "I don't know. There's no doubt he opposes woman's suffrage. So it's odd he's taken up with Amelia Ingle." He looked at Dad and then at me. "He's also married."

My God. That was why Amelia couldn't acknowledge the relationship.

The Chief explained. "I believe the woman he's married to is a suffragist herself. I don't know her name. They separated, according to rumor, because of her activities, and she uses her maiden name—started using it after she got into the movement, probably one of the things they clashed over. But I haven't heard that they've divorced."

No, that would be unlikely for Terence Kelley.

"Perhaps he met Amelia Ingle because of his wife's involvement in the movement. I don't know much more about it. I try to keep up with the gossip when it involves my officers, but that's all I've heard." He smiled at me, for the first time since we sat down. "Until now."

Suddenly, I felt sorry for the two of them. Maybe it explained why Amelia was more difficult than usual. Maybe our seeing Kelley had scared her.

I sighed. "I still don't know what Kelley was doing in either place."

"And we don't know who sent the message to John," the Chief pointed out. "Julia, I have several things to do here. I have to talk to Terence Kelley and see what he says. I have to talk to George St. Martin and get an explanation from him. And I have to find Carl Schroeder and make sure he's safe. Then I have to figure out what to say to get you and Schroeder to lay low until we solve it." He glared at me. "And by 'we' I mean the police, Julia. This is a police matter now. If St. Martin and Kelley aren't the ones to solve it, then I'll put someone else on the case. And you, young lady, need to go home with your father."

I raised my chin. "Are you firing me?"

"Of course not!" He stood up and paced around the desk. "You know I value the work you do here. And if I had to, I'd admit that you did a good job tracking down this Vezjak woman for us. But, aside from the impropriety of it, it's too dangerous for you to be here right now. I want you safe, Julia. And I want Schroeder and McConnell safe." He glanced at Dad. "Your father and I got you into this, and maybe we shouldn't have, but now it's my concern, my jurisdiction, and I'll take it from here. When we figure out who the shooter is, who sent the note, arrest someone, you can come back. And welcome."

This was my chance to leave. The Chief would indeed take over because his officers were involved in either criminal activity or negligence of duty. Neither Carl nor William would blame me. They would think I was following my father's wishes. But I couldn't—or wouldn't—do that. I wouldn't leave the city. I wouldn't leave either Carl or William, and I couldn't keep them safe by dragging them to Fulton with me.

I shook my head.

"Chief Wright, it's my concern, too. I got them into it and look at what's happened. I know more about the situation than George or any of your detectives. I can't help from Fulton. If you want me to stop coming to work, I will. Although, I should think I'd be safe here . . ." I nodded back at my desk, stricken at the thought of not being here everyday.

I wanted to tell the Chief what all I could be doing, like finding more witnesses, but I didn't speak up fast enough.

"Listen to me, my dear. Your only remaining job is to tell me everything you know. If you're leaving something out, I want to hear it right now. I don't want to fire you, but I will if need be, if that's what it takes to get you to go back to Fulton."

I caught Dad's heavy frown from the corner of my eye as I stood. It was going to get worse, if that was possible. I stood.

"I'm sorry, Chief Wright. I love working here. But I'm not going back to Fulton until I know William and Carl are safe, and that won't be until this is solved."

I turned to Dad. "We need to let William know about that note. I need to see what I can find out on Carl's whereabouts. Do you want to go to the hospital with me?"

Chief Wright slapped his hand on his desk. "You can wait for your father outside, at your desk. I need to talk to you, John, if I may." The chief's voice softened only slightly as he turned to Dad. Who nodded.

I closed the door quietly although I wanted to slam it.

I dropped into my chair and cradled my head in my hands. The cut twinged from under its bandage. I wanted to talk to William. I wanted to see Carl walk in any minute now. Please walk in safe, Carl, I said in my head, several times.

◆　◆　◆

I decided I might as well finish up what reports I could. The Chief hadn't actually fired me yet, after all. I tried to concentrate on the typing, because having to erase an error irritated me. But cops who hadn't been there in the morning stopped by to admire the dress. I didn't think my repartee was as clever as usual.

Carl did not appear.

It was an hour later when Jules Blount walked in. He was the *Globe-Democrat* cub reporter who'd been taking on the police beat with William indisposed. Blount had been more than polite, and I'd helped him a couple of times, offering the appropriate files, pointing out the officers he needed to see.

He smiled when he saw me. "You look very nice today, Miss Nye," he said, almost in a whisper, as if he weren't too sure he should let anyone hear him. Of course, several officers did hear him. There was a flutter of comments, including some about me always attracting reporters.

That seemed to freeze young Mr. Blount. He was not a shy

person. He was quiet, perhaps, but shy didn't work for newspapermen. He probably wasn't any younger than me, either. But he was my height and had freckles and curly reddish blonde hair. And just now he looked like a little boy caught opening the pie safe.

He whispered, "I have a note for you."

There was a chorus of oohs from the direction of the squad room. These guys heard everything. My hand shot around the typewriter, and Blount got the idea. He thrust the envelope into my hand, and I pocketed it.

"C'mon, Julia, which boyfriend is it from?" Patrolman O'Neill had gotten close.

"Read it, Julia. We'll look over your shoulder." That was from Willie Long, and there was no way I was touching it with him in the room.

I smiled at Blount and shrugged. "Thanks. I hope it isn't urgent."

He pressed his lips together and headed for the report basket we kept perched on a filing cabinet in the next room. Someone said they hoped McConnell had paid him well, and I shook my head.

But, of course, I was hoping it was from William. It would mean he was well enough to write. And, why else would Blount give me a note? Unless Forrest wanted to know if I had gotten the dress. Lordy, that would be even more embarrassing if the cops saw it.

So, I kept typing and telling men to leave me alone, and they smiled and drifted back to the squad room or out the door to work. A little later, George St. Martin came in, closing an umbrella. He stopped in front of my desk and smiled. I sighed and smiled back faintly. Why not?

"Do you know if the Chief is busy?" he asked, nodding toward the door that often was propped open. It was one of those doors with pocky glass, and you could vaguely see people in there. That should have given George his answer.

"As a matter of fact, he's visiting with my father."

"Your father? I'd love to meet your father." George looked sincere. "I'm going to wait for the Chief, so don't let either of them get away, O.K.?"

Surely, George. If women were supposed to be on pedestals instead of toiling away in offices, as George had once informed me, why wouldn't you say "please"?

He strolled into the squad room. I finished the report I was working on, got up to file it, and fished out the note while I was in the file room.

Julia,

I'd like to talk with you. Would you visit at City Hospital, please?
Yours, Wm. McConnell.

I stuck it back in my pocket the moment I'd finished it. I wasn't sure whether to smile or frown—and may have done both. James O'Neill was passing through and gave me a second look.

"Oh, you read it. I want to read it, Julia." He put his hands on his hips and pouted. Long appeared from the squad room, and George was with him.

"I'm thinking it's from McConnell because the new kid from the *Globe* delivered it," Willie was saying.

George honest-to-goodness had the nerve to say, "If it's from McConnell, it might relate to the case. I need to see it, Julia."

"That's right, Julia," Willie added. "You should hand it over. You could be suppressing material evidence." Willie was fun sometimes, but he had no quitting sense.

"All of you, please let me work."

"Now, Julia, I need to know what's going on with McConnell," George said.

That did it. I didn't know what I suspected George of, incompetence or corruption. But teasing me about William was not his brightest idea.

"You don't need to know about anything personal between William McConnell and me, Detective St. Martin. You need to know who shot him, and you are instead standing around the office teasing me."

O'Neill and Long widened their eyes and backed off.

"Do you really think I can't do my job, Julia?" George asked.

"I think you *can* do it, George. I'm not sure why you aren't."

The teasing evaporated. He fidgeted with buttons on his waistcoat. "I know McConnell, I like him, I care that he was shot. And I do my job. I don't want you to think otherwise, Julia."

"I don't want to think otherwise, George. I truly don't."

He considered at me another moment, then glanced at the Chief's door. "I do need to talk to him. Please let me know when he's free."

He turned and walked away. At least I'd gotten a "please" this time.

It was another long hour before I looked up to see Dad and the Chief emerging from his office. They seemed to be having trouble breaking away from the conversation. A few officers and detectives were leaving about that time, and the teasing resumed.

"Going to see McConnell now, Julia?" It was O'Neill, irrepressible. He dropped a report in my basket. I looked it while I considered my answer. It occurred to me that George had come close and that lots of others could hear my answer.

"No. I'm going out with Dad. I can't make it by the time visiting hours end. Maybe tomorrow."

There was an outbreak of groans and silly comments, and I waved them off. "You guys go see him if you think he's lonely." I tossed that over my shoulder as I headed toward the Chief, trying to motion him and Dad back inside.

There were several hoots at that, but I ignored them. Dad and Chief Wright looked curious, though.

"Could I speak to you?" I asked the Chief as I got close.

He stepped inside the door and motioned us in.

"What was all that about, Julie?" Dad asked.

"Well, the new reporter for the *Globe* gave me a message from William. He wants to see me, it says. They don't know that." I gestured back over my shoulder. "They're just guessing the message is from William and want to tease me about it."

"Does that bother you?" Dad asked.

The Chief answered for me. "If it did, she'd have quit by now."

I shrugged. In the normal run of things, it didn't bother me. Today, I wasn't sure.

"It's not that I'm investigating, Chief Wright. But we do need see William and tell him if there's danger, as Dad's note seems to indicate. And, I don't want to announce the visit publicly." I looked at Dad, and he nodded, thank goodness.

"I was wondering, Chief Wright, if you could arrange to get us in City Hospital after visiting hours."

He stared at me.

"Chief Wright, you said you wanted William to be safe."

"Of course, of course," the Chief said. "I'll call them now, tell them you'll be there . . . when? Eight? That's an hour after visitors closes. That should throw anyone off. Are you O.K. with that?"

"Yes. Thank you."

"I'm surprised you thought of it, Julia." He was considering me, head to one side. "It's an indication you don't trust someone in the department."

"Well, anyone could say something to Kelley or to someone we haven't even thought about. And besides, George St. Martin is standing out there." The Chief's bushy eyebrows went up. "He's eager to talk to you."

"Good. I'll call the Hospital first. Tell him, if you don't mind, that I'll see him in a minute."

He turned to Dad. "You two enjoy dinner or whatever. Good to talk to you, John, and thanks for your advice."

I reached for the door handle, and the Chief added, "I don't want to have to fire you, young lady. I expect you to go home with your Father, and I'll see you back here as soon as it's safe."

I shook my head again but saw no point in repeating my intention.

The Chief seemed to think he'd convinced me of something. "Give McConnell my regards."

I gave George the Chief's message and started to walk off. He looked pained. So, I introduced him to Dad, and Dad was gracious. George seemed pleased, but I could tell he was still hurt by my attitude. So be it. Of course, he might soon be telling Terence Kelley I was on to him. And Amelia.

37

Dad suggested dinner at the new Castella Restaurant on Washington Avenue because he liked to take advantage of the nice places to eat in the City when he visited. That sounded good, but I insisted on stopping twice on our way.

I wanted to try to locate Carl, so we stopped at an office in City Hall, and I convinced a friend to let me use the telephone—so as not to detect from Headquarters. Dad was suspicious but waited downstairs.

I got hold of a man I'd met at the *Post*, by the name of Zimmerman. He told me Carl had made it to Ste. Genevieve, if not Perryville, because he'd called in the story that had run this morning about the arrest. Beyond that, he hadn't seen Carl all day and assumed he was still working on the story, out in the countryside, as he so quaintly put it.

Dad raised eyebrows at me, and I explained I had to know where Carl was, to tell William, who would ask. It was probably true.

Our other stop was to buy an umbrella. It had started raining in earnest, and I'd left mine at home, feeling like an umbrella added to the outfit was both too fashionable and too much trouble to drag around. That's the problem with fashion. I was losing patience with the skirt no matter how good it looked. And most women carried umbrellas for the most impractical reasons. The fact that I needed one now for practicality was unreasonably irritating.

But Dad thought it would be nice for me to have one to go with the dress. I'd told him how I'd come by it, and he wasn't as upset as I'd thought he might be. Sometimes I forgot he wasn't like everyone else's father. That's why I wasn't like everyone else.

And I could do a tad more on the investigation by stopping for an umbrella in the shop where Amelia worked on Olive. She should still be there. Dad could form his own impression of her. Maybe understand my need to keep detecting.

But Amelia had left. I could tell that the husband and wife who owned the small shop were irritated.

Dad bought me a very nice umbrella that would be both practical tonight and fashionable, if I ever had the least inclination to use it so. As he was paying, I asked, "Was Amelia unwell?"

"I don't know," Mr. Braden grumped. "She said she couldn't be here a moment longer and flounced out."

"She's been impossible lately," Mrs. Braden added, hands on her fashionable hips. "I don't know if it's that suffragist movement she's involved in or what. She's missed work all day or a part of a day three times this week." Mrs. Braden tilted her head at me. "But I guess you know that if you live with her."

"Actually, I work as well, and I leave before she does. I wouldn't know if she'd been somewhere else. I wasn't aware that she's ill," I added, almost truthfully. Unless anxiety over your married lover is an illness.

Mrs. Braden considered my outfit one last time and said, "Well, glad to meet you miss, I'm sure."

I was dismissed, and Dad took my arm to guide me toward the door. But I needed to know which days she'd missed—perhaps the days she could have been arranging an assassination attempt or vandalizing my room.

I shrugged loose from Dad and tried Mr. Braden. "Which days did she have to leave?"

He was a bit nicer about it, but said, "Sorry, miss. I'm sure Miss Ingle will tell you if you ask her. Maybe you can help her out." He smiled and dismissed me as well.

We moved out into the drizzle, and I held the umbrella high enough that Dad could share it. He ducked under it and held my arm tightly against him. We wondered out loud about Amelia, and I was nearly through explaining her odd behavior when we reached the Castella.

The Castella was my idea of Spanish architecture. The dining rooms had lots of arches and draping ivy, and little fake balconies protruding from fake windows. I should have enjoyed the place, but tonight I didn't have much appetite, even with my insufficient lunch. I could have been dejected at having to quit work. I could have been anxious about the upcoming fight with Dad over going back home. I was indeed worried about Carl. Maybe Amelia was bothering me, too, as I left good food untouched. I couldn't decide whether I should be worried for her or because of her. But it was the thought of seeing William that made me too jittery to enjoy whatever it was I had on my plate.

Dad asked about my statement earlier that whoever had broken into my room had had a key. I told him my impressions of the incident, complete with my belief that someone had used a hammer to break the doorknob. I sounded like a police report. He said, "You're good, Julie." I felt good . . . and safe . . . for a couple of minutes. He got quiet for a while, and I knew he was detecting, too, in his head.

"Who do you think it was?"

I'd made up my mind while I was pushing food around. I hadn't wanted to say it out loud yet.

"Well, unless it was someone we haven't identified so far—maybe the shooter—I'd say it was Amelia." I put the fork down and gave up on eating. "I thought it odd she was home the day Carl found her there, the day . . . William was shot. And then she took off another afternoon? She was in the right place and had a key, no doubt left over from before I came. If she didn't do it herself, she must've been the one who let the vandal in."

38

I was out of excuses. We made our way to City Hospital, and the people downstairs had indeed been alerted that they'd have a late visitor.

When we approached William's room, I was glad to see two officers there. One was young. I thought his name was Peterson, but I didn't see him often because he was late shift and Fourth District. The other was an older officer, Miles Graham. Another of Luke Arnold's age and years of service. Except that he liked the night shift, he told me once. An old bachelor. It didn't seem as if they were exchanging duties, so the Chief must have put both of them on guard. Good.

Graham knew me from dropping off reports. He shook hands with Dad and said, "Haven't seen you for ages, John."

"How's it going, Miles?" Dad said.

I didn't have much patience with the greetings. I was gripping the umbrella tighter than necessary, and all but jumped when the door to William's room opened. The woman I'd seen yesterday stepped out, looking surprised.

She closed the door behind her, gently, and took in the group. She looked much as she had before, although this time the waist and skirt were in shades of green. Her intensely blue eyes took me again. The intensity was directed at me, no mistake.

She exaggerated a glance at the two-faced clock that cleverly protruded from the hallway wall. "It's after visiting hours."

I walked toward her, toward this woman who must be very close to William to be here at this hour. "I know. We're worried about security."

Her eyebrows tilted from irritation to concern. "Is there some reason to be more worried?"

"Maybe."

She looked around me at the two officers, instead of one, and at the tall stranger she didn't know. She moved back in front of the door. I decided to like her.

"I'm Julia Nye. This is my father. He's gotten a note warning us off the case. I need to tell William about it." I paused. "I'd introduce you to my father, if I knew your name." I tried a smile, and she seemed to be deciding whether to trust me with her personal information.

"Mrs. Evelyn Kinkade," she said, finally and firmly.

It all came together. The eyes, the hour, the name William had given me for his widowed sister and favored sibling. No telling what my face betrayed. She was smiling at me when I said, "Oh, you're William's sister."

She said, "Yes," almost as a compliment that I'd put it together. And then she was smiling more broadly, not in William's style, but in a pretty, ladylike grin, as she must have realized my first assumption. "I don't believe William is seeing anyone at the moment."

I would have liked for my own smile to be more stable, but I was shaking. I introduced her to my father and hoped she could hear me. She didn't seem surprised at the Sheriff part. She simply glanced from one of us to the other and decided we were who we said we were.

She nodded at Dad, took my arm, and moved me away from the

men. "The problem is that you didn't come during visiting hours." Her voice was quiet, although the men likely could hear. "William was hoping you'd come. He was disappointed."

"Does he have news . . . something I should know?"

She breathed out audibly. "No, I don't think so. He just wanted to see you. He's been concerned about your safety, what you're doing . . . he thought you'd visit before now."

We moved past the door, and I was thinking William must be doing better than I had imagined.

Evelyn stopped us and turned to me. "Why haven't you visited?"

My moment of relief turned back to panic. William might not have been so blunt, but here I was, face-to-face with his sister, and I wanted to answer her. And, of course, I had no idea what the answer was. The only thing I could think of was the nagging worry Carl had left with me.

"I know he's angry . . . angry with me, I guess, for what happened. I need to apologize. May I see him now?" I was hoping I'd said enough to get past her. Dealing with William himself seemed easier.

Evelyn's much more feminine dark eyebrows narrowed together over the same dark blue eyes. "I don't think he's angry with you at all. He's grateful for your help and has wanted to tell you." She looked me over again. "I think he's just wanted to see you."

I was going to bend a wire in the new umbrella if I didn't stop gripping it so hard.

She went on. "The problem is, he was disappointed when you didn't come. He said he thought he'd read, but then he laid back and went to sleep. Do you have to see him now?"

"Yes, I do." I was whispering for lack of breath.

"Very well. Give me a minute." She shook her head and hurried inside.

I looked at Dad. He'd heard. Both officers were considering me as if they thought I'd been delinquent in not coming earlier, as well. I turned and looked down the hall at tile and white paint and closed doors. Nurses moved with the rustle of petticoats under stiff-fabric skirts, and the few who got close seemed critical as well. A wave of hospital smells washed over me.

I heard movement inside, Evelyn's voice, William's. He must have fallen asleep within the hour. I'm never at my best when I'm awakened right after I fall asleep. But William was so good at being calm. Maybe that made it easier.

"Julia!" It was almost the same tone I'd heard yesterday, maybe not as agitated, maybe more . . . welcoming.

Evelyn stepped out and looked from me to Dad, maybe unsure if I were visiting first, or if she were inviting my father in, as well.

Dad said, "Why don't you go on in, Julia? I'll meet with Mr. McConnell in a bit." He settled himself on the edge of the cops' table.

Lordy. Evelyn smiled at me and that helped. I felt her hand brush my back. She said, "William, Miss Nye is here"—as if there were any doubt by now.

She had turned on lights, or William had. He was sitting up and could have reached the bedside lamp on his right. The soft glow made the white walls, white curtains, white blanket, mellow. Two books were on the table. One was the new novel by Rex Beach. The one under it was an old copy of an Owen Wister. I was an iota less nervous. You can always trust a man who reads—and rereads—Westerns.

William looked good. Better than I expected. I sighed in relief.

He was smiling, but he was also probing, trying to read *me*, to figure out what was happening, where I'd been.

I managed to say, "William," but I had no idea what to say with it.

Then he gave me that same look I'd been getting all day. He studied me up and down and said, "Is that most fashionable outfit a gift from my employer?" I heard Evelyn do another of those breaths that stopped short of a snort. The attention felt less intrusive coming from William.

He glanced at her and explained to me, "I was irritated with Forrest over his using your name and told him so when he visited. He said he was going to make it up to you, that he'd planned to at least send you some money to repair your wardrobe." He sobered. "I guess you were . . . bloody by the time you got to the *Globe* that night."

I nodded and tried to breathe.

"I told him to send you clothes, not money. He wouldn't have a clue how much a woman's outfit costs." He was grinning again. "Hope that didn't embarrass you."

I shook my head and, finally, gratefully, had something to say. "I did think about sending it back but someone in your office has nice taste." I let go of my double death grip on the umbrella enough to open my arms and show off the line of the dress.

"It looks swell on you," William said.

Evelyn made a noise and moved toward the door. I didn't know if that was good or not. But she nodded to me, and I nodded back, and she was gone.

William held out a hand, and I moved toward the bed and took his hand with my free one. I maintained my grip on the umbrella with the other.

"I was hoping you'd come. I've wanted to talk to you . . . to know for sure you're O.K." He studied me again, checking out the O.K. part, I assumed. "Carl said you were keeping busy, but he was vague and that worried me. You know how unlike him it is not to chatter on about . . . well, he would normally tell me what you were doing."

"I've been busy, that's for sure. One reason I was willing to keep the dress is that I haven't had time to do laundry." I was trying to lighten things up, and William smiled. But he kept hold of my hand, and I still owed him an answer.

"William, I'm sorry. Carl said you were angry, and I assumed you were angry at me, and that seemed reasonable because I feel responsible." I glanced at his left arm, propped on pillows, and realized I'd avoided that so far. "I am so very sorry, William."

I realized I was trembling.

William pulled me closer. We'd been holding hands with our arms extended, like a handshake that hadn't ended. But William pulled me in so that I was next to the bed. "Julia, it's O.K. God, Julia."

He stopped and started in again. "How could you think I was angry with you? Carl said that?" He frowned as he asked, and that made me more nervous in turn. Lordy, why couldn't I handle this situation? I never shook like this.

"Julia, you helped save my life . . . certainly my arm, and I'm grateful. I wanted to thank you, but mostly I was worried about you. Did you stay away because . . .?" Then he simply looked at me.

Maybe I was going to cry after all. "I was so worried about you," I whispered. I didn't intend to whisper. It came out that way because I couldn't get enough breath again. I was pressing the umbrella to my stomach and holding on to his hand as if he'd slip away if I didn't. I realized it and started to loosen my grip, but he held on more tightly.

I had the feeling I sometimes got with William that he was trying to read my mind. And he must have read something. His face smoothed out, his smile went gentle, and he relaxed his grip.

"It's O.K., Julia. I understand." Well, good that one of us did. "Thank you for being concerned. But my arm is healing well. Dr. Potter came by and reminded me that your quick thinking made a difference. He said that if I'd lost more blood, I might not have gotten the use of it back. I'll play the piano again." He was grinning now, teasing me almost. The dimples that lengthened with his grin were twitching.

"Oh, good." I looked at his hand that was still gripping mine and realized I'd sounded a bit flip. "Really. I want to hear you play the piano again."

He laughed. Then he kissed my hand. It was a lot like the gesture I'd made when I kissed his knuckles back in the Station, and I was blushing. Darn, I hated to blush.

William let go of my hand and said, "Pull up a chair, please."

I did, not very gracefully.

"Now. What have you been up to—that's kept you busy?"

I swallowed and started in. I told him about someone searching my room, and he frowned. I told him about Amelia and Kelley and, for a moment, he had that smile all the men had flashed, but then his frown deepened.

"I don't like you staying there."

I paused a moment, trying to decide what I thought about that note of protectiveness. Then I went on to tell him about George St. Martin's pitiful report and my efforts at detecting today. That brought me back to thinking about the shooting, and the breathing problem reemerged. In between pants, I told him about the serendipitous meeting with Mr. Armbruster.

William didn't notice my breathing problem, I assumed, because he was staring at the single window. The rain was heavier now and thudded against the southern exposure. "Kelley," he said and looked back at me.

He offered his hand again, and I stood and took it. He didn't so much grip my hand as hold it and rub his thumb over the back. "You are taking some serious chances, Julia, if it's Kelley. I think you need to get out of that boarding house, maybe out of town. Surely Chief Wright is investigating."

My throat was tight, but I managed to keep talking. "Did your sister tell you my father is here, outside?" I gestured with the umbrella and kept hold of his hand.

"She said there was some kind of safety concern." He half-smiled at that.

"Dad got a note, delivered by someone from the City, he thinks, warning us off the case."

William leaned forward. I pulled my hand away and put it up to stop him. There was a grimace of pain when he moved the bad arm. It wasn't much, but it didn't take much to make me gasp. "Be careful!"

I took his movement to mean he was impatient at being in a hospital bed when there was an overt threat. On top of that, he was looking at me again intently. "I'm O.K., Julia. It doesn't hurt so much as it reminds me that it's healing when I move it. It stings when they clean it, several times a day." Ah, he had put my flight yesterday in context. "But I can get up and be around, and I'm ready to get out of here. Particularly if someone is making threats."

"I should think you're better off here if someone is making threats."

"No, I don't like sitting here, wondering who's outside the door. Especially with Evelyn here. I hadn't thought to be worried about her, but I should be. I need to get out of here, and she needs to head back home."

He was making plans, and I didn't like them. How would he manage on his own—all the worse if someone was after us?

"William, please. Please don't put yourself in danger again." I didn't mind looking like a distraught female if I could convince him of this. "I cannot think of you getting hurt again. I'm already worrying about Carl. At least I didn't think I had to worry about you getting shot again, if you were here."

We were back to gripping each other's hand.

"What do you mean about Carl? Where is he?"

"I don't know. He wasn't at the *Post* an hour or so ago. He'd gone to Ste. Genevieve yesterday and probably spent the night. Zimmerman at the *Post* said he'd called a story in, late." William frowned. "I don't know. He's been looking in on me everyday . . . until today."

William gave my hand a squeeze and let go. "I'd like to talk to your father. We need a plan for dealing with all this."

I nodded. A plan. I needed a plan and more air to breathe. I headed for the door.

◆ ◆ ◆

Dad moved gracefully into the room, escorting Evelyn before him. I could tell William hated being in bed and might have been thinking about getting up. I wondered what he was wearing. I could see a soft flannel shirt without a collar. But I didn't know if it was a nightshirt or if he was wearing a regular shirt and trousers.

Evelyn was saying, "Please don't get up, Will." Dad forestalled him by taking my place beside the bed and offering a hand.

William shook it firmly and said the usual, "Good to see you, Sir," but I thought he meant it. He nodded at the chair, and Dad sat. It would have been more gentlemanly to let me have the metal, upright chair, and let Evelyn settle into the overstuffed chair in the corner. But Dad likely took the chair because he knew William wasn't comfortable looking up at him. I smiled at the back of Dad's head and moved up to put a hand on his shoulder. William was smiling, too, taking in the resemblance again. Dad was quiet, letting him look.

"I understand you've received an unfortunate note, Sheriff Nye."

Dad nodded. "It says that you and Mr. Schroeder and Julia should back off the case before someone gets hurt again. I got it, hand-delivered, this morning. And I hurried on into the City, as you can imagine."

Evelyn moved around to stand beside William, on the other side of the bed.

"Will, you need to come back home with me. Surely that would convince whoever is behind this that you're not having anything else to do with the story." She glanced at Dad on that last one, wanting him to confirm it.

"That probably would do it," Dad agreed. "I'm asking Julia to come home for the same reason."

"But I haven't said I'd go," I felt compelled to say. William and Evelyn were frowning at me, and Dad turned to look up at me.

"Chief Wright has made it clear you're not to go into work until they arrest someone. What are you planning on doing?" Dad asked. "Getting fired?"

William was considering me as if he were trying to anticipate my answer, to see if he knew me as well as he thought he did.

Maybe this was what he had in mind. "Unless Terence Kelley up and admits his involvement to the Chief, I don't think anything is going to get solved anytime soon. I don't want to go sit in Fulton and wonder what's going on . . . or if anyone's coming after me."

Dad was shaking his head, but William was nodding his. I continued. "Whoever this is, is more than concerned about William's story. That note is vengeful. If this is connected with Sheriff Picard, and I can't imagine it isn't, someone has a real bee in his bonnet, probably about prohibition. I don't trust that someone not to keep after us."

Dad was about to say something. I didn't let him. "And there's Carl. We don't even know where he is now. Where's he supposed to hide?" I looked at William. "Carl can't hide off in the country somewhere. For one thing, he'd go crazy."

William smiled and nodded. Carl had made it clear what he thought of William and my rhapsodizing over the joys of country life. Admittedly, we'd been goading him a bit.

William thought a moment and said, "I'm concerned as to Carl's whereabouts, too. And I agree with Julia that someone is unreasonably concerned about our involvement. If someone had only wanted to stop me from publishing that story, robbery, stealing my memo book, would've been as good. Shooting at me—assuming it was me, of course—while I was within inches of the Police Chief wasn't rational."

I hadn't thought of it that way. Of course, when it came to the actual shooting, I'd tried not to think about it at all. Sloppy work on my part.

"What exactly does the note say?" William asked Dad.

Dad pulled it out and handed it to him and reached up to pull the string on the overhead lamp. The mellowness disappeared, and I blinked in the brighter light.

William read the note out loud. It said precisely what Dad had recited.

"... to stop there investigation before another gets hurt," William repeated. "Hmm. That sounds more ominous for Julia and Carl than for me. And whoever wrote it misspelled Carl's name ... and the word 'their.' Common enough." Lordy, he was going to be an editor someday.

I reached around Dad, wanting to see the note myself. William handed it over, asking, "You haven't seen it?"

I shook my head.

I read it, noted the two spelling errors, and then I reread it. Or rather I studied it as if it could talk to me. I studied the typing in particular.

The light from overhead was welcome, and I stepped back so I was directly under it. Then I sat down heavily on the foot of the bed.

William may have winced again, but he also dumped the covers between us as he moved down the bed to grab my arm. Dad was reaching for me also. The noise from Evelyn said she was shocked. Hang it all, I didn't care if I was sitting on a man's bed, but I was irritated that I was having trouble breathing again. Although, it was a different problem, I thought.

"Julia?" William was no more than a foot from my face. "What is it, Julia?"

I was still holding the paper in front of me. I lowered it and opened my mouth, but nothing came out.

William sat back on his heels, still close enough to run his good hand down my arm, blocking Dad. He was holding his other arm close to his body, using a sling that wasn't there. He was also wearing trousers.

"What, Julia?"

I took a deep breath and whispered to him, "I know the typing."

"The typing?"

I cleared my throat. "I know the typewriter it was typed on. And I think only one person types on that machine. All I don't know . . . is whose idea it was."

William was close enough that he looked from one feature to another.

Dad asked, "Is it Amelia's typewriter?"

I nodded. "Yes. The one that Terence Kelley's reports are typed on."

William ran his hand down my arm again and smiled. "I think you've just made progress on the case, Julia. Someone is right to be worried about you. You're good at this."

It echoed what Dad had said earlier, and that made me breathe easier. I smiled at him. "We're all three good at this. And anyone who would write this . . ." I stopped. "Amelia and Terence Kelley can be intense."

I took William's hand without thinking. Dropped the paper and held his hand with both of mine. "Amelia's been telling me I should get out of the boarding house, go home to Fulton—implying that I was endangering the others.

"And last night." I jumped a little, and so did William. I looked at him in regret that I'd jostled his bad arm.

"Forget it. What about last night?" He turned his hand, so he was gripping mine again.

"Amelia was after me about how improper it was that I'd get a dress from a man. I'd had it with her hypocrisy and her implications . . ." I stopped at that, and William shook his head and groaned. I shrugged it off.

"I told her I wasn't the one having a man in my room every night, and she ran upstairs, screeching at me."

"Is that when she said something about Schroeder?" Dad broke in.

I nodded. For William's benefit I explained that she accused me of seeing that "German drunkard."

William snorted and said to Dad, "I hope Julia told you that Schroeder is not a drunkard of any sort." William added, under his breath, "He talks too much to get drunk."

I smiled. "Anyway, she stormed upstairs. Later she left and didn't come back for over an hour." I paused to picture her headed out the door.

"You know, she would've had time to get to Union Station and find someone to deliver this note." I looked down at it again, in my lap. "Meaning, of course, she wrote it on her own. Terence Kelley was no where around, for a change."

39

The debate was whether we should go find Chief Wright or ask him to come here to tell him about Amelia-as-note-writer. It was clear we weren't doing anything without William. He intended to leave the hospital. His plan was to keep Evelyn with him for as long as necessary and telegraph to his brother to come get her. Evelyn wasn't happy with that, and she was no push over.

Dad and I left them arguing and slipped out, Dad continuing on to find a phone. He returned to say Chief Wright was on his way. Furthermore, the Chief had said he had news we'd want to hear. We should all stay put. The hospital staff was going to love it. I had to assume the Chief would be comfortable talking investigation in front of me with Dad there, with men around who might control me.

William had gotten dressed. I thought he was embarrassed enough meeting Dad from a hospital bed. He certainly wasn't going to talk strategy with the Chief lying down. He had skipped the niceties: no tie, in fact, no collar or cuffs. But a decent dress shirt, waistcoat, trousers, shoes, stockings. He could put on a coat and be good to travel. He was using a sling and seemed not to be in pain.

Evelyn went out for coffee, explaining that she knew all the places to get some in the hospital, even at this hour. My eyes must have lit up because she said she'd get several. Dad went with her, saying he didn't want her out, even in the hospital building, alone.

William frowned at that, but then settled in Evelyn's overstuffed chair.

"Are you tired?"

"Just relaxing. Life always gets more exciting when you're around. I should rest while I can."

I humphed. I was worried about a number of things. But I was delighted I'd finally seen William, and he was doing well, and we were back to . . . back to what? Well, I was breathing a lot better than I'd been an hour ago.

I was smiling as I went to stand by the window to listen to the rain. And to roll my thoughts around what the Chief had revealed about Terence Kelley. I considered why a man who hated suffragists would bed Amelia Ingle. Or why Amelia would keep company with a man who opposed even one of her precious causes.

My mother used to say, "Love goes where it's sent, even if it's to a black stump." Like so many things my mother had said, it had confused me. But maybe I understood it now, saw the notion reflected in the inconvenient passion that must encircle Amelia Ingle and Terence Kelley, a passion neither could reveal for reasons ranging from legal to political to moral. Sad. And by the evidence, dangerous for anyone who bumped up against their secret.

I leaned against the edge of the window and sighed.

"Is anything wrong—other than the obvious?"

I turned to consider William, another man who liked tradition, so far as I knew. I was uncomfortable, wondering if his presence had led me to think about Amelia and Kelley's romance. I searched for a safe subject.

I indicated the rain tracking down the narrow window. "I don't want to go home to Fulton. But I was thinking it would be nice to be there, for an hour or so. I miss watching the rain there."

"It rains differently in Callaway County?"

"It rains differently where there are trees. I love to watch the rain when it's falling about this hard and hitting the leaves just so, so that the whole tree trembles." I shrugged. "I wouldn't want to live there anymore. But there are things I miss living in the city."

William got up by pushing with his good arm. I tensed, ready to help, but he shook his head. He leaned on the other side of the window.

"I like to watch the rain on the water. And the river's a lot prettier in Pike County than it is here." He turned to me. "I wouldn't go home, either, although I've had an offer from the county paper. But this is where the action is. It's where my job is, where the music is."

I turned toward him. "What kind of music do you like best? When you're not singing with Carl in a beer garden?"

He didn't blush, but then I didn't think William blushed often. He did duck his head a bit. "I can't believe you walked in Sunday. I knew I shouldn't have let Schroeder talk me into that."

"But I enjoyed it. If I hadn't needed to talk to you two about . . . this mess, I'd have listened all afternoon."

"Do you wish you hadn't gotten involved?"

"No. I wish you hadn't gotten hurt." I stared at the rain. And knew this was the heart of the problem. I had never, in all my daydreaming about detecting, ever considered someone getting hurt, getting shot. Not someone I cared about.

"Well," he said, after a few moments. "I wish I hadn't, either, but I'm fairly sure I was the target, and I'm glad no one else was hurt."

I didn't answer because I couldn't.

He was staring out the window, too. "Whoever it was, was a good shot," he added. "You say he was on the landing, shooting down into a crowd. And we were all close together. If the shooter kept the gun in a bundle . . . I wonder if he could hold the bundle up and fire through it. Wouldn't that be rather hard?"

"No one could aim—and make that kind of shot—through cloth. If the cloth was over the barrel, that in itself wouldn't be a problem, but you couldn't aim with a heavy cloth over the sight, I don't think. I couldn't."

I tried to picture it.

I realized William was staring at me.

"Have you ever fired a gun through a piece of cloth?" Had he been smiling any more than he was, I would've been offended.

I looked back at him evenly. "Yes. I once had a gun in my pocket and didn't have a chance to draw. I fired through the pocket. But I was close. I didn't aim it."

That sobered him up. "And so you fired from the hip, literally. And through a pocket?"

I nodded.

"And did you hit what you were firing at?"

I nodded again.

He leaned toward me. "And what was coming at you, that you didn't have time to pull the gun out of your pocket?"

"Well, it's not easy to pull a gun from a pocket with all that fabric, you know. The hammer always hangs up. Men's pockets are better designed. And I was wearing a pretty full skirt."

That wasn't the answer to his question. He kept looking at me.

I sighed. "A prisoner got loose in Dad's jail. A bad one. I rushed in, trying to help. The man had shot one of Dad's deputies, wounded him, but he was going to have trouble getting out of the building. It was a stand off. When I came in, he thought he had the perfect hostage."

William hadn't blinked.

"Of course, I wasn't going to let that happen. He made a . . . dive behind another deputy, to block the fire, and headed for me. The way everyone was standing, it would have been difficult for anyone to fire at him without hitting me. So, I had to take care of the situation." I shrugged.

"Did you kill him?"

I wondered if my answer would make a difference in how he felt about me. Lots of men couldn't handle the fact that I was very good with a gun. I hadn't intended to make much of it in St. Louis.

I sighed. "No, I didn't. I was aiming low." I was back to staring out the window, because I wanted to finish this before I looked at William. "Dad always told me if I was serious about stopping someone to aim for the torso, but I knew I could stop him. And I'd practiced shooting from the hip a hundred times." The rain blurred as I pictured the scene. "So, I fired at his legs and took him in the thigh. But he still had his gun in his hand. I took time to draw the pistol and aim and fire a second time, as he fell and twisted. I damaged that hand enough for the deputies to move in."

There was an awkward silence. I glanced sideways, and William was looking for something in the rain. The pause got too long for me.

"As it turned out, I had some fabric left over from that skirt. I replaced the patch pocket."

That got him to turn back to me. His eyebrows lowered. "You wounded a man twice. And thought about killing him. And you're telling me about your sewing."

He backed away, as much emotionally as physically, I thought. I couldn't handle his frown. I went back to staring out the window.

"The man was bad, William. They transferred him to Jefferson City, and he broke out of jail six months later. He killed a man and his wife in Boone County after he escaped." If William were never going to speak to me again, he should at least have the whole story. "I should have made the torso shot. But I thought I didn't want to kill him." I hazarded a glance, and William's frown had eased.

"I got more . . . hardened . . . or something . . . when I heard what he'd done. I also heard he was coming after me. Dad was pretty worried. But someone else killed him before he made it back to Fulton."

I stopped and looked for shapes in the rain running down the window.

"I could have made that shot, William, at the Station. I would have hidden the gun in the bundle, pulled it out, balanced the gun on top of the bundle, aimed quickly, and made that shot. Then I would have shoved the gun back in the bundle. A second shot would have been risky. But one shot . . . when people are not looking at you . . . and then the gun is gone. One shot. It would have echoed under the whispering arch so no one would know which side it came from."

I tried to lighten things up. "It's my misspent youth, hanging out with Dad, wanting to be like Dad, being pleased with the compliments on my shooting—instead of my sewing."

I turned to see how he was reacting. I wasn't nervous anymore. This was who I was, and if William were ever going to hold my hand again, he should know what he was getting into. What sort of black stump to expect.

He was looking at me and shaking his head. Darn. I started to turn away, but he held out his good hand to me.

"I knew you had a gun that evening, and I've wondered if you were tempted to draw it."

I took his hand. "I was reaching into my bag for the gun and looking for the shooter. But I couldn't see anyone. There was no target." I looked up at William's serious face. "You said my name. And I looked at you and felt the shawl, and I pulled it out instead."

William raised my hand to his mouth and kissed it, again. I guessed he could live with my shooting skills. A flutter in my tummy replaced the breathing problems I'd had since the shooting. I tightened my grip on his hand and, with difficulty, pulled my thinking back to the shooter.

"William, the shooter could have fired again—if he'd moved off, gone to another spot, another angle. Carl and I were easy targets."

"I know. I've thought about that." He considered my hand. "Had a couple of nightmares about it."

So I wasn't the only one who'd dreamed scary dreams. He let go of my hand and pulled me to him in the one-armed hug I surprisingly needed. I pressed my cheek against his, noting that he hadn't taken time to shave—and not caring. He eased back after several seconds, and I let my hand fall from his chest.

"So, you think Kelley kept the shooter from firing again?" he asked after a few moments.

That was a new thought.

"He may have." I was picturing it. "He was in position to do that—particularly if he knew the shooter and the shooter hesitated because he recognized Kelley."

◆ ◆ ◆

William and I were still considering possibilities about Kelley and the shooter, although it must have seemed as if we were engaged in a close-up study of each other's faces, when Evelyn and Dad walked in, balancing two cups of coffee each. The Chief was behind them with his own cup. They stopped and stared at us, then crowded into the small room as if nothing were happening.

A nurse was right behind them, all starch and authority.

The hospital had rules, it seemed, about how many visitors could be in one room. We were one or two over. And it was past visiting hours. Chief Wright explained the situation, but I wasn't sure she believed him. William explained that he was paying for the room, and he was leaving tomorrow anyway. She certainly didn't believe that.

And she informed William she needed everyone out of the room anyway, so she could clean the wound.

"Not now," William barked. He glared at her, and she glared back. Evelyn pushed her way to the nurse and started whispering in her ear. She appeared to be making some progress in pushing the woman out, when the Chief came to her aid, promising to hurry, declaring it an emergency, and so on. I heard the nurse say she'd be back in ten minutes.

By then, everyone was crowded back into the room. The Chief called the meeting to order and went right to the point.

"I'm sure Kelley was the man on the stairs at the Station the night you were shot, Mac. And by the way, it's good to see you up."

William nodded.

The Chief continued, "I know this because George St. Martin walked into my office and apologized. Said his report was an attempt to stall. All the descriptions fit Kelley." The Chief dared a look at me.

Maybe because I was huffing. "Did he explain his little prevarications? Or the lack of anything else useful?"

The Chief's raised eyebrows and pursed lips said he was glad I worked for him and not vice versa. In an amused way, of course. He couldn't have imagined such a thing for real.

"Actually, he did." The Chief sighed and whatever humor had been there fled. "He said Terence Kelley is his friend, and he thought it suspicious Kelley would be at both Armbruster's and the Station. He was stalling, trying to get Kelley to explain."

William beat me to it. "And did he?"

"Not his presence either place. But he says Kelley denies doing the shooting himself—which we can confirm from what Julia's witness said. And he won't tell George anything about the wheel shop. He insisted that no one got hurt, and that's that."

I couldn't let that stand. "Well, I'd say there was some damage as far as Mr. Armbruster is concerned. He's hiding out of town, for Pete's sake."

"He is?" the Chief asked, and I noticed Dad's eyes widening.

"Yes," William said. "That's according to a message James Ingle got. I didn't put it in the story we brought back," he nodded in my direction, "because I didn't want to put more heat on the man."

He turned to me. "You said someone might be after my memo book when he went through your room. The note about Armbruster is one of the few things in there that wasn't in the story. Could that be why anyone would want it?"

"Maybe, but more likely they didn't know what else might be in it. I think it points to someone who's pretty compulsive to want that book," I added.

"Which reminds me," the Chief said, "I asked George St. Martin about Kelley seeing someone. I think, from his reaction, he knows there is someone, but he said Kelley's private life is his own. If he wouldn't confirm that, I didn't care to use Amelia Ingle's name."

I guessed that Amelia was now in the compulsive category. Which seemed appropriate.

"So," William said, "we don't know who was shooting that night. But Terence Kelley does or at least would have a description."

"Which he hasn't given George," I said.

"Correct," the Chief said. "But," he held a hand up in my direction, "George says he did ask . . . he asked if Kelley saw the shooter, since Kelley insisted he didn't do it himself. He says Kelley didn't answer, walked away. I got the impression George followed him, tried to press him on it, and Kelley never responded. That's why St. Martin came to me." He stopped and glanced at me again. "That, and he said he didn't like people thinking he couldn't do his job. And, of course, he wants to keep his job."

I snorted.

"So, we have to find the shooter," the Chief concluded. "I'll have Detective Smyth on it first thing in the morning."

I couldn't resist adding what I knew. "There were people all over that stair and on the landing and up on the top floor. It's possible someone saw a man raise a bundle and pull the gun out."

"Well, you're not going to go asking, Julia." The Chief sounded certain of that.

I wasn't so certain. In fact, I knew I had come to the decision to stay, one way or another. But it would be smart to change the subject. "We know who wrote the note that Dad got. So, we could take out some of the threat by starting there."

"Who?" The Chief stopped moving toward the door.

"Amelia Ingle."

"Amelia Ingle herself?"

"Well, it was typed on her typewriter. Confiscate it, but I'm sure. And I suppose Kelley could have asked her to do it earlier, and she hadn't gotten around to it." I shook my head. "It's a short note, but she's slow." Grins all around.

"But Kelley wasn't there last night. She stomped out of the house and was gone long enough to take it to Union Station." I paused. "We could look for whoever delivered the note, if we want to confirm who sent it." I glanced at Dad to see if he wanted to go ahead and share anything, like a description of the young man who had delivered the note.

He was smarter than that. "'We' are not investigating, Julia. You've told Micah now and he can do what he needs to do."

The Chief rolled his eyes. "I need to confront Kelley."

William asked out loud what I was thinking. "And you think he'll confess something? It sounds to me as if he's protecting the shooter. Would he tell you if he wouldn't tell St. Martin?"

"He might," the Chief said. "After all, I can threaten him with his job. He may not have thought George would even come to me with what he'd said already."

William started to shrug and caught himself. "Well, I need to figure out how to get Evelyn out of town in safety and get back to work."

"Does that mean you're going to continue looking into the story?" The Chief was curt and frowning, and I figured he knew he had less control over William than over me. At least he thought so.

"I might. First thing I need to do is find out where Schroeder is, and I should think that alone will alert Kelley or whoever."

Dad surprised me. "Isn't that a bit like looking for trouble?"

"Looking for Carl is a lot like looking for trouble," William agreed with a smile.

I made my case one more time with Dad. "I have to find Carl, too. I got him into this, Dad. I can't go running off and hide until I know he's safe." Not after I found him, either, but I didn't say that.

William wanted to tell me he could find Carl by himself and that I should go be safe. I could see all that on his face, in his frown, in the intensity of the look he gave me. But he apparently was too honest with himself—or realistic. We could look together and be safer than either alone. Although that wasn't very safe until we knew what Terence Kelley knew.

40

The Chief gathered everyone, guards and me and Dad and William and Evelyn, into a police coach and headed for his big house out by Forest Park. We left the nurse pushing a bottle of phenol into Evelyn's hand and telling her to use it on William's arm. When I wasn't around, I hoped. The Chief was planning on all of us spending the night with him and Maude.

We scattered into the parlor and a sitting room. Evelyn went upstairs to stow bags. The Chief telephoned and found George St. Martin at home. I was shooed out of the sitting room but from outside the door, I heard the Chief suggest that tonight would be a good time for George to find Terence Kelley and escort him to the Police Department and that he would meet them there whatever the hour. He replaced the earpiece with a thud, and I heard him warn Maude Wright that the evening could get "hectic."

I spent time sitting by a window in the parlor, watching more rain. A thought nagged. George St. Martin and Terence Kelley could be in this together. Gertrude had said that the shooter seemed to be short, at least shorter than her mysterious handsome hero.

Why would George be shooting at William? Because of me? Could he be that jealous because I'd been off with William for two days? No. If affection for me were involved, he wouldn't have risked a shot so close to me. And, romance aside, he wouldn't have talked to the Chief. Unless he were more devious than I could have imagined.

I hated thoughts like that. The odds of George St. Martin being the shooter were almost nothing. But once I admitted the thought, it lingered. The next time I saw George, I'd be wondering if he really cared more for me than he'd said, wondering how good a shot he was. I'd never heard any indication that George was a crack shot—and that would have been something the cops would talk about.

I was pretty sure most of them were just barely competent with a gun. They preferred their nightsticks and their fists. Wading into a situation, not controlling it from a distance, fit their collective image of defending the peace. George, as a somewhat-diminutive detective, might have other skills. But why shoot William? Really, I had never given George reason to believe I would receive his attention.

Of course, I hadn't intended to give Carl that impression either. Looking back, he had likely talked about William's anger to keep me from visiting. Did Carl think our friendship more than it was?

I shook my head hard to dismiss the ideas of romance with Carl or George. I'd have to have a whole lot more to go on to even suggest something like George's involvement to Chief Wright. My fear of making a fool of myself, alone, would keep me quiet, although I knew pride could make a bad situation worse. In this case, it was too farfetched to be worth it.

And, to be honest, Henry Ingle was a lot more likely as the shooter. I didn't want to believe he'd done it. I didn't want to believe I was so wrong and Carl so right.

Then it was my turn to use the telephone in the sitting room, and I called the boarding house. By great good luck, Mary picked up.

"Oh, Julia!" She sounded so relieved that I felt guilty. "Where are you? We were worried. And," she lowered her voice, "you've got a telegram here."

"A telegram?" My voice rose sufficiently to get Dad's attention.

"It came about two hours ago. We haven't opened it, of course."

"Can you open it and read it to me without anyone else hearing?"

"How did everyone like your dress?"

The non sequitur made me pause until I realized she must be trying to lull any listeners to boredom.

"They liked it fine."

"Oh, well, that's nice." There was the sound of paper ripping, and then she whispered, sounding breathless, "I've got it, but I'll have to do this quick."

I felt bad for putting her in the difficult position.

"It says, 'Meet me at Station stop midnight stop Carl.' And here comes Claire . . . and Fran."

"That's it? The Station at midnight, Carl?"

"Yes."

"And there's nothing unusual about it?"

"Like what?"

Good question. I thought for a second. I wanted to see the telegram, but I also didn't want to take the chance Amelia would see it.

"Can you just put it in your pocket? And keep hold of it until I get there?"

I couldn't tell if she'd done that, because suddenly there were women talking loudly. It sounded like more than Claire and Fran.

"What's happening?"

"Well, everyone is wanting to know if this is you, and why I read it."

"Tell them it was personal, and I asked you to. What's Amelia doing?"

"Being sweet."

"Well, that's suspicious, isn't it? Listen, Mary, I appreciate it, and I'm sorry to leave you with everyone yapping at you."

"It's O.K., Julia. I hope it isn't trouble."

"Me, too." But, of course it was trouble of one sort or another. Maybe the sort we needed to clean up this mess.

I heard Amelia say, "Where is she? Is she coming home?"

Honestly. She wasn't being that sweet.

Mary said, away from the mouthpiece, "There's no problem."

"Mary, thanks a million. I need to go. I may be by tonight, and I may not. Watch out for the terror."

She laughed, but there wasn't much humor in the sound. Apparently she didn't think the evening was going to be all that much fun. That made two of us.

◆　◆　◆

When I hung up, William was in the room, and Dad must have said something to him while I was talking.

"Carl? You've heard from Carl?" Evelyn followed him with the medicine bottle, trying to do nursing duty. *Good luck, dear.*

"Well, I don't know if I have or not." I explained that a telegram had arrived, but I didn't know if it was really from Carl.

William joined Dad in seeming more than nervous about me meeting Carl at midnight in Union Station.

"But where else would he be arriving if he's coming back from Ste. Genevieve?" I said. "I mean, it could be legitimate."

"Why you?" Dad asked.

"Who else? He thinks William is in the hospital. He doesn't know the Chief is all but personally investigating." I shrugged. "Really, who else?"

"Well, he doesn't have to have anyone meet him," William pointed out. "He can go to the *Post*. Although he'll never get the story in if he doesn't arrive until midnight. In fact, if he does have a story, he'll have to have called it in, or at least let them know about it. So, we should contact the *Post* and see what they've heard."

William made the call. While he was getting someone he knew to talk to, the Chief came in and we told him the latest—facts that is, not my speculations. Evelyn had settled into a chair, frowning. I suspected she thought anything that called for action tonight was a bad idea.

William hung up and turned to face us, thoughtful. "They have heard from him, and he is headed home tonight. He told them he'd found out a few things but not enough for a Sunday story."

"What does that mean?" the Chief asked. "Not enough for a Sunday story?"

"We'd all have a chance to read the story at our leisure and follow up on it. If you don't have a big enough story, and if no one else has anything at all, you might as well wait until you can put more together."

"I'd bet that's what Carl is doing," I said. "Holding off on whatever he found out until he can pick up some more here in the City. And it would make sense that he would want to tell me whatever he's found out, even if it's not enough for a story."

They all looked at me. As one, the three men said, "No."

"No? What if he's in trouble?"

"Then there would be two of you in trouble," Dad said.

"What kind of trouble would he be in?" William asked.

"Let some of my men meet him. If he's in trouble, he'll have a police escort when he gets off the train." That was from the Chief, of course.

"Well, I think I should at least go to the boarding house and check that telegram. If it's from Amelia's typewriter and she paid someone to deliver it, that puts his arrival in a more dangerous light. Amelia is the key. We have to find out where she's been and what she knows."

William settled with care into an exposed-wood-and-leather chair. I didn't think he'd sit in front of the two older men unless he was hurting. I frowned at the thought.

"If she sent it, trying to draw Julia out, how would she even know Carl was coming in? That would be the excuse to get Julia there." He looked at me and widened his eyes. "What, Julia? Are you thinking she knows Carl is coming back and wants both of you there?"

Oh. He thought I was frowning at him because of his logic.

"No, no. I was just thinking . . . well, yes." I'd act confused, instead of solicitous. After all, he had Evelyn for that. "I guess if she, or Kelley, or whoever, wanted to hurt us, and she could find out where Carl was—somehow—she could let the shooter know she had both of us lined up at the Station."

"How would she find out about Schroeder?" The Chief paused in chewing his mustache again.

"Maybe the same way we did. Maybe she ran around looking for him. We do know she wasn't at work this afternoon."

"How do we know that?" William asked.

"On the way to dinner, I needed an umbrella. So we stopped in the shop where she works. She wasn't there. The owners said she'd left during the afternoon. In fact, they said she'd missed work, at least part of a day, three times this week. Interesting, no?"

The Chief said, "You can't let this be, can you, Julia?"

"I needed an umbrella. Dad could have judged Amelia. I expected her to be there." I saw three exasperated faces. But Evelyn was smiling to herself.

I started to say more but decided to stop. I had these three difficult men to convince yet tonight, and I didn't need to irritate them.

Because I intended to go to Union Station at midnight. And time was passing.

William was looking at me, but he was thinking things through. "She might know Carl was returning, if someone in Ste. Genevieve alerted her."

"Are you thinking James?" I asked.

William nodded.

I sighed. "I suppose James could have mentioned it in passing. We went and talked to Henry, and I believed his . . . indignation. But maybe I was wrong."

Maybe I shouldn't have added the part about our visit. Now I had the three of them frowning again.

"What? It wasn't my idea. I went along to keep Carl from starting a fight on the Ingles' front porch."

William got up and started a slow pace. "This is why I need to be doing something besides sitting in a hospital. You and Carl will go poking in the Prohibition bushes to see if anyone will aim a gun at you."

Dad and the Chief offered a variety of snorts and nods that signaled their agreement. But the more I thought about it, the more I realized that I was scared not to poke about.

"Well, maybe that's not a bad idea."

"What in the world do you mean, Julia?" The Chief asked as he sat heavily in the chair William had vacated.

"I'm not thrilled by the idea of being in my room at the boarding house or out walking down the street, thinking someone has me in his sights. I want to meet Carl tonight—and see who's behind this."

"That's called being bait, Julia, and you're not going to do it." Dad was sounding a lot like a father, not a sheriff.

"If we get there in time, we could have your men everywhere," I said to the Chief. Despite his attitude, he was still my best bet. If this were a trap, my presence could help him catch the killer.

William said, "Julia, you cannot be serious."

I turned to him—on him. "I certainly am. Do you want to walk around knowing that someone has threatened you . . . and you aren't even sure who it is? We can end this tonight. We need a plan for watching the Station, that's all."

They stared at me. "You have to have police there anyway," I reminded the Chief. "You said you'd protect Carl, and he may well be coming through then."

The room fell silent. The men glared at me and, one by one, looked away. That left Evelyn smiling at me. Shaking her head, but smiling. I wanted to get to know her better. Maybe I could if I survived the night.

The Chief pushed himself out of the chair.

"Well," he said, "on the possibility Schroeder might come in on the midnight train, we'll have people in place. I'm going to get that organized right now." He picked up the telephone. "You, however," he pointed the earpiece at me, "are not going anywhere. You are staying right here, or you're through at the department."

I sensed movement from both William and Dad, but I couldn't manage the words to say anything, to them or to the Chief.

"It's the only thing I can say to stop you. And I mean it. You and McConnell stay here, and I'll make sure Schroeder makes it someplace safe. If a shooter is lurking, we'll have him."

I raised my chin, turned on my heel, and left the room. Maude

Wright had said Evelyn and I could share a room, so upstairs seemed a likely destination to be by myself. To worry. To plan. To find the back stairs.

Looking out an upstairs window, I saw Chief Wright leave with Miles Graham. Maybe the Chief had left Peterson to make sure I didn't follow. Or to guard me and William. Same thing.

A clock somewhere in the house chimed half past ten.

If Amelia were still at the boarding house, I would confront her there. I figured she'd be leaving for the Station at some point, wanting to see the result of her handiwork. If I couldn't get the information out of her otherwise, I'd accompany her. She couldn't stop me.

If she weren't there, I would take my time changing clothes and get to the Station on my own. And what would I do at the Station? Be inconspicuous. I hoped the police would see someone suspicious, maybe someone targeting Carl, and arrest the shooter before anything could happen. I did not want to be the heroine of the evening. I did not want to shoot anyone tonight. I wanted the shooter arrested so the three of us could get back to work. Maybe rearrange our relationships.

I found the back stairs. They led to a kitchen, and I knew there was a covered space, a porte cochere it had been called when horses were involved, over a kitchen door, to allow people to get in and out of the house in the dry. Luckily, I'd dragged the silly umbrella with me, because once I left the porte cochere, it would be a wet slog to a streetcar.

The kitchen itself wasn't lit, but a glow spilled in from the dining room. I hadn't taken more than a few steps toward the door when William's voice stopped me.

"Julia? You're headed out?"

"I'm going to the boarding house."

He took time to find the light, and I was immediately concerned. Not only was my father standing behind him, but I also thought the evening's activity was catching William up. His eyes looked darker in a paler face.

William moved slowly toward me. "You felt bad that I was hurt, Julia. But you think it's fine if you go to the Station, maybe set yourself up as a target. That's not O.K. with me. Because I don't want to feel bad if you get hurt."

That stopped me for a moment. I wouldn't want him to feel as I had when he was bleeding in the Station, when I was so afraid he would die there. But this was the argument for me going and being aggressive. He could get shot again—or I could—by not going tonight. By not being there myself to make sure.

I tried to explain that to him. "I don't want either of us to get hurt. I don't want Carl hurt. If we let this opportunity get away to find out who's shooting, if the cops protect Carl but don't get the shooter, I think the odds go up of one of us being a target later. All of us, maybe."

Evelyn walked in, the phenol bottle in hand.

"Please, William," I said. "I will be careful. But, I have to go."

Well, that sounded too close to asking permission. I couldn't let that stand.

"Please understand, William." That's what I'd meant.

William considered me for several beats, expressionless. Then he turned to my father. "Are you going, too, sir?"

Dad had his hands on his hips, a sure sign of furious thinking. "I'll go to the boarding house with you, Julie. No going to the Station. I agree that Amelia Ingle is a key, and we need to find her, make sure she's there."

"I'm coming along," William announced. It was my turn to protest, but I knew he would win. He couldn't stop me. I couldn't stop him. More's the pity, because now anything I decided to do would be harder. I would worry about his presence, about his safety, about his weakness. It was almost as if this were his payback for my stubbornness. He smiled at me and quirked an eyebrow, as if he knew what I was thinking.

Evelyn was saying, "No," and whispering her objections in his ear. I would never be able to face her if anything happened to William because I had insisted this be the night. I would never be able to face myself.

41

Dad found Peterson and somehow convinced him to take the three of us to the boarding house. We climbed in the big police coach under the porte cochere, with Peterson up on top driving—in the rain.

Dad looked out the window and rubbed an index finger over the top of his lip, his usual sign of silent worry. William sat very still and looked out the opposite window for a block or so. The silence was approaching awkward when he said, "I need to do something normal, relaxing, enjoyable."

A streetlight illuminated his face for a moment, and he was gaunt.

"Well, maybe you and Carl can do another performance. I promise I won't interrupt this time." I smiled and hoped he could see it.

"It may be a while before I can play." He inclined his head toward his left arm.

I caught my breath and looked away. We turned onto the west end of Laclede.

"I was thinking maybe a baseball game."

I turned back to him, noting a dimple.

"Would you care to take in a game Sunday week, Julia?"

Dad jerked beside me. William had just asked me for a date,

almost the old-fashioned way—in front of my father, if not of him.

William was studying me. I could tell by the way he held his head, even though he had the shadows now.

"Browns or Cardinals?"

He pretended to study that in turn.

"The Browns, if they're in town. It may be a while before I can applaud either."

I gasped in mock outrage. Dad burst out laughing and smothered it.

Peterson stopped in front of the house, and I realized William had timed his question well. He stepped out of the coach the minute it stopped and held out his good hand.

I was delighted to take it. I leaned toward him and said, "I can't wait."

William held my hand to keep me close a second. "Good. I'll be careful if you will, then."

◆ ◆ ◆

Dad's hand was on the revolver in his pocket when we walked in the front door of the boarding house. That was funny. These were the women I lived with. Of course, I may have prejudiced him by asking William to stay in the coach with Peterson. I didn't want Amelia to scream and produce Terence Kelley to shoot him right there in Miller's.

To my surprise, William had agreed to wait outside, confirming my fear that he wasn't ready for this particular outing. In the morning, some doctor at City Hospital would be complaining that McConnell shouldn't even be out of his bed.

Four of my housemates said hello to Dad, and no mayhem

ensued. Ruth had a date. Amelia had gone out earlier, and no one had seen her return.

Dad and I examined the telegram. I didn't think it had been typed on Amelia's typewriter. It lacked the uneven strokes. But I also didn't think it was from Carl. I couldn't say why.

In my room, I peeled off the new dress and dug to the far side of the armoire to retrieve the outfit I hadn't worn since I'd arrived in St. Louis. It was time for the bloomers.

I'd looped my braid into a chignon to be a little more fashionable for the new dress. Now it was out of my way and worked well with the golf cap. From a distance, everyone would think me an eccentrically dressed young man—or an overgrown boy. Probably not the image the shooter would be looking for. Nor the cops.

Most importantly, my Hopkins & Allen fit in the jacket pocket, as designed. I had weighted the edge of the jacket so it stayed modestly low. It made the gun easier to pull, as well.

Climbing out my window onto the fire escape was so much easier in the bloomers that I felt confirmed in my plan. I was careful on the wet metal but made it to the bottom easily enough. I managed to turn and hold onto the bottom step, and then it was more a matter of letting go than jumping.

With William and Peterson sitting out front, I made my way through our back yard and a neighbors' and then through a side yard onto Laclede. Once on Grand, I picked up a streetcar that would take me toward downtown. I kept my head down and ignored the people who were staring at my outfit. And considered what I'd done. Would William would be so angry that he'd beg off the ball game date? Dad's anger bothered me a bit less. And the one I should really care about was the Chief and his threat of firing me. I so hoped I could stay hidden.

I got off the car at Twentieth Street, on the west edge of the Station, and moved into the Midway foot traffic, still considerable though the hour was closing in on midnight. I located the gate that Carl would pass on his way from the train platform—the route we had all three used so often now. I stowed any regrets and moved slowly about the area, watching first one and then another group of passengers move through the gates, into the Midway, and beyond. So close to midnight, many of the local trains were out in the hinterland, ready to make milk runs into the City early in the morning. Still, there were plenty of trains about, including the transcontinental lines.

My plan was to follow Carl—if indeed he arrived this evening—down the Midway toward the 18th Street exit if he went that way or into the waiting room if he chose the Market Street exit. The latter was more likely if he intended to meet me. I didn't know why I still debated the validity of the message. Carl either would or would not be walking toward me in a moment.

And then he was there. I was pleased to see him safe so far, but my hands turned clammy as I thought of him walking into the waiting area where he'd met us Wednesday.

I realized he wasn't moving. He was looking back, toward the steps. A second later, Henry Ingle stepped into the light. How cunning, to have Henry accompany Carl. If, of course, Henry were going to turn on him.

Carl and Henry talked as they crossed the Midway and headed to the waiting room. The air of shared intent surprised me. After their confrontation at the Ingles's house, I didn't expect even civility between them. It made me more suspicious of Henry in an odd way.

My decision surged through me like a shot of energy. If Henry was already beside Carl, he could be steering him toward the shooter. Or maybe Henry was a good guy after all and might be in danger as well. Either way, I needed to be behind the shooter, not walking up behind Carl and Henry.

Steps rose from the Midway to the Station's carriage concourse. I dashed up them and through the space, ignoring several shouts, presumably about juvenile behavior. From the corner of my eye, I thought one of the carriages looked like police property, but that wasn't a problem if I didn't stop.

With the freedom of the bloomers and sensible boots, I was out and rounding the foot of the sweeping outdoor terrace that led to the next level in seconds. I ducked under the Station's own, much grander, porte cochere. Two redcaps were helping folks from an auto, and another three were helping load people and luggage onto a wagon. I dodged them. A sixth redcap tried to stop me with a, "Here, young man, slow down." I honest to goodness said, "Got to meet Mother," and kept moving. I burst through the vestibule and onto the landing—where William's assassin had probably stood.

The scene below in the waiting area stopped me short. Some dozen police officers were moving people away from Carl and Henry. Several other officers were standing closer to the two men and looking around for a threat. The Chief was directing men and glancing toward the pair. Carl and Henry had stopped. They were listening to Amelia, who stood, back turned to me, of course, maybe ten steps down. I stopped across the stairway from her, against the opposite banister.

Even with a dozen people between us on the stairs, I could hear her say, "What are you doing with him? Where have you been? He's . . . he's the enemy, Henry. He encourages people to drink. He writes filthy articles urging votes against prohibition in some outrageous language, Henry, you can't—"

"He's not the enemy, Amelia." Henry's voice was soft enough that

I moved a step closer. I could hear the pain. "We need to talk. Will you come upstairs with me, have a cup of coffee?"

"Coffee? At this hour?" Amelia stopped, and I wondered if she'd flashed the Amelia smile. "Why don't you go on up, Henry? I'll be there in a moment."

"No, Amelia. I want you to leave Carl alone and come upstairs with me. Or come home."

Henry stepped in front of Carl. The top of Henry's head would barely brush Carl's chin, but I applauded his courage.

Amelia turned away to pick up something lying against the banister on the step just above her. I drew an abrupt breath. It was a blanket, folded and tied with cord. Folded with a seam, a pocket, along the top. A bundle. She balanced it on her left arm.

Cops still moved travelers, as before. The Chief was on the job, as before. They wouldn't think anything about a bundle. Or about Amelia as a shooter. None of the cops were bothering with the stairs, which were emptying out fast, leaving me exposed. I drew the Hopkins & Allen.

Amelia was saying, "He had no right to drum up support among his immigrant, beer-drinking readers for that bootlegging sheriff and his distributor."

I watched her and cursed myself that I had made the same stupid mistake all the men had made: I'd assumed the shooter was male.

I'd have to find time to upbraid myself later. Amelia said, "Where's Julia? She's supposed to be here." Amelia stamped her foot as she moved a step down, and her blonde strands shuddered.

"You're not going to shoot anyone, Amelia," Henry said.

"Oh, and you could stop me? You're not half as good as I am."

As if that might be true, and to give himself the advantage, Henry drew a gun. The Forehand Hammerless glinted in the light.

316

"Oh, Henry, no," Carl said. The Chief turned toward them.

"Shut up!" Amelia said. And Carl did. I was amazed he'd been quiet this long.

"You can go home, or go to your boyfriend, or whatever, Amelia, but this is over now." Henry was getting angry, I thought.

"You won't tell me what to do!" Amelia said.

I thought for a split second that she yelled for "Terry" next. But the voice was wrong.

I looked across the waiting room to see Terence Kelley being chased by George St. Martin, who was calling his friend's name. Cops backed off at a command from their detective sergeant and looked to the Chief for confirmation. The Chief was yelling, too, but he simply added to the confusion as the crowd began to react. The more frightful tried to move faster, stymied by cops blocking the way to the stairs. The more curious tried to see around the cops to locate the heart of the action. Lordy. The odds were not good that any of the cops would fire at a woman or even want to rush her.

Amelia turned to watch Terence Kelley run toward her and listen to him scream, "No! Wait, Amelia!" She turned back to face Carl. And pulled a pistol from the blanket roll.

"No," Kelley screamed again.

Amelia raised the pistol and tried to aim for Carl. Henry darted back and forth in front of him and yelled at Carl to get down, to stay behind him.

Cops, including the Chief, moved toward Henry. Unfortunately, they were on the wrong side of the action, in the line of fire.

I aimed, but Amelia was shifting, moving her body instead of her arms. A miss now on my part could take out one of the bystanders, an officer, Henry, or, less likely, Carl, now in a crouch behind him.

And then Terence Kelley jerked to a stop close to Amelia,

shielding the men for the moment. Luckily, he focused on her and didn't glance up the stairs.

"Amelia," was all he said. He was out of breath, and she lowered the gun. He touched her cheek. I strained to hear him say, "I told you I'd take care of everything."

He turned and took a step down toward Henry and Carl, who'd gotten to his feet. Kelley said something I couldn't hear to Henry. Carl moved to Henry's side, maybe assuming the threat was over.

I saw Amelia move, and I started to move myself, to get to a lower level for a safer shot.

Kelley heard her move as well and whirled to face her just as she fired.

Amelia's shot set off a round of screaming.

Kelley went to his knees and slipped to the next step, clutching his gut as best as I could see. Amelia stared at the gun in front of her, as if she were trying to figure how to take the shot back. George St. Martin moved up to support Kelley, as cops started to close in.

Kelley struggled in George's arms to turn, put a hand up and say, "No, it's O.K." to the cops. I didn't hear what he said to George, but George backed off to the floor level.

Amelia fell back onto a step and crouched behind Kelley.

"Look what you've done, you bastard," she yelled, presumably at Carl.

A chorus of "noes" went up. Her next shot hit a marble pillar and ricocheted. 'Noes' turned to screams. Chief Wright was yelling at Amelia and pulling Carl away.

She was still aiming from behind Kelley—in good competition style—when another shot took me by surprise. I jumped when the bullet hit the banister on the other side of the stairs and tried to see who had fired.

Amelia's response, along with several other voices, told me. "Henry!"

I could hear Carl saying, "Henry, don't."

Henry Ingle aimed his pistol directly at his sister. "I won't let you shoot anyone else, Amelia." His voice was shaking. Miles Graham was moving toward him.

I could see Amelia's hair moving and imagine the fury on her face. "Shoot me? You'd shoot me in defense of that German drunkard?" She crouched lower behind Kelley. I could see him swaying and thought she was going to lose her cover soon. She was moving her pistol to and fro, one instant trying to aim for Carl, who couldn't seem to stay behind a pillar, and the next instant targeting her brother.

I started to take another step toward her. I could call out to her and fire before she could even aim. I could protect Henry, Carl, and even George St. Martin, who clearly wanted to move closer to Kelley. For that matter, I might save Kelley if a doctor could get to him.

I was ready to call her name when a voice spoke behind me. "A decision," the man said.

I gasped, fearful that there was another shooter other than Amelia and that I hadn't glanced back for at least a full minute. I backed against the banister and swung my gun upward.

I was aiming at William, who was breathing heavily enough that I hadn't recognized his voice.

"Shoot to kill or shoot to wound. Does it always come down to that?"

Lordy.

"William. Thank God. But get back up the stairs. Please."

As I turned back to Amelia, he said, "No." I spared one more glance at the bitter smile on his face and saw he was pulling his own pistol out.

I didn't have time to say more as Amelia fired again. The shot took Henry in the shoulder. I didn't think it was bad, as he stayed on his feet, but he dropped the gun. I had a glimpse of Graham's white face as he pulled Henry away.

The cops crowded closer, but Amelia managed to use Kelley to her advantage. I could hear him saying, "No," still.

It would have been so convenient if any of the cops had thought to come up behind Amelia, but it was only me and William on the stairs. I hadn't wanted to get behind Amelia for fear of Henry or an officer shooting in her direction. Now, Henry was out of the picture, and it didn't look like the cops would fire—or could fire around Kelley. And William's question about shooting suggested another option.

I pocketed the H & A and rushed down the steps.

Amelia turned her head quickly at the pounding of my boots, and her hair flared. That made it easy for me to grab a good handful just as I put a knee in her back and grabbed her gun hand.

She screamed, and I recognized her anger as well as pain. Voices in front of us called my name as the Chief, Carl, George, maybe others, recognized me. I felt Amelia go still for a second, and then she gave up using her left hand to protect her hair. She flailed at my face.

"Julia, you bitch!"

She was gasping. I heard, ". . . all your fault . . ." and another screech as I pulled on her hair.

I said the predictable, "Let go of the gun, Amelia," and knew she wouldn't.

She still had a finger on the trigger.

The best I could do was force her wrist up. The barrel was nearly vertical.

She fired. From our spot near the bottom of the stairway, the bullet was traveling at least three stories to the top of the Grand Hall.

I tightened my grip and thought I could control her aim. But I couldn't let go of her hair to actually take the gun away from her. Although I was sure she wouldn't waste her last shot or two on the ceiling, none of the cops were coming to help.

"Enough shooting, Amelia. Give it up." I shook her arm to emphasize my control. She responded by trying to twist away, "bitch" coming through the panting. She had grabbed my left arm with her left hand, but she couldn't dislodge my grip on her hair.

I felt a hand on my shoulder and realized William would help. I knew he shouldn't. Wrestling a gun from someone would surely sap what little strength he had. And I didn't want him that close to Amelia's weapon. I shifted slightly to block him.

At which moment, a cop did step in. I hoped it was to help.

Terence Kelley had fallen forward when I pulled Amelia backwards. Somehow, maybe with George's help, he had turned and crawled up the two steps to Amelia. He shifted his left hand to clutch his gut and used his bloody right hand to reach up and grab Amelia's gun.

He squeezed hard, I could tell, and I wondered that he had the strength. Blood dripped from their intertwined hands onto mine. Amelia was trying to kick him, gasping, "Terry. No. Don't."

He managed to get his own bloody finger under her trigger finger and pry it away. With a sudden jerk, he pulled the Forehand Hammerless from her hand. He would have fallen over from the force of his action if George hadn't been right behind him.

Chief Wright was beside us in the instant. He reached in and grabbed Amelia's arms and pulled her away from me. Two officers helped him push Amelia against the far newel post and handcuff her.

William's hand was on my shoulder again, and I wanted to sag back against him. But I didn't. He offered a handkerchief, presumably for the blood. I ignored it, the better to give all my attention to Terence Kelley.

He had Amelia's gun in hand. Awkwardly, he managed to stay on his knees and balance on his left hand. Blood dripped from his wound, and I wondered crazily if the marble would absorb any of it. He looked up. To find me.

We locked onto each other, and we were back at my desk, each daring the other to make a move. I slipped my hand in my pocket to grasp the Hopkins & Allen, ready to offer a demonstration on how to fire through fabric.

I did not want to shoot Terence Kelley as he knelt there bleeding, hearing Amelia scream for him in her litany of blame and protest. But I held his gaze, knowing I couldn't back down.

Around me the noise level rose and fell. I heard Dr. Potter, running to treat whomever the latest round of mayhem had provided him, saying, "Is that you, McConnell? For God sake, sit down."

I wanted very much for William not to see me shoot anyone. I wanted Terence Kelley not to fire with William right behind me. The Chief stood close by, saying, "Give us the gun, Terence. Back off, Julia," and I knew we had everyone's attention.

I trusted I would read in Terence Kelley's eyes when he could aim the gun sufficiently to fire. He grimaced and smirked at the same time, and then he jerked. I almost fired before I read surprise and more pain.

The Chief and George hadn't known what to do with us back at the office. George had it figured out now. He grabbed Kelley's shoulder and his arm, bent his wrist up, and worked the gun from his hand, much as Kelley had done with Amelia.

Kelley didn't say anything. He gave me a last glare and collapsed.

EPILOGUE

Carl pushed his way through the crowd on the stairs to get to me. I thought for a moment he was going to hug me, but he stared at my outfit instead. William said, "Thank God you're safe, Schroeder," and that distracted Carl more. And then he saw Dad, who was behind William on the stairs. I wasn't sure how long Dad had been there, but I could see a smile working through the stern face he was trying for.

Chief Wright tried to organize the chaos and confront me at the same time. I sat on a step, just to get William to sit as well. Dad stepped in and suggested the Chief could use the police carriage parked on Market, presumably with Peterson waiting in the rain, for Amelia. Attendants came running in from the Eighteenth Street end of the Midway, and Henry and Kelley left in the same ambulance. The scene cleared out amazingly fast as janitors cleaned and travelers unaware of the drama repopulated the waiting room and the stairs. I wanted to hold William's hand again, but I settled for sitting close.

Later, Carl paced in the Station's closed lunchroom and explained to us how he and Henry and James Ingle and Paul Carrey had put the story together. Henry was anxious about Amelia's behavior and had gone to Ste. Genevieve to confer with his cousin. Carl had gotten there at the perfect time to join the Ingles and Carrey as they sat Tom Caruthers down and finessed his confession.

It seemed Amelia and Henry had visited James and his wife for several days around Easter, and James happened to mention the smuggling operation. Amelia had stomped outside to vent her anger, and that's where she ran into Caruthers, who'd appeared looking to do some task about the Ingles's house. Caruthers admitted that he'd fallen under the spell of the fiery new woman. However she managed, he saw her off with the promise to derail the next beer shipment and maybe embarrass Claude Picard in the bargain.

He'd cabled Amelia when he heard the Sheriff was making a delivery. Apparently she'd had Terence Kelley call and alert Paul Carrey to look for the beer.

Caruthers couldn't resist going out to look at the spilled beer so he could tell Amelia about it. But like Sheriff Carrey—and before Sheriff Carrey arrived—he found Sheriff Picard instead.

Carl said the man was agitated as he explained that he'd picked up the money belt and run. It wasn't so much guilt that he'd taken it, according to Carl, as continuing anxiety over Amelia's response. She'd telegraphed him to ask about the money, and he'd told her the truth by return. She'd cabled again—Caruthers still carried the tattered paper, Carl said, shaking his head—to declare it blood money and that Caruthers should throw the belt in the Mississippi. He hadn't had the nerve to do that. But he had tried to burn the beer at the Klines's to appease Amelia.

James Ingle had forced Caruthers to reveal the hiding place and then returned the belt to Marjorie Picard with the payment intact.

I was impressed. Ingle could have done any number of things with the money, but apparently he knew it was the last bit of income Marjorie Picard might see for a while. Even Carl said it was a square thing to do.

On Sunday, the Chief phoned to ask me to come in to talk to him. We glared at each other over his desk, but it was hard for him to criticize as much as he wanted. Clearly his officers had been taken by surprise by a woman shooter and had done little to control the situation. He dismissed me with a command to show up for work Monday as usual. I caught his smile as I left.

Henry was back at his parents' home, nursing the arm grazed by his sister's bullet. The word was not so good on Terence Kelley. The gut shot was serious, and he'd lost a lot of blood.

Amelia was in jail and would be for a while. She was going to face numerous charges. I wondered if her attorneys could enter an insanity plea that involved obsession with a cause.

The Ingle family dealt with their hurt and grief. I told Carl and William what Mrs. Ingle had said about not taking your causes too seriously. Carl did not admit any guilt along those lines. I thought about it a good deal.

Carl and William and I debated, off and on over the next week, if Terence Kelley would continue to be a threat when he got out of jail—or if he'd even go to jail. If he didn't confess, the arson charges in St. Louis might not stick. We were sure he'd set the fire, as a way to head off any charges that might be aimed at Amelia. Given how it had turned out, he might well feel like coming after me. Truth be told, there was a small part of me that felt sorry for him. Of course, the whole discussion would be moot if he didn't recover, and by week's end that was not a given.

At work, George didn't talk to me about the events at Union Station. I smiled at him when he came near, because I felt guilty for having suspected him. I think he was distressed about Kelley, maybe feeling bad he hadn't talked to the Chief earlier.

William was back to work, but at a slow pace. Evelyn left halfway through the week, satisfied with his progress or simply resigned.

Carl was happy with our efforts. He said we'd helped nudge justice along. I wasn't so sure. The papers were debating the whole matter on their editorial pages, and it was clear to me St. Louis was not going to be a happy place until the prohibition issue went away. Too many jobs, too much identification with beer, too much emotion.

And two lives, maybe three, wasted. The papers didn't mention that. I debated with myself if I had done the right things, given all that had gone wrong. I might be thinking about that for a while, as well.

On the domestic scene, I got enough laundry done to wear clothes I wanted to wear, not clothes I had to wear. I started work on a new skirt for Elizabeth, promised the week before, and had thoughts about making myself another suit like my new one. In fact, by Sunday, I thought I might as well wear the new outfit again. It had been more trouble than it was worth at work. But William had seemed to like it.

There was a stir in the house when I strolled down the stairs late Sunday morning. Ruth said she thought I'd save the outfit for something special. I thought I had.

We were in a dry spell again. We would be most of the summer. So, it was a nice, hot, sunny, St. Louis baseball day.

William and I had lunch first and made our way to the ballpark at a leisurely pace. William didn't want to move too fast, and I couldn't, in the slender skirt.

It appeared that William could get seats anywhere. A *Globe* sports reporter would be on the job, but the owners liked good relations with the newspapers, regardless. William had picked up tickets for not two, but four, good seats. So his arm wouldn't get jostled, he said.

We were along the first base line, just a few rows back from the Browns' dugout. I loved baseball. I'd enjoyed the boys' games back home, and the first time I walked into a park in the city and looked out at the green and precise field, I'd fallen in love. I loved the ballparks. I loved the game. I didn't always love the other fans, because I hated the smell of beer, but sometimes, if the game was rip-roaring along, the people around you could be fun.

I'd come to games by myself, if need be. I had, several Sundays, braving comments and advances. But today was perfect. Baseball and William.

I was smiling. William looked over at me and smiled, too, but it turned to a frown.

"What? Is your arm hurting?"

"No, Julia, my arm is fine. It's only . . . why was I so stupid as to . . .?" He stopped, and I interpreted the twitch of his eyebrows as an apology.

"Stupid to do what? What is it?"

He gestured with his good arm, which was between us. I looked back and heard as much as saw what he had picked up on.

It was Carl. He was talking, of course. He was greeting people. How could he know so many people in a city this size? He was making his way down the steps with two beers.

I turned to William, trying for dismay. "What have you done?"

"I told him we were coming to the game today. I never dreamed . . ." He grinned. So did I.

Carl acted as if we'd been waiting for him. "Here we go. Figured you'd have trouble carrying the brew, Will."

I said, "If you splash any of that swill on my skirt, I will throw it in your face, Carl."

He burst out laughing but was careful when he handed the mug over to William, who twisted around to put it down on the other side of us. We were taking up the four seats just fine.

Carl handed out bags of peanuts, which William also put down in front of the vacant seat. Carl didn't seem to notice. And then he launched into a discussion of the game, asking along the way why we hadn't gone to see the Cardinals, who were playing in town today as well, a few blocks away. People nearby muttered.

William hadn't had to say a thing yet. He raised an eyebrow, deepened the dimples, and offered a hand. I took it. Carl must have noticed, but he just kept talking.

From the **St. Louis Globe-Democrat***, Monday, June 16, 1910*

> The Browns pulled out a close victory against the rival Chicago White Sox Sunday afternoon. The final score, 7 to 6, breaks a five-game losing skid for the hometown team.

AFTERWORD

Historical Note

I have met people who think Prohibition began in 1920. That, of course, is the date that national prohibition took effect—became "the law of the land"—as a result of the Eighteenth Amendment, approved by Congress in 1917 and ratified by the final state in 1919.

But the prohibition impulse was almost as old as the country and accelerated in the second half of the nineteenth century. The Prohibition Party was formed in 1869. One strategy of prohibition proponents was "local option," which meant the voters in a governmental unit could choose wet or dry.

In 1887, 83 of 114 Missouri counties approved local option. Missouri was one of the states that allowed both town and county local options. Within two years of the legislation, 61 governmental units (towns or counties) used the local option to vote dry. Spread throughout the years that followed, another 35 governmental units voted to go dry.

The prohibition vote our characters see coming up in November of 1910 was real. To get a little ahead of ourselves, Missourians voted down statewide prohibition, two to one, some four months after our story ends. (The vote takes place during the events of the third book in the series, *Heaven Will Protect the Working Girl*.)

So, what about Ste. Genevieve and Perry Counties? There had to be adjoining counties with differing votes on prohibition, but I could not find the status of these two counties—which are located perfectly for purposes of the story. It is the situation historical fiction writers face when we conclude that history *could* have played out a particular way, and if we don't stop doing research, we will *never* get around to writing fiction.

That was my thinking many years ago when I set up the structure of this book. About two months before it was first published, I did a search using just the right words and found a map of wet and dry counties about this time period on a site featuring the exploits of prohibitionist Carrie Nation. Both Ste. Genevieve and Perry counties were wet. The county just south of Perry was dry. I did not rewrite. The dynamic could have been shifted south, but the train trip would have been too long! I did assume that Perry County had electricity in 1910 and found out otherwise in time to make the change.

Thanks go out, as always, to the libraries and historical societies in towns and cities, both for their help in person and for their engaging websites.

If you would like more insight into what life was like in St. Louis and the rest of the country in 1910, please see my website on the topic, 1910-stlouis-by-jallison.com. There are sections on styles and landscapes and issues of the day—including the link between prohibition and suffrage. You can find citations there for the facts above.

Book Titles and Music Titles

The books in the Julia Nye series carry titles that reflect the music of the day. In this case, the title reflects a popular ballad, *In the Good Old Summertime*. Aside from the fact that the story takes place in summer—and that a young woman in the crowd at Weider's Garden requests the song—its lyrics reflect the different standards of physical contact between men and women at the turn of the last century. The chorus goes:

> *In the good old summertime,*
> *In the good old summertime,*
> *Strolling thro' the shady lanes,*
> *With your baby mine;*
> *You hold her hand and she holds yours,*
> *And that's a very good sign*
> *That she's your tootsie-wootsie*
> *In the good old summertime.*

The music was written by George Evans and the lyrics by Ren Shields. It was published in 1902 and became popular in a stage musical that year. It is also the title of a 1940s film starring Judy Garland. There are lots of versions of it on YouTube. I prefer the contemporaneous recording by the Haydn Quartet (provided by Nathaniel Jordon on YouTube as of this writing.) It is typical of the three-quarter-time ballads popular before the world started to turn to ragtime and jazz.

Preview of the next Julia Nye Mystery

Speaking of ragtime, the next book in the series is *St. Louie Slow Drag.* (A slow drag is a kind of ragtime tune.) The novel opens when William asks Julia for a date to see ragtime master Scott Joplin in St. Louis's seedy, prostitution-laced Mill Creek Valley. The rag club erupts in flames, and a Negro musician is found dead in the alley. Julia realizes she can make a contribution to solving the crimes because the police are unlikely to find out anything from the young Negro woman Julia has befriended.

Meanwhile, Chief Wright wants Julia to use her other skill—with a rifle—to tame a potential race riot. His demand may mean a loss of what Julia holds dear, her suffrage activities and her romance with William. What she doesn't see coming is that her involvement puts her in someone else's cross-hairs: she has become the woman whose death could spark the race riot.

And more on the Julia Nye series . . .

Please check out my website at joallisonauthor.com. On it, you will see the synopses for all the books in the series. You will also find a book of short stories and vignettes that take place before and between the novels of the series. One (award-winning) story explains why Julia left Fulton to live in St. Louis and sets the context of her particular skills—and her relationship with her father. (That book is

I hope you have enjoyed the start of this series. If you have, please leave a positive review on Amazon or other sites. If you have issues or questions, please contact me through my website.

Made in the USA
Columbia, SC
19 June 2018